"I should hate you," Kerry moaned. "That place—"

"It's over, " Craig murmured.

He narrowed the space separating them and gathered her in his arms. Without saying a word, he held her against him, stroking her hair and uttering a soothing "Shhh." Then he planted a kiss on the top of her head.

"It's over," he repeated. He rocked with her. "I'm sorry," he said softly. "But there was no other way."

She wasn't a crier. The last time she'd allowed herself to cry in front of anyone had been at her mother's funeral. Now she was powerless to hold back the tears. She sobbed for several minutes before finally pulling back enough to look at him with red-rimmed eyes.

She had to touch him again, had to feel his warmth and strength. She pressed herself closer and heard the drumming of his heart.

"You did the right thing," she told him.

Dear Reader,

Most of us have at least one relative we're not particularly fond of, someone we'd just as soon not associate with, but with whom we're inexorably bound by ties of blood or marriage.

And let's face it—every family has its black sheep.

The First family is like that, too. Kerry Durgan, née First, is an alcoholic who has sold her share of the family ranch, thereby destroying a heritage that goes back more than 170 years. She doesn't seem very likable, does she? Yet Craig Robeson discovers, after nineteen years of separation, that he's still attracted to her. And perhaps because of his own flawed background, he sees the pain behind her bravado. The question is whether he can help her tap the core of goodness he knows is within her, and whether in doing so he can put his own troubled past behind him.

Family sagas have always been among my favorite reads, because the dynamics of families fascinate me. I hope you find this First family story and the ones to follow equally interesting. (The previous story is *The First Family of Texas*, which appeared last year.)

I enjoy hearing from readers. You can write me at Box 4062, San Angelo TX 76902, or through my Web sites at www.superauthors.com or at www.outreachrwa.com.

K.N. *Casper*

The First Daughter

K.N. Casper

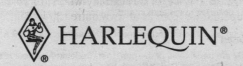

HARLEQUIN®

TORONTO • NEW YORK • LONDON
AMSTERDAM • PARIS • SYDNEY • HAMBURG
STOCKHOLM • ATHENS • TOKYO • MILAN • MADRID
PRAGUE • WARSAW • BUDAPEST • AUCKLAND

ISBN 0-373-71006-2

THE FIRST DAUGHTER

Copyright © 2001 by K. Casper.

This edition published by arrangement with Harlequin Books S.A.

® and TM are trademarks of the publisher. Trademarks indicated with
® are registered in the United States Patent and Trademark Office, the
Canadian Trade Marks Office and in other countries.

Visit us at www.eHarlequin.com

Printed in U.S.A.

To Janet Branson, Jan Daugherty and Susan Vaughn.
Thanks for your help, insights and inspiration

To Lori Kerr and, of course,
Mary Casper for your encouragement and patience

CHAPTER ONE

"FIVE, FOUR, THREE, two..." The director pointed to the regal woman sitting in the high-backed gilded chair in the middle of the brilliantly lit stage.

"This is Leslie Fischer coming to you live from Big D. Dallas, Texas. Welcome to the 'Tell Leslie Show.'"

Canned orchestral music swelled at the same time the audience cheered and clapped wildly in response to the neon signs that were flashing Applause.

"Did you know that one of the two most dangerous situations for the police to respond to is a domestic disturbance? Sometimes the violence and emotion escalate so much that both sides of the dispute turn on the peace officers who are trying to stop it. In a few moments, we'll talk with two women who can give us further insight into this tragic world and fill us in on what we can do about it. So don't go away."

Kerry sat on the couch at an angle to the show's sparkling host. She wanted to fidget—actually, she'd like to get up and run—but this public announcement that she was establishing a foundation for battered women and children was too important. Not for her. She'd been through therapy, come to face her demons and develop coping mechanisms. Now it was time to help someone else.

The cameras glided soundlessly around her. She'd never been on TV before. The experience was fascinating and exciting. Scary, too. Her hands were sweating, and she was making a conscious effort not to look down to see if stains showed on her teal dress.

"Relax," Leslie said with an endearing smile that in no way matched the commanding tone of her voice. The mike was off, but the camera was watching, and the veteran of stage, screen and now talk TV was clearly in her element.

Kerry wanted desperately to smile back, but her eye caught the last of the show's introductory credits rolling on one of the monitors, and panic was setting in. *I can do this. I can do this.* Her favorite mantra had gotten her through alcohol rehabilitation—twice.

The director held up five fingers and slowly folded each in a silent countdown. Three, two... The finger pointed at Leslie.

"Today we're privileged to have as our special guest Kerry First. I know you all recognize the name. If you've ever dined on prime steak or a simple hamburger, there's a good chance the beef came from the Number One Ranch in West Texas. The famous First Family spread is one of the biggest cattle producers in the Lone Star State and in the country." A camera followed the wave of her bejeweled hand toward her guest. "Welcome, Kerry."

This time the cameras didn't move, but Kerry knew one of them was focused on her. At least it couldn't see the beads of sweat breaking out between her breasts.

"Thank you, Leslie—" her smile felt completely unnatural "—it's a pleasure to be here with you."

Leslie looked past her, no doubt into another camera. "Kerry First is maintaining an honored family tradition of supporting worthy causes. In a few minutes, she'll tell us all about hers. But before that, let's meet my other guest, Charlene Higgins. Family abuse takes many forms, ranging from shouting and verbal intimidation to physical torture. Charlene knows all about it. She's experienced it firsthand. Welcome to the show, Charlene."

"Thank you." She was dressed less stylishly than Leslie and Kerry, more befitting the stereotypical image of a victim. "It's good to be here."

"Tell us your story, Charlene. How did the abuse start and how did it end?"

Kerry was only half listening to her best friend. She'd heard Charlene's story before—her marriage to a great guy whose strength and protectiveness soon turned into demands and brutality. Kerry had had her own term in hell with a man, in addition to the years of alcoholism.

"The first act of violence was a slap," Charlene said, "followed instantly by a fawning apology and a promise that it would never happen again."

Mine wasn't a slap. And there was no apology, Kerry thought. However, this wasn't the time to be thinking about herself. She'd been too selfish for too long.

"I was sure," Charlene was saying, "that he loved me in his own way. We'd just gotten off track."

Isn't it strange, Kerry mentally commented, *how we confuse pride with love? Or let it get in the way of love.*

"He had me convinced it was my fault he got so upset," Charlene explained. "If I'd learn to do better, things would be all right."

"What usually set him off?" Leslie wanted to know.

Charlene huffed. "Everything. Anything. Later, I came to realize none of it was about me or what I did. It was about him—his inadequacies, his need to be in control." Her voice was steady, but she was gripping her hands so tightly in her lap that her knuckles were white.

"Was the abuse always physical?"

"A lot of it was, but the mental torture was worse."

Without thinking, Kerry reached forward and snagged a tissue from the dispenser on the coffee table in front of her and crumpled it in her lap.

"What kind of torture? Can you give us an example?" Leslie asked, eyeing Kerry suspiciously.

Charlene nodded. "Brad demanded absolute order. Everything had to be in precisely the right place. If it wasn't—or if he said it wasn't—he would tear the entire house apart, rip up clothes and bed linens, shatter pictures, pour all the flour and sugar on the kitchen floor, along with the spices. It would take me days to clean up and reestablish order. Then he'd do it all over again a day or a week or a month later." She spoke with a kind of fatalism that was frightening—as if she were someone else.

Kerry wiped the palms of her hands with the tissue.

"Then there were the Hummels I'd inherited from my grandmother. It had taken her years to collect all the pieces. Some of them were quite valuable. Brad knew how much they meant to me. Piece by piece he destroyed every one of them, along with the bone china my parents had given us as a wedding present."

"I know everyone in the audience, here and at home, is asking the same question," Leslie observed quietly. "Why did you put up with this, Charlene? Why did you stay with him?"

Hands folded neatly in her lap, Charlene lowered her head for several seconds, then faced her inquisitor. "Because I felt trapped and totally alone. Because I had a mental image of how things should be and tried to make life fit that picture. Because it's easier to do nothing, to put off action. Because I wanted to believe he really loved me."

She paused to take a deep breath. "I also had no idea where to turn. I had no family close by, and we had three small children only one year apart in age. Two boys and the little girl I'd been praying for."

"Did he ever abuse them?"

Charlene glanced down and bit her lower lip, her eyes growing tearful. "Yes, but I didn't recognize it. Brad insisted that all kids need discipline. And of course that's true. But I refused to see when he crossed the line. I'd become so inured to physical violence, so convinced I was worthless and incompetent to do anything on my own, that I couldn't see I was endangering my children's lives.''

''How bad was it?''

''Black and blue marks. Occasionally open cuts. Once, my six-year-old son broke his arm. We told the people at the hospital that he fell, which was true, but only because Brad shoved him so hard, he tumbled down the stairs.''

The audience was deathly silent.

''So nothing was done?''

''The hospital made the required call to social services, and they investigated but they had no proof. Brad was a charmer with a glib tongue, and like true victims, we closed ranks behind him. Isn't it amazing that even abused children will protect their abusers? Brad was always contrite and, like after that first time, always promised never to do it again. He could be very affectionate when he wasn't beating one of us, and he constantly told us what he was doing was for our own good.''

As she again wiped her hands with the tissue that was now in tatters, Kerry was sure she heard a sniffle in the audience. How many women out there were in situations similar to Charlene's? They were the ones she had to reach.

Leslie spoke very softly, very dramatically. ''How did you finally manage to break this cycle, Charlene?''

''Seven years ago I saw a program about family violence on TV. In fact, it was a show very much like this one. As I sat there listening to these women talk about what they'd gone through, something finally clicked, and for the first time, I recognized myself.''

"Did you leave Brad immediately?"

Charlene shook her head. "No. It took me another three months."

"Why did you wait so long? If he was hurting you and your children—"

"I was afraid, Leslie. Afraid to make a decision. Afraid of the unknown. And I was ashamed to admit how bad everything had gotten. Most of all, I was terrified of the prospect of being alone. You see, Brad swore if I ever left him, he'd take the kids away from me, and I believed him. He was a respected businessman. I was nothing."

A feeling of restlessness emanated from the audience, like breaths being held.

"What finally gave you the courage to leave him?"

"The next beating." On a shuddering breath, Charlene added, "The one in which my daughter ended up in the hospital, almost dead."

The audience gasped.

"What happened when you did leave?" Leslie asked sympathetically, and Kerry suspected this time the show's host wasn't acting.

"I went to a shelter. They fed and clothed me and my children and helped me with legal advice. I swore out charges against Brad. Eventually he was arrested and served jail time."

Leslie leaned back in her chair, relieved. "So the story has a happy ending."

"There are no happy endings in domestic abuse situations," Kerry said on the cue she and Leslie had worked out beforehand. "Most of the external wounds heal, but the internal scars don't go away. Touching them is always painful. Charlene was fortunate because she was able to find a shelter that had room for her. Unfortunately, the one she went to had to close its doors soon afterward because of lack of funds. Which is why I'm establishing the First Family Foundation.''

''There are so many worthy causes, Kerry,'' Leslie commented earnestly. ''Yet you've chosen this one to support and give your name to.'' In a calculated glance, she stared for a moment at the two shredded tissues on the coffee table. The camera moved closer. ''Have you experienced this type of tragedy in your own life? Is that what motivates you to establish this foundation?''

The observation caught Kerry completely by surprise. They hadn't discussed this earlier, and for an anxious moment, she wondered how much of her background the show host knew. She should have been prepared for this. Shock questions were what had produced some of Leslie Fischer's most electrifying and memorable shows.

Kerry kept her chin up and shook her head in denial. ''This isn't about me, Leslie,'' she said pointedly, ''but about the plight of women and families like Charlene's. Her story is only one of thousands. We can't stand by and let violence and substance abuse continue to destroy lives without holding out hope to the victims. So many people could get out of the hellish situations they're in, the way Charlene did, if they knew there was someplace to go, someone to help them—if they knew they weren't alone. That's what the First Family Foundation is all about.''

The camera moved in. Kerry struggled to focus on her message and not be distracted.

"I want to provide a haven for battered women, to help them discover the joys of life. But it's the children who are the most tragic victims of abuse, Leslie, because they're the most vulnerable and defenseless. Only cowards beat up women and children." She looked directly into the camera. "How much more cowardly are we if we stand by and fail to do everything in our power to defend and protect them?"

"So you're providing a refuge," Leslie prompted, "not just for women but for whole families."

"Exactly. A sanctuary where people who are the victims of domestic violence—regardless of age or gender—can begin the long and sometimes painful road to reclaiming their lives and their dignity."

The show's host remained silent for several seconds to let the words sink in. "Kerry, how can people help in this noble effort?"

"In so many ways, Leslie. First of all, by understanding that the victims of abuse need help and compassion. Especially the children, who are truly innocent. People can also help by contributing clothing and toys. But the most precious gift anyone can give is time, something no one seems to have enough of these days. Nothing mends a broken body or a broken heart better than a gentle touch. A soothing hand. A warm embrace. A patient ear—to listen and console, not to condemn or judge."

"We all need love, don't we?" Leslie asked rhetorically. "How about financial contributions?"

"Yes, those, too. Even with generous contributions

of clothing, toys and time, it takes money to feed people, build facilities, to furnish and maintain them, to pay for utilities and other essential services. And in many cases, to provide health care for broken bodies."

Someone sniffled loudly enough for it to be picked up by a mike. The camera panned the audience, revealing set jaws, glistening eyes and hankies held to runny noses.

"Where can people send their contributions?" Leslie inquired.

"To the First Family Foundation at the address on the screen. No contribution is too small. And of course," Kerry added with an ironic smile, "no contribution is too big. Whatever you can give helps victims become victors." The camera returned to her, and she spoke directly to it. "I hope we can count on your support."

"Cut!" shouted the director as the audience clapped and the theme music took over. The hot overhead lights dimmed, and Kerry wilted in her seat.

"Good show," Leslie said as she rose from her chair. "Too bad you didn't have a personal experience to relate. It would have been the perfect touch. But don't worry. Contributions will be rolling in in no time."

"I'll have you to thank for that," Kerry replied, grateful the session was over. "It was very generous of you to have us on." *Even if you did try to ambush me.*

"Tearjerkers always raise ratings," the former movie star turned talk-show host said flippantly, though Kerry suspected the great Leslie Fischer's motives might go beyond ratings. There had been rumors years ago of violence in her third marriage, to screen idol Nestor Pride. Never confirmed, of course. What leading woman would want to brag about being a victim?

"By the way," Leslie continued, as she removed a pearl choker from her neck and handed it to her wardrobe lady, "I ran into an old friend of yours who said he'd stop by and observe the broadcast." A stagehand gave her a bottle of French mineral water.

"An old friend?" Kerry accepted a chilled bottle, as well.

Without elaborating, Leslie led Kerry and Charlene to a small break room. The single occupant was a man facing the coffee machine.

Kerry was puzzled. Leslie had said old friend. Considering the man's size and build—he had immense shoulders that tapered to a narrow waist and hips—she felt she should recognize him, even with his back to her. Yet there was something uncomfortably familiar about him.

He turned around, took in the three women with a sweeping glance and locked on Kerry.

Oh, my God. Kerry froze. Her past had come to haunt her.

"I understand the two of you went to high school together," Leslie said, obviously pleased by her little surprise.

Craig Robeson.

Icy panic rippled through Kerry as he moved toward her.

He stopped a few feet in front of her. "Hello, Kerry."

His quiet, almost shy smile was both appealing and unnerving. He extended a hand palm up, to hold hers rather than shake it.

In *The Wizard of Oz* a bucket of water had undone the Wicked Witch of the West—which was who Kerry felt like at this moment. Maybe, she decided, if she poured her water over her head she could melt into the soiled carpet. A lifetime had passed since she'd last seen him…since she'd humiliated him—and herself.

In an automatic gesture, she brought her hand up and placed it on his. Did he notice that it was clammy? Blame it on the water bottle. Could he feel her trembling? How could she explain that?

She lifted her gaze and studied the man whose warm fingers continued to hold hers. He was every bit as tall as she remembered him. Maybe taller. More mature in build, too, but then, he was nearly two decades older than the last time they'd met. The teenage pimples were gone without a trace. The boyish angles of his even-featured face had morphed into striking handsomeness.

"Hello, Craig." Kerry managed to squeak the words out. "How are you?"

Leslie glanced from one to the other, twisted her mouth in a semblance of a smile and quietly wandered over to the coffee machine. Charlene, looking both awestruck and bewildered, followed her.

Craig gave Kerry a lazy grin that brought out the dimples in the hollows of his cheeks. "Very well, thanks.'' Those dimples had been cute in the high school boy. They were killers in the man. "It's been a long time.''

His voice had deepened, and like his eyes had acquired a self-assurance that was pure male. *Dear God,* Kerry thought, *if I had known you'd turn out like this, I would never have...* She refused to finish the thought.

"A very long time,'' she agreed and, like Craig, lapsed into silence.

Good grief. Were they going to stand around staring at each other, saying nothing? There must be a more intelligent way to pass the time, polite questions they could ask. But for the life of her, she couldn't think of a single one.

He released her hand but continued to hold her gaze. The air of quiet confidence in his hazel green eyes stirred a distracting flutter in the pit of her stomach. She was thirsty. That was the problem. She lifted her small water bottle to her lips to take a sip and caught herself upending it.

"Can I get you something else?'' His glance flicked between her mouth and eyes. Without waiting for a response, he relieved her of the empty bottle. "Coffee, okay?''

She began to salivate, but she was sure it had nothing to do with the prospect of coffee. "Thanks.''

He smiled again, damn him. "Be right back.''

He'd been a basketball player in his junior year, tall and gangly, quick on his feet and uncommonly accurate with his shots. But he'd quit the team in his senior year. Apparently, he needed to work to help support the family. There'd been a shyness about him, too, that had been not sexy exactly, but definitely appealing.

Kerry's attention was riveted on him as he made his way to the stand in the corner of the room. His masculine movements screamed a self-assurance that had been missing in the shy teenager.

He returned and held out a moderately full cup of black coffee. "I should have asked if you put anything in it."

For a second, their fingers touched and Kerry felt suddenly tongue-tied. "This...is fine." Using both hands, she took a shallow sip. Despite its color, the brew tasted unnaturally bland. It needed a good shot of Irish whiskey to give it an edge.

"I saw your picture in the *Dallas Morning News* last weekend," Craig commented. "It didn't do you justice, Kerry. You're more beautiful now than you were in high school."

She'd received compliments before and knew how to accept them graciously, but something about this one disconcerted her. Other people's flattery was genuine enough, but the sincerity in his struck a deep chord.

"That's very kind of you, Craig. Thank you."

He made a gesture with his hand—a big, square, powerful hand—toward a cluster of chairs at the other end of the room, where Leslie and Charlene were already seated. It must be the caffeine, she decided, that had perspiration breaking out on the back of her neck.

"Thanks for letting me stop by, Leslie," he said after they were seated. "Your show has really taken off. When you started three years ago—"

"Nobody thought I had a chance," Leslie scoffed proudly. "Not against Oprah."

"They underestimated you." He grinned triumphantly at her and raised his cup in a salute. "Interesting program today." He turned to Kerry. "So you really are into good works."

Was he mocking her? Considering how she'd treated him the last time they'd met, perhaps he had a right to. "We all have to do our part," she said, trying to match his breezy tone.

"With Leslie's endorsement, I'm sure you'll accomplish miracles."

For a fleeting moment, anger flared like dry grass touched by a glowing poker. Was he suggesting she couldn't do anything on her own?

"And you?" Leslie asked him. "Will you contribute to the cause?"

"I'll give it consideration." He addressed Charlene. "Your story was very touching, Ms. Higgins. What became of your ex-husband?"

"He owns a major car dealership now, makes a ton of money and is remarried with two kids."

"And your children?"

Charlene glanced at Kerry. No one else had even asked. "My oldest is starting high school next fall. He's a bit rebellious, but basically a good kid. The middle boy is doing fine."

"And your little girl?"

"This year, she's determined to be a ballet dancer." She smiled proudly. "Thank you for asking, Mr. Robeson."

He shifted his attention to Kerry. "Do you mind if I pose a few questions about your foundation?"

She tried to relax, but the intensity of his gaze was disconcerting. "Fire away."

"Have you had much experience running shelters?"

"I've been associated with several in the past year." She smiled, fully aware she was dodging his question—and that he knew it. "But you're correct. I haven't actually run one. That's why I plan to surround myself with experienced people—like Charlene."

He grinned back. "Smart move under any circumstances. Are you personally contributing capital to this venture?"

She drew back and arched her brows. "I wouldn't put my name on it if I wasn't."

"Then why do you need contributions?"

She took a deep breath. "Because I want this endeavor to go beyond me. I'm endowing a perpetual trust fund, but I don't want it to stop there. Inflation can take a terrible toll on fixed resources. If we have a constant influx of new money, we can grow and expand. Getting people to contribute also means getting them involved. That's vitally important. We can't cure domestic violence, Craig. Our mission is to offer a refuge for its victims."

"Noble sentiments," he said without a trace of sarcasm. "You might want to reconsider the title of the foundation, though. The First family name is so well-known and its wealth so legendary that the public's immediate reaction is likely to be that you don't need their support."

Kerry simmered. She'd reverted to her maiden name specifically because of its renown and because she wanted to finally do something to add to its prestige.

Seeing her scowl, Craig added. "No offense. Just a thought."

She had an urge to ask him who the hell he thought he was, preaching to her. He might be tall and carry himself with the grace of an athlete, but he was no millionaire basketball star. She followed sports and had never seen his name—or face. The old Kerry would have gone for his jugular. Fortunately, the new, sober Kerry was less volatile.

When she gave no response, he asked, "How long will you allow people to stay in your shelter?"

As long as it was necessary. But that wasn't the answer he wanted to hear. It wasn't the right one, either. "We haven't worked out all the details yet. Our primary concern, naturally, is for their immediate safety."

"Speaking of which—" he plodded on "—shelters themselves can be extremely dangerous places—as you undoubtedly know—because they become targets for disgruntled abusers who feel they've been robbed of their property. What provisions will you make to protect your guests?"

"We'll employ standard shelter security procedures. Initial contacts through third parties. Knowledge of the location of the house limited to police supervisors. And access strictly controlled."

"What about on-site guards?"

He made it sound like a prison instead of a refuge. "We haven't decided yet whether they'll be armed."

"When do you plan to open the first one?"

"I'd like to have it up and running within three months."

"Three months?" He pinched the bridge of his nose. "As I understand it, you don't even have a facility yet."

His critical tone was increasingly irritating her. Most contributors sent in their twenty-five-dollar checks without asking all these questions. "We're considering several potential locations."

"But that's only the beginning. Even after you find a suitable site, you still have to negotiate the deal. The building will undoubtedly have to be modified to meet your specifications. A zoning change may be required. Then there's the paperwork that has to be filed for a tax-exempt enterprise. You'll need to run background checks on your staff and train them." He shook his head. "I think your schedule may be a bit ambitious, Kerry. I've had a little experience in property management," he commented. "Perhaps I can help."

Ah, real estate. So that was what he was after, a juicy commission on a commercial sale. "That's very kind of you, Craig. I'll keep it in mind."

The note of dismissal brought raised eyebrows and dropped jaws from both Leslie and Charlene.

Craig's mouth twitched in a burgeoning smile. "I wish you the best of luck." He rose easily from his chair and extended his hand to Leslie. "Thank you for inviting me, Les. It's always a pleasure to see you." Charlene stood up. He offered her his hand. "Take good care of those kids, Ms. Higgins."

"I will, and thank you for coming, Mr. Robeson," she said sincerely. "I've enjoyed meeting you."

He stepped over to Kerry and again lifted his hand the way a gentleman would if he was going to kiss a lady's. "Nice seeing you again, Kerry. Please give my best to your dad."

Leslie escorted him to the door, received a peck on the cheek and closed the door behind him.

"Well, Kerry, you certainly blew that." She settled into one of the worn easy chairs, her elegant hands draped over the armrests. "He called me the other day, explained that he'd lost track of you since high school and asked if he could drop by to say hello. Said he might also be interested in contributing to your foundation. Talk about golden opportunities. I couldn't have staged it better if I'd tried." She threw up her hands and dropped them with a shake of her head. "Craig Robeson, for God's sake. And you give him a brush-off."

Kerry was genuinely taken aback by the woman's rebuke. "What's so special about Craig Robeson?" Back in Coyote Springs he'd been as poor as a bronc rider on a losing streak.

After a moment of stunned silence, Charlene glanced at Leslie, and they both burst out laughing.

"Lordy, lordy." Leslie peered at the ceiling and rocked her head from side to side. She broke into an amused grin. "You don't know who he is, do you?" The knot in Kerry's belly tightened. Leslie shook her head and asked slowly, "Have you ever heard of the Robe Corporation?"

Kerry's breath caught in her throat. Her head

pounded. "Robeco? Craig Robeson is Robeco?" It was one of the biggest land development companies in the world. She plopped down on the couch across from the movie star and came as close to tears as she had in a very long time.

"My dear," Leslie said, "you just flubbed getting financial backing from one of the wealthiest men in the country."

CHAPTER TWO

SO THE NAME Robeson meant no more to her than the guy she'd ditched in high school. He shouldn't be surprised. Over the years, he'd made it a point to keep a low personal profile, but it was humbling nevertheless. He chuckled at his own vanity.

She'd been a knockout as a teenager, with her long black hair, peach-blossom complexion and violet blue eyes. None of that had changed, nor had his male reaction.

He'd often wondered if she ever felt regret for running out on him at the prom. Even now, recollection of that night brought an empty feeling, a sense of failure. She'd made a fool of him, or rather he'd allowed her to make a fool of him, which amounted to the same thing.

At the end of summer, after he'd graduated from Coyote High, he'd driven out of town and never looked back. There'd been no close friends to see him off, and what few acquaintances he'd made he'd left behind.

Two years earlier, the telephone company had transferred his father from Los Angeles to Coyote Springs. The small West Texas town was laid back enough that for a while Craig had thought things would improve, but he'd been deluding himself. The problem wasn't geography, it was the baggage they took with them from place to place.

During that first school year, he'd managed to cope with the situation. By the second, it meant staying home every evening, giving up virtually all social activities, even the sport he loved—basketball. His coach had insisted he was a shoo-in for an athletic scholarship if he applied himself. Quitting the team early had jinxed that. He'd never developed into the star everyone had expected. The professional career that had once seemed so promising never came. Responsibilities took priority.

He turned off FM 1171 onto an access ramp for Interstate 35W and went north toward Flower Mound. Traffic was almost as bad as an L.A. freeway. Normally, he enjoyed the challenge of whipping around cars and trucks, secure in the knowledge that he had the power to gun away from hazardous situations.

Kerry had been a year behind him in school, but he'd definitely noticed her. He'd considered asking her out a few times, but he was afraid to leave his mother at night—alone and vulnerable. Besides, what girl would want to go on a date in a broken-down old pickup with seats held together by duct tape and an engine that sounded ready to die at any moment? The Number One Ranch was a long trip from town, and while the idea of their getting stuck all alone on a deserted country road sounded very romantic, Craig couldn't risk the practical consequences of his father's wrath—or hers—if something went seriously wrong.

He wasn't experienced with girls, but he did know about the birds and bees.

He'd hardly talked to Kerry, much less been a part of her crowd, yet he'd had the audacity to ask her to accompany him to the prom. He'd been totally prepared for her to say no, but to his utter amazement, she'd said yes. He'd gone home with a smile on his face and air under his feet. For a while, life was good.

He'd spent some of the money he'd managed to squirrel away from his lawn-mowing jobs on a rented tuxedo and a corsage. Asking his father if he could borrow the family station wagon had crossed his mind, but he'd decided against it and used the rest of his hard-earned cash to rent an economy car rather than take his rusty old truck.

The big night finally arrived, and he made the long trip out to the Number One. He felt like a knight on a quest as he climbed the side of the mesa to the impressive ranch house. Kerry's father met him at the door. Adam First said he'd seen Craig play basketball the previous year and complimented him on his hook shot. Then he made it clear he expected his daughter home by 1:00 a.m.

"Yes, sir," Craig had answered dutifully.

When he and Kerry entered the lobby of the country club, everyone stared. She was wearing a long satiny sheath with slits cut up the sides. Craig's hands were damp when he took her out on the floor for the first dance.

They danced for two hours. Most of the rock-and-roll numbers were fast, which meant no physical contact, but sometimes there was a slow lyrical tune, and he was able to hold her in his arms. Between dances and during the breaks, he tried to fit in with her crowd. She was the life of the party, jovial and a bit boisterous. He smiled a lot but didn't say much, content simply to be with her, to watch her throw back her head and listen to her laugh. Sometimes she would touch his hand. Her contact was pure sensuous torture, and he spent most of the evening on the verge of an erection.

Then came the band's second break, and the crowd migrated from the sweltering ballroom to the refreshing coolness of a torch-lit open patio. A few people smoked by the rail while several couples quietly necked in dim corners. Craig wondered if Kerry would let him kiss her, or would she slap him?

He had his arm around her waist and was coaxing her toward a shadowy alcove of the single-story building when the rough, rumbling sound of a motorcycle shattered the night air. A big shiny Harley-Davidson materialized on the lawn beyond the stone fence. The events that followed rolled like a slow motion movie in Craig's mind.

Rafael Durgan called Kerry's name. She grinned excitedly, pulled away from Craig and raced to greet the leather-garbed cyclist. Stunned, Craig stood stock-still, not quite sure what was happening. He called out and ran after her, but by the time he caught up with her, she'd already hitched up her long skirt and climbed onto the back of the motorcycle. Her expression was defiant as she wrapped her arms around Rafe's waist. Craig reached for her just as the two of them went speeding off into the night.

He could still remember the sinking sensation in the pit of his stomach and the strange feeling of unreality as he watched them disappear. This couldn't be happening. The most beautiful girl in school had agreed to be his date. They'd danced. He'd soaked in the sweet, alluring scent of her skin and perfume, felt her feminine curves rub against his body. Now she'd taken off with another man, abandoned him with hardly a backward glance. It was too unreal. Even the other people at the party didn't seem to know what to say. They gawked at him, then averted their eyes, embarrassed for him. Thank God nobody laughed.

Craig stayed on the patio. What was the point of going inside? He was alone, and he couldn't face the pity he knew would greet him there.

Should he try to find her? He moped with his hands in his pockets, unsure what to do, secretly hoping she would come back, knowing she wouldn't. Finally, after the last number was played and she hadn't returned, he walked to the car he'd foolishly hoped would impress her, climbed in and drove alone to the Number One Ranch.

Adam First answered the door. "You're right on time." He checked his watch. "A few minutes early, actually." He peered at the small car.

"Kerry's not with me, sir."

"Not with you? Where is she?" His eyes widened. "She's not hurt?"

"No, sir." Then he explained about Rafael Durgan showing up and Kerry going off with him.

Craig wasn't sure what to expect. He saw the rancher's hands curl ominously and prepared himself for a blow. It wouldn't have been the first time he'd felt the impact of a man's fist, and for once he would deserve it. Adam First had entrusted him with his daughter's safety and he'd failed that trust.

But the swing didn't come. Would he take it out on Kerry? Craig wondered. Had he made a terrible mistake by telling this man that his daughter had run away with the town's bad boy?

They stood under the entry light. The heat of the day was spent, the night air cool. It seemed to crackle with tension. Finally, Adam First raised his left hand to Craig's shoulder and held out his right.

"Thank you for coming out here to tell me personally. You could have phoned or said nothing at all. I appreciate your being man enough to face me."

"I'm sorry, sir."

"You have nothing to apologize for. Go home and forget about her."

He went home, but he couldn't forget her. He saw her on campus the following Monday. He didn't confront her. Like a coward, he avoided her.

That summer so long ago had been the worst of his life, so bad that the humiliation of being ditched at the prom by the prettiest girl in the school paled by comparison. When it was over, his mother moved to Dallas to live with her sister, and Craig left for college, never to return to Coyote Springs. Never to see Kerry First again. Until today.

KERRY SANK onto a butter-soft leather couch and kicked off her high heels. She threw back her head and wriggled her toes. "That's better."

Charlene plopped down on the sofa opposite her. "I need a drink. Something other than stale coffee or designer water."

Kerry chuckled. "How about a double bourbon on the rocks."

"Nah. Scotch was my potion of choice."

"Not you," Kerry chided good-naturedly. "Me."

"Coming up."

Charlene climbed to her feet and made her way to the bar, where she filled two old-fashioned glasses with ice from a silver bucket, opened a fresh bottle of root beer, poured, added a slice of lemon to each and brought them to the couch. She handed one to Kerry. "Bourbon and soda."

Kerry accepted the glass, held it up and examined it. "Hmm. More like black rum."

"Whatever."

They'd met at Betty Ford's less than two years earlier on Kerry's first visit to the famous detox center. Charlene had begun drinking when she was still married, in a foolish attempt to bond with her volatile husband. She'd taken the pledge after leaving him and hadn't touched a drop since. She was still the person Kerry called when temptation began to overwhelm her.

"Your old high school sweetheart sure is a gorgeous hunk."

"He wasn't my sweetheart. He just invited me to his prom. It was sort of a last-minute thing. Besides, he wasn't all that good-looking back then. How come you knew who he was?"

"He attended a real estate convention at the hotel

last year," Charlene replied with her head back and eyes closed. As a publicity consultant for the Hawthorne Hotel chain, she helped organize big meetings and trade shows. "I didn't actually get to meet him. I heard he's not the easiest guy to deal with. Not necessarily unreasonable, but demanding. Meticulous about every little detail. Still, if he were in the market for a wife, I might be willing to violate my vow of celibacy."

Kerry's eyes bugged open. It hadn't even occurred to her to ask any personal questions, the kind old acquaintances would naturally ask. She had noticed he wasn't wearing a ring, but that didn't mean anything. "He isn't married?"

"Confirmed bachelor." Charlene snorted. "What a waste." She lifted her head off the couch. "You really didn't know who he was?"

"No idea at all." Kerry lay back on the sofa. "In high school...as I recall, he came from a rather modest family."

Snickering, Charlene noted, "We're not all born with silver spurs on our heels."

Kerry had told her friend about growing up on the Number One Ranch. At the time, the eight-hundred-square-mile spread was one of the largest privately owned ranches in Texas—or the country. "What do you know of his career?"

"Hmm. From what I heard, he sold tract houses part-time while he was in college...graduated from Texas Tech with a degree in business admin...delved into residential and commercial real estate full-time after that and made his first million. Within a few years he had his own brokerage, expanded into property development and hasn't stopped since.''

''Poor boy makes good. The American dream,'' Kerry said flippantly, though in truth she admired his achievements very much. They also reminded her of how little she'd accomplished with her life.

''An American dream, all right.'' Charlene brushed a stray wisp of hair from her face. ''Maybe I ought to just have an affair with him. To hell with picket fences and apple pie. On second thought, I like apple pie, even if it is fattening.'' She sighed. ''I guess I'll have to leave him to you.''

Kerry pictured prom night and the soft glow of his eyes in the moonlight when he took her outside for a kiss. She could still remember the way he'd held her in his arms when they'd danced. Not possessively, exactly. Proudly. As if she were a delicate prize he couldn't believe he'd won. Of course, she'd disabused him of that notion all too quickly. How different might life have been if she'd let him take her home that night.

''GOOD MORNING, Mr. Robeson,'' Karen Douglas said as Craig passed through the double glass doors to the executive suite of Robe Corporation. Dark-haired with a sprinkling of gray, Karen was in her late forties, tall and slender. Her brown eyes smiled at him.

''Good morning, Karen. Call Schneider and ask him to stop over when he gets a chance. Today, if possible.''

''Yes, sir. Your calendar for the day is on your desk. I rearranged Covington's and Haley's appointments. I didn't think you'd want to meet with Haley right after lunch."

Craig laughed. "Bless you." Haley was a developer who had a penchant for talking people's ears off. His monotone was hard enough to endure before lunch and an absolute invitation to a siesta after.

"Sid Richey called a few minutes ago. He's running into problems with the council in Arizona."

Craig looked at his watch. It wasn't yet eight o'clock, which meant it was going on seven o'clock in the Copper State. "He's up early. Get him on the phone for me."

Fifteen minutes later, after working out a strategy with his representative on a new housing development being constructed on an Indian reservation, he hung up the phone. It immediately rang.

"Mr. Schneider is here, sir."

"Send him in."

Alvin Schneider, Craig's chief of security, was a retired Marine officer. Now in his late fifties, he still ran several miles a day and worked out at a gym three times a week. He was undistinguished in appearance since he'd let his hair grow to civilian length, but he still had a sharp analytical head for details.

"Morning, sir," he said as he strode across the thick carpet toward the desk. "What's on your mind?"

Craig picked up a copy of the Sunday *Dallas Morning News*, the society section folded open to show Kerry's picture. "Do you know anything about this woman or her charity work?" He handed over the paper.

Schneider speed-read the article. "Can't say I do."

"She's trying to drum up support for a shelter for battered women and children. I'd like you to find out what you can about her—her background, where she got her money, what kind of causes she sponsors."

"Thinking of contributing?"

"Maybe."

Al had investigated other enterprises Craig had been asked to support. Not all of them proved legitimate. Those that didn't soon found themselves under scrutiny by several government agencies. Craig didn't like to think Kerry might be involved in anything shady, but other so-called friends had tried to bamboozle him on occasion, and this woman hardly qualified as an old friend. Did she really not know who he was? Or had she played dumb because she was aware of his reputation and was afraid he'd poke too deeply into her affairs?

"Priority?" Schneider asked.

Craig considered for a minute. As much as he wanted to learn everything about Kerry First immediately, he recognized there were other matters more pressing. In the world of high-risk investments, intelligence on whom you were dealing with was vitally important, and Craig had a lot of irons in the fire. He didn't want to get burned.

"Routine. How long do you think it'll take?"

"High-profile personality like her," Schneider mused, "probably not very long, unless we run into something suspicious. I can give you a preliminary report in a couple of weeks."

"Fine." Craig waved his hand, then changed the

subject. "What have you found out about Donnelly Corp?"

KERRY WAS at the dining room table poring over proofs of brochures the printer had delivered. She spread them out in frustration. What did she know about fonts and colors and photo placement? She'd send them to Charlene to evaluate. Char had offered her expertise in advertising and promotions to the First Family Foundation free of charge, but Kerry insisted on paying her from her personal funds.

She enjoyed Char's company, their wild shopping trips, hectic lunches and quiet girl talk. Kerry admitted to envying her friend, too—her success in the business world and the close family ties she'd reestablished after her divorce.

The phone rang in the next room. Evelyn, her day maid, would pick it up. Now, where was she? She fanned out the different colors of paper stock. The yellow would catch the eye, but it was too loud and definitely inappropriate for the message she wanted to convey. The buff was more dignified, but it also disappeared in a stack of other papers. The gray had a sort of elegance, especially with the cursive black type, yet it, too, seemed to fade into obscurity. She liked the blue. Maybe it was too dark, though. A lot of her prospective contributors were older people who preferred clarity to artistry. Perhaps if she made the font larger...

"Excuse me, Ms. Durgan. Your son is on the line." Evelyn brought over the cordless.

"Thank you." Kerry accepted the instrument from

the uniformed maid. "Brian, honey, is everything all right?"

"Oh, Mom. You ask me that every time I call."

Kerry laughed quietly, pleased at the happy sound of her son's voice even if he was feigning annoyance. "That's because you call so infrequently, darling, that when you do, I'm sure it must be an emergency."

"I called you two weeks ago," he reminded her with a note of irritation.

"Two weeks," she moaned. "Sweetheart, do you realize how long two weeks is in the life of a mother?"

"Probably about the same as it is in the life of a son—fourteen days."

Kerry couldn't help chuckle. "Smart mouth. No respect. Okay, young man, so why are you calling your dear old mom now?"

"To let you know about my plans for spring break."

Spring break. Was it March already? The months were speeding by. When she'd lived on the ranch, she'd noticed the seasons, but she'd also had time on her hands, time that had gotten her into trouble. Keeping busy was better. Fewer temptations, for one thing, and a newfound pride in resisting the ones that still existed. "You are going to come here, aren't you?"

"Actually—" there was a pregnant pause "—I'm not. Stan's dad has invited Ryan and me to go scuba diving in Florida."

He was telling her, she noted, not asking her if he could go. "Isn't that dangerous?"

"Heck, no. Stan's been doing it for years. He says it's a cinch. You don't mind, do you?"

On one level, she minded very much, but it wasn't Brian's fault she'd missed parts of his growing up. Her father had played a part in that. She hoped Brian didn't resent her too deeply for failing him. "No, I don't mind," she assured him. "It's just that...I was looking forward to seeing you."

"You'll get to see me this summer, or part of it. I told you, didn't I, that I'm trying to get hired on at that new construction site in Colorado?"

Another disappointment. She'd been hoping they could spend the whole summer together, do some traveling. Maybe even drive the Alcan Highway to Alaska. "Yes, you told me. When your flight lands at Dallas-Fort Worth Airport," she went on, "I'll meet you there, and we can at least do a meal together. Stan and Ryan are welcome, too, of course, but you're the one I want to see."

"Well," he drawled.

She didn't like the sound of that. "Don't tell me."

"Our flight doesn't go through DFW."

"Everything goes through DFW." Doesn't it?

"They've got this new airline service here in Lubbock. We'll fly directly to Houston and then on to Fort Lauderdale."

"You mean I won't get to see you at all?" She couldn't disguise the disappointment in her voice.

"'Fraid not, Mom." He did sound contrite. "Not this time. But I'll see you the end of the semester. I promise."

"Promises, promises." She paused. Her little boy

was all grown up. He didn't need her anymore. "You really want to go scuba diving?"

"Yeah. It'll be awesome, Mom."

"You won't get bitten by alligators."

"This is saltwater, Mom. Alligators live in fresh water, in the Everglades."

"Okay, sharks, then."

"No sharks, Mom. We'll be careful."

She didn't want to leave him feeling guilty about not spending time with her. After all, he was eighteen. Old enough to vote. A man. He shouldn't feel obligated to spend time with his mommy. "Will you send me a postcard?"

"Absolutely. Some pictures, too."

"Okay, kid. Have a good time."

"Thanks, Mom. You're the greatest."

Oh, honey, I wish I were. I wish I could be all you deserve of your mama.

TEN DAYS LATER Schneider was back with his report. "You didn't tell me you went to high school together," he commented dryly.

Kneading the upholstered arms of his executive leather chair, Craig leaned against its high back. "Briefly. She was a class behind me."

Schneider nodded. "So you know she's the daughter of Adam First, who owned the Number One Ranch."

Craig waved him to the chair across the desk. "Past tense?" This sounded like it might take a while.

The P.I. removed a small notebook from his inside coat pocket and balanced it on his massive thigh. "The drought of the fifties forced Kerry's grandfather to cede forty-five percent interest in the ranch to the Homestead Bank and Trust. Of the remaining fifty-five percent, Adam retained thirty and gave each of his five children five percent ownership.''

Schneider crossed his legs. Characteristically, he didn't bother to refer to the notes in his hand. ''Three years ago, the youngest son was killed in a car accident. Adam and his four surviving children split his share, each receiving an additional one percent. So Mrs. Durgan had six percent ownership—''

Craig held up a hand. ''Al, hang on a minute. Did you say Mrs. Durgan?''

''She uses First in her public life, but her legal name is still Durgan,'' Schneider confirmed. ''Her husband's name was—''

''Rafael,'' Craig said. ''I remember him. He was a senior the same time I was, though he was a year or two older.''

So she'd married the son of a bitch. Craig was surprised by the violence of his reaction. Could she have loved the leather-jacketed hoodlum? Her running off with him that night had seemed more like a lark, an act of rebellion, than one of romantic devotion. Could Rafe Durgan have been a better guy than people thought?

''You used the past tense again.''

''They divorced fifteen years ago,'' Schneider said. ''Seems he was physically abusive. He was killed a few years later when a car he'd stolen crashed and burned.''

Physically abusive. That explained her interest in

setting up a foundation for battered women. With all her advantages, life hadn't been so easy, after all.

"According to my sources," Schneider went on, "she wasn't the one who wanted the divorce. Apparently her father forced it, threatened to have their son, Brian, removed from their custody if she didn't file papers. Mrs. Durgan never forgave him. When she sold her six percent interest in the ranch to the bank, Adam First lost control of the place."

Craig's brows lifted. "She sold out her own father?" His jaw tightened at the depth of her hatred. Yet, Craig asked himself, wasn't he guilty of worse?

Schneider nodded. "By then she was drinking pretty heavily."

"Drinking?" Craig's insides sagged, his thoughts zeroing in on the past. Had she been drinking that night? He knew one of the punch bowls had been spiked, and he'd been very careful he served her the untainted variety. The last thing he wanted was a drunken date on his hands, or being accused of getting her that way.

"A little while after the bank took over," Schneider continued, "a tornado ripped through the ranch. Kerry was injured, though not seriously. While she was in the hospital, however, her son apparently put pressure on her to go into rehab. She went to Betty Ford's, came out, fell off the wagon a few months later and returned for a second session."

Unconsciously, Craig closed his eyes. Not just a drinker, but an alcoholic.

"That's not unusual," Schneider explained. "About three months after taking the pledge, recovering alcoholics often try to prove they're cured by having another drink. Just one. The rest, of course, are inevitable, since the first shot deadens the frontal lobe, which controls good judgment. That was over a year ago. She's been dry ever since.''

Yeah, but for how long? She'd stuck to mineral water and coffee at the TV station. But then, she didn't have much choice. Did she have a private stock of gin—or more likely vodka, since it was odorless—stashed away somewhere? In her purse? The ladies' room? Alcoholics could be ingenious in hiding their addiction and their booze.

''How much blood money did she get for her sellout?''

The investigator raised an eyebrow at his boss's choice of words and pinched his lower lip between his fingers. ''Fifty million.''

Craig whistled. ''Not bad. How has her father handled the situation?'' He remembered Adam First very well from his two brief meetings with him the night of the prom. He seemed like the kind of man Craig had always wanted for a father. Or had that been a facade? Harry Robeson, too, had been a charmer to his neighbors.

''A few months later, the old man sold his thirty-one percent to the bank for cash and clear title to his great-great-grandfather's original sixty-thousand-acre land grant. From all indications, he cut a pretty good deal. Took all the competition horses, a share of the cattle and had a provision written into the contract that gave him first option on the sale of any of the remaining Number One property.''

An astute businessman, Craig decided. "Has he exercised the option?"

Schneider crossed an ankle over the other knee. "The bank hasn't offered any land yet, but word is they're about to. The drought is taking its toll on the cattle business."

If Adam didn't exercise his option, Craig decided he'd explore buying a chunk of the Number One himself. He didn't know how much would be offered or what rights would go with it, but the location might be perfect for a retirement community à la Sun City.

"What else can you tell me about Kerry *Durgan?*"

"She's on the board of a homeless shelter and a charity hospital, but they're essentially sinecures—not much to do but rubber-stamp management decisions."

"No practical experience?"

"Some. Mostly at a soup kitchen. She works there on weekends and has a reputation for being very generous and a good listener."

"Handouts?"

"Occasionally."

A soft touch, Craig concluded. "And her personal life?"

"She never remarried. Has an eighteen-year-old son attending Texas Tech."

"How do they get along?" The relationship between a child and an alcoholic parent was inevitably complicated. Some children rejected their parents at the first opportunity. Others felt bound to them in a pact of guilt.

"Pretty well. He had a drinking problem of his own about a year and a half ago but appears to have overcome it. He's a good student, goes to the usual parties on campus but sticks to soft drinks now.''

Call it nature or nurture, the truth was that alcoholism was often passed from one generation to another.

"What about her friends?''

"Charlene Higgins, who's a consultant for the Hawthorne Hotel chain, seems to be her closest friend. She's also a paid adviser to Mrs. Durgan for this foundation she's establishing.''

Craig suppressed a smile. So Kerry's battered-wife poster girl was a successful businesswoman. He wondered if the mousy victim wardrobe and demeanor was her idea or Leslie Fischer's.

"Aside from Higgins, Mrs. Durgan keeps pretty much to herself,'' Schneider went on. "No men in her life that we've been able to discover.''

After the private investigator left, Craig mulled over the report he'd received on Kerry. He was still attracted to her physically. There was no denying it, and he acknowledged that his curiosity about her went beyond her obvious beauty. Even in high school, he'd been enthralled by the mysterious person behind the carefree affability. Despite the tension of their meeting at the TV station, that hadn't changed.

Nonetheless, his inclination to get involved with her was radically altered. He didn't like what he'd heard about her selling her share of the family ranch. It had the ring of pure malice. He would have given her the benefit of the doubt temporarily, however, if not for the other, more devastating aspect of her personality. She was an alcoholic.

Having lived with one, he knew how selfish and

self-absorbed they were. How much they lied. How mentally and physically cruel they could be. He would never willingly entangle himself with an alcoholic. Never. Any secret hope he might have entertained that he and Kerry might, after all these years, get to know each other better was completely shattered.

CHAPTER THREE

SEVERAL WEEKS went by, and Kerry found herself caught up in the complex world of establishing a major enterprise. She realized Craig was being diplomatic when he said her plan to open her first shelter in ninety days was ambitious. *Impossible* would have been a more accurate term. Giving herself away as so naive was annoying, but it didn't discourage her. On the contrary, it ignited a fire. With Charlene's help, she put together a small staff to deal with aggravating government agencies and bureaucratic regulations while she redoubled her efforts to find a suitable property for her shelter. She probably should have called on Craig Robeson, but pride made her want to pull off the deal herself. Having never been a businesswoman, she was only now beginning to understand the attraction, excitement and incredible sense of achievement in meeting a challenge.

And for perhaps the first time in her life, she was beginning to feel good about herself. Her days were filled with activities that gave her a sense of purpose and satisfaction, and in the evenings, when she was alone, the reclusive part of her was able to lean back and be content. At the age of thirty-five, she was finally growing up.

On this particular Saturday morning, she shunned the professional attire of suit or dress that had become a kind of uniform. Today she wouldn't be working but relaxing on an old-fashioned train to Fort Worth. Casual was appropriate. She pulled on a pair of stone-washed black jeans and was surprised when she didn't have to suck in her belly to button them. In spite of business lunches and fast-food meals on the run, she was managing to keep the weight off. The aerobics sessions she attended three times a week probably helped. She'd hated calisthenics in high school and had sworn she'd never do them again, yet now she was paying a personal trainer to watch her sweat her buns off.

She twirled in front of the full-length mirror in her dressing room. Well, maybe the exercises were worth it. They were pretty nice buns. Not that her figure made any difference. For all her socializing, there hadn't been a man in her life in years.

After buttoning her blouse and putting on slender turquoise drop earrings, she called downstairs and asked to have her car brought around. She enjoyed driving the Ferrari she'd treated herself to, enjoyed snaking around crowded freeways and the city streets of the sprawling Metroplex. Assuming traffic kept moving and she wasn't stopped for speeding, it shouldn't take her more than half an hour to get to Grapevine, twenty miles away.

The railroad station was a small turn-of-the-century wood-frame building with characteristic overhanging hip roof and tall, narrow windows. A vintage 1896 steam locomotive, complete with cowcatcher and smokestack, hissed and fumed at the head of a special four-coach Tarantula excursion train. The eighteen-mile track leading to the Fort Worth Stockyard area was a mere remnant of the spokelike web of rail lines converging on what had once been the nation's cattle Mecca.

Kerry greeted several people she recognized and found a seat in one of the passenger coaches. The rich decor of polished wood and shiny brass fixtures harked back to an age of seeming gentility. That this luxurious ambience had only been experienced by a select few was all but forgotten in the passage of time, and perhaps that was just as well.

"Good morning."

She turned from the raised window at the sound of a man's voice and knew even before she looked who it was. Her pulse quickened, and she felt a strange tremor ripple through her. Not an unpleasant sensation, but one that was decidedly unanticipated.

"Hello, Craig."

He smiled, and his dimples flashed in the sunlight slanting through the windows as the train began to roll away from the station. "May I join you?"

She extended her hand in invitation and watched him slide onto the seat across from her. He, too, was wearing jeans, subtly faded blue denim that hugged his narrow hips and muscular thighs. The black knit polo shirt wasn't tight, but it couldn't disguise the breadth of his shoulders or the thick contours of his chest. A few dark hairs peeked over the V of the collar. Altogether a very distracting man. Kerry felt uneasy about wanting to stare for the pure pleasure of it.

"I have to admit," she observed, "I didn't expect to see you here."

The train had been specially chartered to take wealthy contributors to Fort Worth for a day of shopping. The proceeds from the thousand-dollar price of the ticket, roughly five hundred times the normal fee, went to a rehabilitation center for crippled children.

He grinned, making the dimples flash. "I support a variety of worthwhile causes."

She studied him critically. The jeans weren't designer. There was no chic monogram on the shirt. But she already knew it wasn't the clothes that made this man, and it was definitely the man that made her feel defenseless and vulnerable.

"White knight to the rescue?"

Unfazed by the hint of sarcasm, he chuckled, a deep throaty sound that conjured up images of intimacy, of touching, of tasting. Of sex.

"Don Quixote." He bowed grandly forward from the waist. "At your service. I'm also a sucker for trains." Still smiling, he added, "They've got things to drink in the next car. Would you care for something?"

A mimosa, champagne and orange juice. Heavy on the bubbly. "A cup of coffee would be nice," she said.

The touring coach was an open-air car that imparted a nostalgic sense of adventurous travel. The train didn't reach modern speeds, and the breeze blowing in was gentle and invigorating. The clack-clack of the wheels on the tracks and the throb of the old steam piston engine set a soothing rhythm. Time slowed but didn't stop, like the unconcerned tick of a grandfather clock.

A white-jacketed waiter brought them a tray with a silver pot, two china cups and saucers and a dish of dainty butter cookies.

"Do you go on train trips very often?" Craig asked after the waiter had moved on to serve someone else.

She laughed. "Hardly. My parents took me on one when I was a little girl. They said they wanted me to have the experience before the iron horse went the way of the buggy whip. We boarded in Coyote Springs and rode all the way to Dallas. It seemed to take forever. We stopped a lot, in Abilene and a bunch of small towns. I can still remember my father hoisting me onto his shoulders as we made our way among the crowds at the end of the line. I kept gazing up at the skylights and feeling as if I were floating. The inside of the Dallas terminal was an adventure in itself, as colorful as a circus because of the sun shining directly on the stained-glass windows."

It was all a long time ago. A lot had happened since then. Kerry tried to fold the fond memories away. Another world. Another age. She wouldn't dwell on it.

Craig sipped the steaming coffee. "What've you been doing since high school?"

She stirred cream into her cup and narrowed her eyes, her lips smiling. "If you read the article in the *Dallas Morning News*—"

"Newspapers tend to distort things. I'd like to hear it from your perspective."

Kerry regarded him curiously, sensing a hint of censure in his challenge, as if he were asking her to justify herself. Or perhaps it was her paranoia.

"I'm divorced."

"From Rafael Durgan."

"The marriage was a mistake." She placed the spoon on the saucer and lifted the cup between her fingertips. "It lasted only a few years," she said before taking a sip.

"That's too bad," he said, and quickly added, "but you have a son."

"Brian." She regretted *how* she'd conceived her one and only child, but she didn't regret *that* she had. "He's a freshman at Tech."

"My alma mater," Craig noted in a kind of disbelief. "The time has flown, hasn't it? But you didn't go to Tech. I would have seen you there. So where did you go? The newspaper article didn't mention."

She could use her normal evasions, change the subject or make something up, but for some unaccountable reason, she didn't want to with this man. "I didn't go to college, Craig. In fact, I didn't even finish high school." A few years ago, she would have said she never missed it, that it didn't matter, but she'd matured enough to know it wasn't true.

"Why not?" he asked.

She couldn't decide if it was surprise or disappointment in his expression.

"You were one of the smartest kids in school, though I suspect you didn't study much." He offered her a smile to take some of the sting out of his words. "You could have been accepted anywhere if you'd put your mind to it, and your father certainly had the money to send you to the best.''

Deep-seated guilt rocketed through her. ''If you must know, I dropped out of school because I was pregnant. A good old-fashioned shotgun wedding followed.''

''I'm sorry.''

''No need for you to be.'' *It wasn't your fault I ditched you at the prom,* she wanted to tell him, but acknowledging it to herself and saying it to the man she'd humiliated were different matters. ''Nobody could see the good in him, but I did.'' She lowered her voice. ''He's dead now, killed when he crashed a car he'd stolen. That was a couple of years after our divorce.''

''I'm sorry,'' Craig repeated softly.

''Stop apologizing. It has nothing to do with you.'' She paused long enough to get rising emotions under control. ''The truth is Rafe was neither a good husband nor a good father,'' she said more temperately.

Craig narrowed his gaze. ''What I meant was that I'm sorry he hurt you,'' he explained. ''Was he violent? Is that why you're setting up your foundation?''

Kerry took a steadying breath and withdrew defensively into the brocade-upholstered seat. ''If you must know, yes.''

''You avoided discussing it on the air. Too bad. It would have gained you a lot of sympathy and probably garnered more contributions.''

Her jaw dropped. She wasn't looking for pity, and the idea of baring her soul to strangers was terrifying.

Baring it to a friend was almost as bad, and this man was certainly not a friend.

"I consider my private life to be just that, Craig. Private. And the response to our appeal has been very good."

He nodded without taking offense at her tone and sipped his coffee. "You ought to get your GED and go to college. It's never too late, you know. I think you'd do well. You obviously enjoy a challenge." When she made no comment, he asked, "What's Brian taking in school, or hasn't he decided yet?"

Kerry's mood lightened. "At the moment he has his heart set on becoming an architect, but I suppose that could change."

Craig laughed. "The math may dissuade him."

"Actually, he was always pretty good at numbers. Didn't do particularly well in his other subjects, but took to geometry."

"That's certainly a point in his favor. But why architecture? Why not one of the other sciences?"

"He helped his grandfather and uncles rebuild the old homestead on the ranch last year and really enjoyed it."

"Point two in his favor—practical experience. Does he have any idea what he would like to specialize in? Residential, commercial, institutional?"

Kerry sipped her coffee, then carefully placed the cup on its saucer. "I doubt he's thought that far ahead."

Craig shrugged. "He's got time. I wish him well. We can always use good architects."

They rode on, past Colleyville toward North Richland Hills, once known as Smithfield.

"Charlene tells me you're not married," Kerry commented.

His hazel eyes twinkled with amusement, maybe because she had the audacity to pry after so vehemently demanding her right to privacy. "No, never have."

"Why? There must have been plenty of candidates auditioning for the job."

He threw back his head and laughed, apparently not in the least offended by her blatantly indiscreet statement. "Are you a cynic, Kerry, or are you calling me a womanizer?"

She had the decency to look away, at least for a moment. But she'd gone this far on the road to honesty. No point in retreating now. "Maybe a little of both," she admitted with a grin.

The dimples remained in place. "I've met a few women I thought I might like to share my life with—"

"But it didn't work out," she concluded for him.

"Let's say we discovered our incompatibilities in time."

"Was your money a factor?"

"In one case."

"And the others?"

He shrugged. "Religion. Politics. Careers."

"You make marriage sound like a merger rather than a matter of love. Was there never a fire, a need?"

He pursed his lips and gazed up at the ceiling. "There were sparks, but no fire. A desire, but no need."

"That's too bad."

They chugged on for another half mile. Craig finally broke the silence. "Did you love him? Rafael, I mean."

She'd left herself wide open for this and should have seen it coming. She surveyed the suburban countryside going by, as if all the middle-class homes with their basketball hoops over garage doors and bicycles scattered in the middle of driveways held a hint to the secret of love and happily ever after.

"I wanted to," she admitted. "Our marriage wasn't all boozing and fighting. There were moments...." She paused, unwilling to reveal too much of herself, to confess that sometimes she thought she saw genuine affection in Rafe—the good part of his soul that she was never able to completely draw out. Maybe if she hadn't trapped him—if her father hadn't forced him to marry her—Rafe could have entrusted her with his better nature. But he never had.

Another silence fell.

"Can I ask you something?" Kerry inquired.

"Sure," he said brightly, but he was studying her.

"I know you're a busy man, Craig. So why did you come to the TV station last month?"

One corner of his mouth curved up, revealing those killer dimples. "I guess you don't realize how charismatic you are." He slanted her a crooked grin, then chuckled softly. "There's no mysterious agenda, Kerry. I wanted to see you."

"Why?"

Amusement played across his features. He shrugged almost shyly. "For old times' sake."

She wasn't sure if it was a statement or a question. "And your being on this train today?"

"I told you," he said with a wide grin. "I'm a sucker for choo-choos."

Kerry laughed to hide her disappointment that he didn't say again that he wanted to see her. "From what I've heard, you could probably buy this or any other train if you really enjoyed hearing the whistle blow."

He arched a brow. "A slight exaggeration."

"Not according to my sources. I know you're a generous contributor to various charities. Is there a special reason you're interested in this one?"

"It's a good cause," he replied blandly.

"And that's all?"

"My reasons are complicated," he said, "and like yours, private."

Having skirted his probing with a plea for privacy, she could hardly reject his.

She raised the cup to her lips and sipped the cooling brew. She could feel him watching her.

He waited until she returned the cup to the saucer. "I understand you sold your share of the Number One Ranch."

Kerry's growing sense of comfort and goodwill shattered like a piece of glass. "How did you hear about that?"

"Meeting you after Leslie's show piqued my curiosity," he said, apparently unfazed by the change in her tone.

"You...you've been spying on me?" she sputtered.

"Spying, no, but I have been doing some research."

Kerry's discomfort shifted to annoyance and was

well on its way to anger. "I don't like people checking up on me, Craig. My personal life is none of your business."

He seemed unmoved by her outburst. She wondered if he ever got angry. Even when she had walked away from him at the prom, he hadn't shown the kind of fury she would have expected. He'd run across the lawn after her, but when Rafe burned rubber getting out of there, Craig hadn't stomped the ground or tried to pursue. Yet the concept of passivity didn't match the image of the man sitting across from her, and it certainly didn't jibe with his becoming a multimillionaire on his own initiative. So, what did make Craig Robeson tick? What stirred his juices, got him excited? And how dangerous was he when that happened?

"Not checking up, Kerry," he said mildly. "I'm not your father or your husband, and I haven't been spying. No one is following you around and chronicling your every move. Matters of public record aren't too difficult to uncover."

Her pulse was accelerating. "It's still none of your business. What was the point of asking me all these questions if you already knew the answers?"

"I've upset you," he said with detached calm. "That wasn't my intent. All I know is that you sold your share of the ancestral ranch, and I wondered how your father and the rest of the family felt about it."

Heartbeat drumming, she glared at him, agitated by his direct assault. "For your information, Craig, my father's forgiven me and is living quite happily on the Home Place, and I get along fine with the rest of my family."

"The subject makes you uncomfortable," he said, "so let's drop it."

His easy dismissal of the matter only served to infuriate her more. If they weren't on a moving train she would get up and walk away. She could still move to another car, she realized, but it would look petty rather than final.

They lapsed into silence as the train slowed and glided into the station in Fort Worth. Neither made a move to rise until it had stopped completely.

"I know you don't like apologies, but I do offer one for upsetting you," he said.

She would have preferred him to leave her alone, but he was forcing her to respond. With a small shrug, she said, "Let's forget about it, shall we?"

He stood up from his seat and held out his hand to her. She accepted it. So simple an act shouldn't have an effect on her, but it did. She liked the tug of his large, strong fingers, the sensation of his skin touching hers. Awareness left her shaken and uncertain.

"If you can tolerate my company for the next hour and a half," he said as they walked to the door at the end of the car, "perhaps we can see the sights together."

She wondered why he would be interested in *her* company. She'd made a fool of him when they were younger and recently rejected what she now knew was an overture to support her foundation. Clearly, he didn't approve of her selling her share of the family ranch. Yet he still wanted to be with her. Why? And why did she want him along? He was very nice to look at, no question about that. But there was an indefinable something else, a quality that went beyond his being an attractive male and made him an intriguing man.

THEY DISEMBARKED onto a platform at the Fort Worth Stockyard Station, a monstrous terminal that had once furnished temporary housing for cattle, sheep and hogs. Those days were gone. The aromas that greeted travelers today were those of fine restaurants and boutiques. The Western theme was everywhere, for this was where the West began.

After wandering in the shops and pavilions, they stepped into an art gallery and stared at an imitation of a Remington oil painting of cowboys and Indians.

"Do you miss the ranch?" he asked, not sure if he was igniting another explosion.

"Nope. Not even a little bit," she insisted. He wondered if she protested too vehemently. "My mother was a city girl. I must have inherited her genes."

"Apparently. Do you ever go back?"

"No," she mumbled, and sidestepped to another painting, this one of a prickly pear cactus in bloom. "Do you miss Coyote Springs?"

"We moved around a lot, so it wasn't really a hometown for me," he answered evasively. "Maybe one day my travels will take me back there."

They were standing in front of a stone pedestal on which stood a life-size bronze sculpture of a cowboy in chaps holding a lariat at his side, gazing into the distance.

"Do you think he's looking at the horizon or the cow that got away?" she asked.

"Hard to tell, isn't it?" He flashed a grin that added an extra beat to her pulse.

He extended his arm and was about to place it gently on the small of her back and usher her to other paintings and sculptures, when she turned abruptly and glanced at him.

"Let's go somewhere else."

"Is something wrong?"

"I'm just not in the mood for cowboys right now."

It had been her idea to come here. He wondered what had happened to make her uncomfortable, because she definitely was.

"How 'bout the zoo?" He wagged his eyebrows. "Up to some monkey business?"

She laughed as they retraced their steps to the main entrance. "How about the snake house?"

"Sounds fascinating—as long as they're behind glass. Thick glass."

But there wasn't enough time before their return trip, so they drifted without any discernible aim or pattern among concession stands. He bought them frozen custards, and they continued their stroll. They didn't talk about anything personal. Not about the family ranch or battered women or charity drives. He talked a little about some of the places he'd been. She mentioned places she wanted to go.

At last, they climbed aboard the train. They could have spent the hour's leisurely trip discussing almost anything. Instead, they were perfectly content to ride in silence, occasionally catching the other's eye and smiling.

"It's been a very enjoyable day," Kerry said when

they reached the quaint little station in Grapevine. "Thank you for sharing it with me."

"My pleasure."

The moment lingered, neither of them quite sure how to say the final goodbye—or perhaps unwilling to.

Finally, Kerry wet her lips with the tip of her tongue. "I don't know if you already have plans for this evening...but if you don't, would you like to join me for dinner?" She gave him a self-deprecating smile. "I'm not much of a cook, but perhaps we could go out somewhere."

Craig took a moment to consider her offer. He had a stack of paperwork on his desk at home and he always made his duty call to his mother on Saturday evenings. "Thank you for the offer," he told her, "but I'm afraid I can't make it tonight."

She seemed disappointed and a little embarrassed at being turned down, or was it relief? "Perhaps another time, then."

He handed her into her sports car and waved goodbye, then wedged himself into his Saab. Spending an evening with Kerry Durgan might have been pleasant, so why had he refused her invitation? He knew why. Because he was afraid. Of getting too close. Of admitting she still did crazy things to his nervous system. Afraid she would hurt him again.

KERRY WAS more disheartened at having her invitation rejected than she was willing to admit. Craig Robeson intrigued her, and she would have liked being with him again. After their initial testy moments, they'd settled into a pleasant companionship. Did he really have something to do tonight or did he just not want to spend any more time with her?

She pulled into the circular driveway of her luxury condominium and stopped under the concrete awning. The doorman stepped out of the lobby and opened her vehicle door.

"Good evening, Mrs. Durgan. Will you be needing the car again?"

"Hello, Earl. No. You can put it away." She left the keys in the ignition.

He darted ahead of her and opened the glass door to the lobby.

"Were there any messages or visitors?" she asked. She didn't feel like being alone tonight. Maybe Charlene had called to say her kids were out for the evening, and they could go to dinner and maybe a movie.

"No, ma'am, not today."

"Good," she commented as she walked to the elevator. "It'll be nice to have nothing to do for a change."

"Yes, ma'am. Have a pleasant evening."

She thanked him and inserted her card into the slot for the penthouse. On the way up, she contemplated what to do for dinner. She didn't feel like cooking, and her maid was off on Saturday night. A quiche from the freezer, followed by a long, soaking bath, then one of the movies she'd bought but hadn't gotten around to watching yet, sounded good.

The elevator door opened, and she stepped into the foyer. There were two penthouse apartments. She used her plastic key to enter the one on the left. The hall lights inside were on. She was sure she'd turned them off. Maybe Evelyn had come by for some reason. That would explain it. The doorman wouldn't bother to mention the maid.

Snorting at her stupid paranoia, she deposited her bag on the side table, stepped into the living room and stopped dead in her tracks.

Lounging casually on the couch, a smile creasing his dark face, was her late husband, Rafe Durgan.

CHAPTER FOUR

KERRY STAGGERED down the three carpeted steps into the sunken living room to the chair opposite her dead husband. Digging her fingers into the knobby dark green upholstery, she stared at him openmouthed.

"But..." She gulped.

"Hello, babe." He held up a half-filled old-fashioned glass in a salute and gave her an alligator grin over the rim.

"But..." she repeated. She hung on to the back of the chair like a drunken sailor in a storm-tossed lifeboat, moved around and sank into its soft cushions. "But you're dead," she finally managed to enunciate.

His skin was weathered to a burnished bronze. He'd put on weight, and there were distinct lines fanning from the corners of his eyes. He sported a full, bushy mustache. Only his pitch-black hair was as she remembered it—thick and lustrous. But the man before her was Rafe Durgan. There was no mistaking his eyes. Dark. Mysterious. Dangerous. They'd once excited her. Now they made her stomach churn with fear.

"Oh, baby." He smiled and gazed at her with what might have been affection. "I assure you," he said lecherously, "there ain't no part of me that's dead.

Flesh and blood, *querida*. Every bit of me. I've missed you.''

Kerry tried desperately to focus, to think coherently, but the man sitting across from her in black jeans, black T-shirt and scuffed black boots had her heart racing out of control. She'd put this man behind her a dozen years ago. A piece of her heart had mourned him—no, not him so much as her fatal attraction to him. He'd taken his pleasure from her and given her pain in return.

She'd hated herself that Monday morning when Daddy showed up at their house on the Number One Ranch to check up on his grandson. She'd called the day before to say she and Brian weren't coming to Sunday dinner as usual because the baby was running a fever. It wasn't true, but she couldn't admit to her father that her husband had beat her the previous evening in a drunken rage. She'd despised her weakness in letting him treat her with such contempt, but what alternative did she have when he threatened to hurt her baby, their son? She would endure anything to protect the child she'd borne. She knew she should have gone to her father the first time it happened, but she was too humiliated. And the longer she delayed, the more difficult it became. When Adam First arrived that morning, he found her cut and bruised. He rescued her and Brian, and she rewarded her father by making him the victim of her unbearable guilt.

''Are you glad to see me, *corazón?*''

When had he started speaking Spanish? she wondered.

''What happened?'' Her voice was a near whisper.

She forced air into her lungs, held it there and released it. Her heart was still thumping but at a more steady rate. "They said you were killed in a car accident," she added more firmly. "The police identified your body."

He stood up and stretched. The ice in his glass tinkled musically. His T-shirt was sweat-stained under the arms. The worn cotton pulled against a wide chest that was thicker than she remembered. Where had he been? In prison where he worked out with weights every day? Or had he received his deep tan as a laborer toiling in the sun?

"Nice place you've got here."

How did he get in? The doorman said there had been no visitors. She would have to talk to Evelyn. Perhaps she'd let him in through the service entrance. No, her housekeeper wouldn't admit a stranger into the house or go out and leave him here alone.

"Answer my question," she demanded. "What happened in the car accident? Whose body was it and how did they identify it as yours?"

He lowered his arms and sucked in a belly that wasn't nearly as firm as it had once been. Obviously feeling very good about himself, he stared at her with a smirk and said, "Become pushy now that you've moved away from Daddy, haven't you?"

Her mouth was suddenly dry. She needed a drink and was tempted to go to the bar and pour herself a generous shot of bourbon. But no. She wouldn't let this ghost drag her down to the depths she'd struggled so hard to crawl out of.

Rafe's white teeth flashed. "Not the sweet, compliant little mouse so eager to please you used to be."

Kerry almost sputtered. The image shocked her nearly as much as his presence. She'd never thought of herself as sweet, much less compliant or mousy. She'd been a rebel, defying her father, flaunting her independence, her strength and individuality.

Rafe tossed off the last drops in his glass and strolled to the wet bar by the bookcases. He lifted a bottle of Scotch and examined the label. "First class," he noted with approval, then snickered at the pun on her maiden name. It was an old joke. He seemed to never tire of reminding her that she was no longer a First, that he'd reduced her to his social level.

He put the whiskey back. "Never did like that highbrow stuff. I'll take cactus juice every time." He picked up the already open bottle of tequila and raised it to eye level. "No dead worm. I'm disappointed in you, babe."

A current of panic shot through her. She remembered those words too well. They were often the prelude to savage terror.

He poured a couple of ounces into the crystal glass and started to the couch. "Oops, where are my manners?" He paused and gave her an ingratiating smile. "Can I get you something, sweetheart?"

She took a deep breath, not sure if it was his presence or the offer of a drink that had her pulse racing. "No, thanks."

He swallowed a mouthful of the yellowish liquor, his eyes squinting at her over the rim. "Betty Ford's really did a number on you, huh? Too bad."

How did he know about her rehab? But she dismissed the question almost immediately. He'd found her here, so he obviously knew a lot about her.

"I always enjoyed a good drunk with you," he added with a narrow-eyed sneer. "That's when you were at your best in bed, babe. Going at me every way but Sunday."

Kerry wanted with all her heart to close her eyes against the image his words provoked. She couldn't deny they'd shared some exciting sex, but they'd never made love. He'd stimulated her flesh and brought her to physical climax, but he'd always left her feeling empty rather than fulfilled, used instead of pleasured.

"You still haven't answered my question," she reminded him sternly.

The grin he gave her this time was one of pure lechery. "You know, I think I like the new you better than the old one. More spunk, more fight. I like a woman who puts up some resistance. Bet now you'd be a real tiger."

He still knew how to use words to make her feel small, like a thing instead of a human being.

"Who was in the car, Rafe?" Maybe a specific question would distract him from his current line of thought.

"A buddy." He said the word reverently with a faraway look in his eyes. She'd never thought of Rafe as sentimental, but that was the only word she could think of to describe the change that seemed to suddenly come over him. "You remember José?" he asked softly.

She nodded. A skinny kid a couple of years younger than Rafe. He was shy and reticent and spoke with a stammer. He also bore several scars, purportedly bequeathed by his sadistic mother and uncle. José had seemed an unlikely companion for Rafe, yet whenever they were together, Rafe had treated him like a kid brother.

"I sponsored him into the Sabers, so we both had the tattoo." He pulled up the sleeve of his shirt and revealed the crossed swords behind the skull on the tip of his shoulder. It had been a turn-on once. It struck her now as juvenile and ridiculous.

"That doesn't explain why his body was identified as yours. What made them think he was you?"

Rafe resumed his seat on the couch and propped his legs on the shiny coffee table. "Evidence," he murmured, then seemed to break out of his reverie. He emitted a vicious laugh. "I guess you could call it circumstantial evidence."

He took another swallow of tequila, and Kerry realized he didn't so much savor its taste as need its analgesic effect. For a moment, there was a haunted expression in his eyes.

"We'd hot-wired this new Suburban and were taking it to Mexico. Good market for SUVs down there," he told her. "José was driving. Or trying to. I guess he'd had a little too much beer. He hit a telephone pole. Got himself impaled on the steering column."

Rafe sampled a smaller, more thoughtful taste of his tequila. Again, he seemed to take several seconds to snap out of his melancholia.

He chortled. "For one of the few times in my life,

I happened to be wearing my seat belt. Remember how you always used to bug me about it?'' He hoisted the drink in a toast. "You saved my life, babe." Grinning, he sipped again, then rested the glass on his thigh. "Naturally, I was a little shook up, but not hurt."

He raised the heavy crystal glass once more, apparently fascinated by its sparkling facets. "It took me a few minutes, but then I figured out what I had to do. We were on a deserted road at night. Not a soul around and probably wouldn't be for several hours. It was simple, really. I removed poor, dead José's wallet and gave him mine. Then I cleaned out everything that could be traced to him. Setting the wreck on fire was the scary part. I was sure the damn thing was going to blow up and take me with it."

He polished off the rest of the tequila and went to the bar to replenish it. "Fortunately, I was able to get a good quarter of a mile away before the van finally exploded," he said over his shoulder, then wheeled around and leaned on the counter to face her.

"Between the fire and the explosion, I guess there wasn't too much left of him to make a positive identification, except for my driver's license in his hip pocket and the tattoo on his shoulder."

Kerry shuddered. She'd told Craig only hours ago that she'd seen something redeeming in Rafe. Now she wondered. What demons and angels possessed a man that he would love a friend, then use his body in such a calculated fashion? "Where have you been all this time?"

"Moved down to old Mexico."

She wished he'd stayed there. Her life was complicated enough without Rafael Durgan coming back into it. "How did you find out that I live here?"

He beamed. "Hey, babe, if you want to hide, you shouldn't let them put your picture in the Sunday paper. Good picture, too. I cut it out and taped it over my bed."

The image wasn't one she wanted to dwell on. As soon as she got rid of him, she'd have to take a long, hot shower. Maybe two. "I bet your girlfriends love that," she muttered, and instantly regretted it. His female companions were none of her concern, and it wasn't wise to give him ammunition to use against her, as he instantly did.

"Jealous, babe?"

She jumped to her feet, took a few steps away from the chair and spun to face him squarely. "What are you doing here, Rafe?" she demanded. "What do you want?"

His eyes crinkled with merriment. "What do you think?" When she didn't respond, he said, "Money, of course."

She wasn't surprised. "You've wasted your time."

"A husband and wife are supposed to share things. Fifty-fifty."

She strode to the bar, reached into the under-the-counter refrigerator and removed a bottle of spring water. The initial shock of Rafe's return was wearing off, replaced with anger and outrage, which always gave her strength. She unscrewed the plastic cap with a vicious twist. "We're not husband and wife. We were divorced a long time ago."

"Not in the eyes of the church."

It was her turn to laugh, and she did, barely managing to cut it short before hysteria took over. "We weren't married in church, remember?" She almost added, *Because I couldn't wear a white dress.*

He climbed to his feet and moved close to her, his eyes narrowed, his full lips pouted ever so slightly. It had been a playful expression when they'd been together. He probably still expected it to turn her on. "It doesn't matter." He ran a finger along the side of her jaw. "We swore before God in the company of witnesses to have and to hold till death do us part."

She slapped his hand away. "You forgot the part about love, honor and cherish." She nearly shouted, retreating a pace. "You sure as hell didn't do much of that."

Clearly pleased that her composure was beginning to crack, he smirked. She inhaled deeply and faced him, her eyes locked on his. "You're not getting a nickel from me, Rafe. Not now. Not ever. I don't know how you got in here, but I suggest you get the hell out before I call the cops."

She should have been prepared for the blow, but she wasn't. His meaty, callused hand sprang up so quickly she didn't have time to react. The slap came hard across her face, sending her staggering. His other hand grabbed her firmly by the forearm, his fingers curling painfully into her flesh. When she instinctively squirmed to get away from him, he tightened his grip and pulled her against his body. She could smell the liquor on his breath, the musky stench of unwashed flesh. Bile rose, filling her mouth.

"Let's get a few things straight, sweetheart." He

twisted her arm enough to make her wince. "I'm in charge here, not you. You can forget about calling the cops, too. I'm dead, remember? I don't exist. I have no record." He placed his free hand on the side of her neck. "The statute of limitations ran out on them old warrants a long time ago." He sneered and pushed her away.

She bumped against the side of a chair, clung to it and crawled spider-like around it to sit down. She looked up, wishing there wasn't fear in her eyes, knowing there was. From his feral expression, she could tell he knew he'd frightened her. It only added to his enjoyment.

Still watching her, he picked up his glass, took a drink, then strolled around the room. He examined a carved jade box and studied an amorphous sculpture of swirling pink and gray granite with as much disdain as curiosity.

"You got fifty mil for your share of your daddy's ranch. I want half."

She sat up straighter and rubbed her arm where he'd held her. There'd be a bruise tomorrow. Already she could see the skin discoloring. "Rafe, you—" She was about to say he must be crazy to think she'd give him that kind of money. But maybe he *was* crazy. Maybe the years of rough living and hard drinking had destroyed enough brain cells that he was no longer capable of rational thought. "Rafe, be reasonable. There's no way I can give you that kind of money without raising suspicions."

"Suspicions of what? You're setting up your own

charity thing, right? Well, babe, it's time to be charitable to your dear hubby.''

''Ex-husband,'' she reminded him. It was a small
defiance, but she was hell-bent on regaining some
semblance of self-respect.

He snickered. ''Whatever, sweetheart.'' His voice
took on a cold cutting edge. ''Just get me the money.''

He continued to examine objects. A figurine. An oil
painting. He came back to the small jade box, pursed
his lips and stroked it with a coarse finger. For a moment, she thought he was going to slip it into his
pocket, but he didn't. He moved on, halting at last in
front of a photo of Brian in his high school cap and
gown. Kerry's heart hammered.

''Good-looking kid.'' He picked up the picture and
examined it. ''Takes after his papa. My eyes and
mouth. Bet he doesn't have any trouble getting laid
whenever he wants.''

''He's a good boy,'' she blurted before she realized
what she was saying. She loved her son, was proud of
him and couldn't stand by while he was cheapened.

''Boy?'' Rafe raised an eyebrow. ''He's what, sev-
enteen, eighteen? I read somewhere that a kid needs a
male role model in his life. A father. *His* father.'' He
held the photo at arm's length, either for a more objective view or because he needed glasses. She wasn't
sure which.

''I feel real bad about neglecting him all these
years,'' he continued with a guilelessness that made
Kerry's blood run cold.

''He thinks you're dead, Rafe. Leave it that way.''

When he set the portrait down and faced her, she

detected no trace of sentimentality, no sense of wonder that this young man was his son. His indifference infuriated her until she realized she should be grateful for it.

"I'll give you a week, Kerry," he said in a very sober voice, and put his glass on the coffee table. "In the meantime, I'll be watching you, so don't try running to the police...or back to Daddy." He chuckled at that. "Fat chance, right?"

He sauntered to the front door like a man without a care in the world and opened it. "One week." He stepped out and closed the door quietly behind him.

Kerry slumped in her chair and stayed there for several minutes before she began to shake. And then she couldn't control herself. Her hands trembled. Her legs were too weak for her to stand up. She could feel tears building and hated herself for her weakness. Biting her lips, she pressed her eyes closed and inhaled slowly, held her breath and exhaled with equal concentration. Finally, she steeled herself, made it to her feet and walked to the bar. The bottle of tequila stood invitingly open. Cursing the need surging through her, she glared at it. Rafe had touched it. Maybe she ought to keep it. Turn it over to the police for fingerprints.

But he was right. There wasn't anything they could do. Even with proof that he was still alive, she was helpless. At best, they could warn him off. A lot of good that would accomplish. He wasn't afraid of the cops.

What could she do? Change the locks on the doors and alert the doorman to strangers. But she couldn't lock herself in her penthouse. She refused to go into hiding.

She wasn't about to give Rafe money, either. He'd never be satisfied. Wasn't it ironic? She could actually afford to give him twenty-five million dollars and not have it affect her lifestyle. Yet she knew it wouldn't end there. It wasn't only money he was after. Money was secondary to him. What Rafael Durgan craved was power. Power over her.

CRAIG REGARDED his weekly calls to his mother as an obligation and his monthly visits as a chore. When he could reasonably avoid them, he did. He felt guilty about it, but she never gave any indication she missed them. Gina Robeson had still not reconciled herself to her husband's death or to her son's role in it. Even now, more than eighteen years after the police had come to announce finding Harry Robeson's body, Craig wasn't sure if he'd done the right thing. Had there been an alternative to the way he'd dealt with his father's abuse? What weighed most heavily was the realization that, right or wrong, he wasn't sorry Harry Robeson was dead.

Gina refused to answer the phone on the first ring. Craig wasn't sure why. And if she didn't pick up by the third, she either wasn't there or wouldn't answer at all.

"Hi, Mom." He made it a point to sound cheerful, the way a loving son was expected to greet his aging mother.

"Hello, Craig," she responded formally, making no attempt to match his enthusiasm. For the thousandth time, he wondered why he made the effort when it was clearly neither required nor reciprocated. "I didn't know if you'd call this evening." Her usual comment. Craig was well aware it was an invitation not to call, that she wasn't interested in talking to him, but she was his mother. He owed her his life, even if she regretted having given it to him.

"How was your week?" he asked, though he knew what the answer would be.

"Quiet. Yours?"

"Busy." Should he tell her about seeing Kerry again? He'd debated mentioning her when he saw her at the TV station but decided against it. His mother watched a good deal of daytime TV, but she was a devoted fan of Oprah, so she probably hadn't seen Leslie Fischer's show that day. She hadn't commented on Kerry's picture in the paper, either, though she could hardly have missed it. They scrupulously avoided talking about their time in Coyote Springs or the people they'd met there. Gina had left everyone in her life behind when she'd moved to Mesquite to live with her unmarried older sister. When Aunt Dorry died four years ago, Craig arranged for his mother to move into the Mesquite Hills Retirement Village. She'd put up only token resistance. Gina lived alone in a small patio home surrounded by neighbors her age. She received social security, but every month Craig transferred a generous amount to her checking account. After all the years of scrimping and saving, of sometimes working two jobs, his mother was comfortably well off. She didn't thank Craig for the money and never asked for more. He often wondered if she regarded it as her due, or perhaps as blood money.

"Mom, I may be out of the country next week on business, so I can't be sure if I'll be able to make it over Sunday."

"Don't worry about it. I won't go hungry." She could have said it lightheartedly, as an inside joke, a subtle thanks for his generosity, but she didn't. The words came out as a statement, a blunt reminder of reality.

Their routine was for him to take her out to dinner when he visited, usually to a very fancy and very expensive restaurant. She wouldn't admit it, but he knew she enjoyed dressing up and having waiters cater to her every wish. Most of the time she ordered the most expensive item on the menu, unless it was something she truly disliked. Craig wondered if she thought she was punishing him with the huge bill that came at the end of each meal. He wasn't sure if she knew how enormously wealthy he was. Besides, talking about the food, the service and the decor was easier than talking about themselves.

"I'll make it up to you next time," he added. "Do you need anything?"

"No."

"How's the car running?" He'd bought her a Mercedes, which she rarely drove, preferring to take taxis. Just as well. She wasn't a particularly competent driver.

"It's fine. Ham drove me to the cemetery the other day."

To visit Aunt Dorry's grave, no doubt. Harry was buried in Coyote Springs. "Ham?" he asked.

"Hamilton Oglethorpe. I told you about him. He moved here a couple of months ago after his wife died. MS."

"Oh, yes. I remember now."

"He has a nice little Ford, but it's been giving him trouble lately. Something wrong with the radiator, I think he said. So we took my car."

"I'm glad you were able to get out."

There was a brief, strained pause, as if his mother didn't know what to say next. "I've got to go, Craig. Ham is coming over in a few minutes. He's taking me to the movies."

He couldn't remember his mother ever going to see a movie, partly because it cost money, but also because it took her out of the house, where Harry had insisted she belonged. Perhaps she'd fallen into the habit and just hadn't bothered to tell Craig.

"What are you going to see?"

"One of those new techno thrillers, I think. I don't know the name of it."

Techno thriller? Not her style. Was this a date she was going on? He resisted the temptation to ask or to chuckle. "Well, enjoy yourself. I'll call you and let you know what my plans for next weekend are as soon as I work them out."

He hung up a minute later. Duty done. What was this Hamilton Oglethorpe like?

Gina had never shown interest in another man after Harry died, and Craig wondered what had happened to change her mind. He was also curious about the kind of man who would want to keep company with such a sour woman. She'd made a few friends at the Hills, so maybe her bitterness was directed toward him exclusively.

His mother with a beau. It surprised him how pleased it made him feel. She'd done her time in hell. Maybe the years she had left would be more blessed. He hoped so.

He rearranged the papers on his desk. The work piled in front of him was important but not critical, and he didn't have the concentration this evening to probe it effectively. He fingered his personal telephone book. It wasn't exactly a bachelor's little black book; the hundreds of entries were predominantly business contacts and ordinary friends. Only a few were women with whom he occasionally spent an evening—and less frequently a night. A night of mindless, pounding sex was what he needed. He started flipping pages.

Then stopped. He liked sex. He had no objection to the pounding variety, either. But mindless? No, he thought grimly, it wouldn't be mindless. He'd be thinking of Kerry.

His friend Hank said he thought too much. It was an ironic statement from a man Craig considered one of the most caring and attentive people he'd ever met. But there was, no doubt, some truth in it. Craig liked to analyze, to understand, and there was a lot he didn't fully comprehend, such as his continuing fascination with Kerry.

Why had she invited him to dinner? Loneliness? A need for companionship? Everyone envied the glamour of having wealth; very few appreciated the isolation it caused. Unless he'd misread the sadness in her eyes, those were definitely elements. She was unmarried. Her son was away at college. Schneider reported her best friend was Charlene Higgins, but even if Charlene wasn't available, she must have other friends. If she wanted companionship, why not call one of them? Why choose him to spend an evening with?

Attraction, obviously. And he was attracted to her. Except she was an alcoholic. She might be dry now, but for how long? Alcoholics called themselves recovering, not recovered. They couldn't say they'd never take another drink. They lived one day at a time, always wondering if this was the day they'd give in to the urge for self-destruction.

He didn't want to risk that kind of relationship or deal with the pain and disappointment it would inevitably bring. Yet, in spite of his solemn vow to shun her, he was drawn to Kerry. And it terrified him. If she fell off the wagon again, there was a distinct possibility he wouldn't be able to walk away—because he'd be in love with her.

KERRY'S HANDS shook as she poured tomato juice from a small can into a glass and added a plentiful dose of Tabasco. Maybe with enough pepper to burn her tongue, she wouldn't miss the vodka. She took a mouthful and nearly choked. Okay, she'd overdone it a little. That was all right. It distracted her from the problem at hand sufficiently to get a more objective view of it. The first thing she needed to do was talk to someone about the situation. Charlene was her AA counselor, the person she called when the draw of the drink started to really get to her. As busy as she was, Charlene always took the time to talk her friend out of that first sample. It rarely took much. A sympathetic voice was usually enough. A few words of encouragement.

She picked up the portable phone on the end of the kitchen counter and punched in Charlene's home number. An answering machine responded. Saturday night. She was probably out somewhere with her kids. Kerry considered leaving a message for her to call back as soon as possible, but decided against it. Let Charlene enjoy her weekend with her children. Kerry decided she could get through this shock by herself. She hung up when the beep sounded.

Clutching her fiery cocktail, she returned to the living room, eyed the bar and the bottle of Stolichnaya. A shot of vodka would thin the pepper nicely.

Okay, Charlene wasn't available, but her wise counsel was. Kerry tried to compose the conversation she would have with her friend if she was there.

Rafe is back, Kerry would say, and explain his sudden appearance.

Charlene would hold her in her arms and call the SOB worse names. *What are you going to do?* she'd ask.

Fight him.

Good, Charlene would reply. *Guns or knives? How about a cattle prod where it will hurt the most?*

Kerry laughed at the bawdy suggestion.

Remember, God never tempts you beyond your ability to resist. It didn't make any difference how she defined God as long as she recognized that there was a power stronger than her and that she could draw on it for help.

By the time the conversation was over, the idea of pouring a drink and tossing it down her throat would be regarded as so much foolishness.

Foolishness, Kerry reminded herself. She didn't need a drink to fight Rafe. She wouldn't let him win by making her fail.

It would have been nice to talk to Charlene, but she didn't need her this time, after all. Unexpectedly, Kerry felt encouraged. She'd slain her dragon by herself. She really didn't need anyone else.

CHAPTER FIVE

THE UNIFORMED DOORMAN at Kerry's condominium greeted Craig with formal friendliness and asked whom he wished to see. Security. Craig lamented the need for it, but the wealthy and powerful were prey to predators.

"Craig Robeson to see Mrs. Durgan."

"Yes, sir. One minute please."

The doorman hit a fast-dial button on his desk phone and announced him. He eyed the visitor suspiciously during the moment's delay before he received a response. "Yes, ma'am. You can go right up, sir." He escorted Craig to one of the elevators and inserted a key card in a special slot to grant him access to the top floor. The push of a button would allow him to come down later.

He glided up. When the door opened, he faced a gilt-framed mirror above a faux French provincial credenza topped with an eclectic arrangement of silk flowers. Kerry was standing in the doorway on his left. Her brows were raised.

"Craig, what are you doing here?"

"Sorry to barge in on you unannounced." He stepped toward her. She was wearing jeans beneath an oversize man's white oxford shirt, the sleeves rolled back at the cuffs to her wrists, the tails draping her hips. Casual attire, the kind for lounging comfortably in solitude at home. "I hope I'm not interrupting anything. If you have company I—"

"It's all right. I'm alone." She paused as if weighing the wisdom of the admission. "Please come in." She stepped back and let him precede her into a spacious entranceway, then slipped the bolt behind them. Her security consciousness seemed curiously inconsistent with her initial hesitation to invite him in.

She led him the short distance to carpeted steps that descended into a wide, open, sun-filled living room. The furnishings were not exceedingly modern but displayed a simplicity that pleased him. There were personal touches—framed photos, small pieces of sculpture scattered about—but no clutter. The paintings on the walls were bright and cheerful—colorful florals, sunny landscapes. No dark Rembrandts. No obtuse Picassos.

He didn't miss the fully stocked wet bar in the corner. Alcoholics dealt with the issue of having liquor around one of two ways. Some banned it from their homes. Others kept it available as a reminder that they didn't need it. Craig had met a few bartenders who were alcoholics. They served liquor for a living but hadn't touched a drop in years. They admitted, though, that the temptation never completely went away. It took courage to resist, but every time they did, it made them stronger. Was that why Kerry had booze in the house, as an exercise in flexing her temperance muscles?

"Can I offer you some coffee?" He heard other

questions lingering in her voice. *Why are you here? What do you want?*

He turned to her. "Actually, I came to invite you to brunch."

She bit her lip, unsure of herself.

"They have a very nice spread at the Mansion on Turtle Creek," he added, hoping the name of one of the most exclusive hotels in the Metroplex might help persuade her. Brunch there cost a hundred dollars a person.

"I don't know." Avoiding his eyes, she continued to the oversize, dark brown leather wing chair in front of the wall of windows that looked out on a well-tended roof garden. The bright sunshine streaming in behind her cast her in shadow. "I hadn't planned on going out."

"Did you eat dinner last night?" Why was he asking? It was none of his business. Or did he want her to tell him that since she couldn't have dinner with him, she hadn't eaten at all? *Talk about vain and arrogant,* he chided himself. Yet secretly he hoped it was true.

"I wasn't very hungry." She motioned him to a seat.

"Then you need a good meal, and I owe you one after declining your invitation yesterday."

She raised a hand to push a strand of hair from her cheek, then changed her mind. "You don't owe me anything, Craig."

She was friendly, but she wasn't at ease. Something was definitely wrong. If she didn't want his company, she could have refused to see him. There wasn't any reason being alone with him should make her uncomfortable. Besides, she'd bolted the door.

"I owe you good manners," he said. "Please. I'd enjoy your company." He could feel rather than see her staring at him. This shouldn't be a difficult decision to make, yet she seemed to weigh it carefully.

"Please," he repeated.

She shrugged, and he spied the curve of a smile. "You say it so nicely, how can I resist?" She stood up. "You'll have to give me a few minutes to get ready, though." She started across the room and did an about-face. "There's a pot of coffee in the kitchen." She pointed down the hallway opposite the front door. "Juice and soft drinks in the refrigerator, if you prefer. Help yourself." The bounce had returned to her step. "I won't be too long." She disappeared around the corner.

The kitchen was large and more institutional than cozy, but there were touches of warmth. A potted geranium. A few herbs growing in little containers on a sunny windowsill. Sparkling copper pots that hung from an iron framework over a cooking island. How very different from the cramped little kitchen in which his mother had prepared meals. He went to the coffeemaker, found a mug in the cabinet above it, filled it halfway, sipped and wandered to the living room.

Sitting on the baby grand piano by the plate glass window affording a sweeping panorama of the city was a silver-framed studio portrait of a young man. Craig picked it up.

"My son, Brian," Kerry said from behind him.

Craig turned, still holding the picture. She was buttoning the cuff of a blue-and-white paisley print blouse. In a tantalizing flash of awareness, he imagined the process being reversed, and it wasn't she who was securing the cuffs but he who was unbuttoning the front of her shirt, his hands poised between her breasts. Desperate to gain control of his overactive libido, he focused on the photo.

He could easily see a resemblance to Kerry in the boy's high cheekbones and fine nose, but the broad jaw and full mouth were unmistakably those of his father, Rafael. A handsome combination, Craig concluded, and tried not to resent the man who'd fathered the boy.

"I bet he has to fight off the girls."

She chuckled. "Yeah, but he assures me he tries not to break their hearts in the process."

"Very honorable of him." He wondered how much of his father the boy remembered, if he knew what kind of person Rafe had been. Did Kerry ever talk about him? Did she describe him as the ideal dad?

"You look very pretty," he said, and was amused when the compliment seemed to make her uncomfortable.

"Thank you. Ready?" she asked.

He placed the picture on the piano and left the coffee mug on an end table. "Let's go."

They drove in near silence to the hotel, intermittently exchanging snippets of small talk, but even that was forced and seemed to amplify the tension between them.

With its wood-inlaid ceiling and murals on the walls depicting scenes of Italy, the dining room of the Mansion had the sophisticated charm characteristic of the Old World. Well-dressed diners talked in muffled tones while a string quartet played chamber music.

"Would you prefer a window or a booth, Mr. Robeson?" the silver-haired maître d' asked.

"Window," Craig responded at the same time Kerry said, "Booth."

"Make it a booth, Nick," Craig corrected himself.

The tuxedoed headwaiter didn't bat an eye at the mixed signals but checked off a square on the floor plan atop his podium. He led them to a richly upholstered booth that was slightly raised and gave a full view of the room as well as the precisely manicured gardens beyond a long wall of windows.

Napkins were shaken out. Water was poured.

"May I offer you some champagne, ma'am, or perhaps a mimosa?"

Kerry shook her head. "Just orange juice, please."

"And coffee," Craig added.

Two glasses of orange juice arrived. Coffee followed.

"Shall we?" Craig asked, nodding toward the huge circular buffet richly set among potted plants and vases of freshly cut flowers.

A waiter followed them, carefully placing modest servings of their selections on plates he carried for them. There were delicacies aplenty, but Kerry ordered sparingly. A bit of poached salmon with a dab of lemon dill sauce. A thin curl of Westphalian ham. A few spears of asparagus vinaigrette. Fresh fruit compote.

Craig eyed her meager selection as they resumed their seats.

"Warming up." She smiled. "Don't worry. I intend to get your money's worth."

They ate in silence for a minute. Between bites of beef Wellington, Craig observed his companion. She seemed far away, preoccupied, morose. He noticed other things, as well. More makeup today, for example, than she had previously worn. It might be because she was wearing Sunday clothes, but he didn't think so. Kerry had the kind of clear complexion that required little or no augmentation, and she hardly struck him as the type of woman who fancied powder and blush. She was also wearing a long-sleeve blouse that seemed inappropriate for the warm spring weather.

"How's your love life?" he asked bluntly.

She jerked, nearly dropping a piece of strawberry on its way to her mouth, and lowered her fork. "I beg your pardon?"

He cut into a perfectly browned rissole potato. "Is there a man in your life, someone you're seeing?"

Wide-eyed, she didn't seem to know whether to be vexed or amused.

He stabbed a piece of roast beef. "It's none of my business, of course."

Her eyes twinkled. "Then why did you ask?"

He speared a piece of sautéed salsify. "Just curious." He continued to eat as if it really didn't matter, but the glances over her fork were like radar beams.

"As a matter of fact, no," she informed him. "No plans to have any in my life, either."

Funny, he thought. Yesterday, he didn't get the impression she was down on men. What had happened in the meantime?

He didn't expect her to tell him, of course. She was showing all the classic signs of a battered woman, but if someone had hit her, asking questions would be fruitless and might make matters worse. Silence and denial were the bulwarks of the abused.

"This food sure is different from what I grew up on." He tore off a piece of crispy roll and buttered it. "Meat loaf and spaghetti were more our fare."

"Nothing wrong with either one," she commented.

"I bet you ate steak every night."

A small chuckle followed. "We had our share, but it was hardly every night. Maybe once a week."

He snorted. "That's about fifty times more often than we had it."

"I guess living on a ranch makes a difference," she replied between bites of salmon.

"Having money to buy groceries does, too."

She looked up. "Were you really that poor that you went hungry? I had no idea, Craig. I knew you weren't rich, but..."

"My father worked for the telephone company. On the engineering staff. He was quite well paid, actually."

"Then why—"

"He drank most of it. My mother worked, not because she wanted to or because she had any special skills. Clerked in a grocery store. The discounts she received helped."

He watched Kerry's facial expression. She continued to eat, slowly and methodically, but she kept her eyes averted from his.

She had finished what was on her plate, and a waiter asked if she would like something else. She requested several items and watched him go off to get them before she asked her question. "If he drank so heavily, how did he hold on to his job?"

Craig smiled and forked up a piece of feta from his Greek salad. "As I think you know, different people handle alcoholism differently. Some get rip-roaring drunk and stay that way. Others are part-time drinkers. A few are so subtle they go for years without being detected. When their friends find out, they're inevitably flabbergasted. They didn't have any idea."

He noticed her stiffen when he referred to her familiarity with the disease, but she didn't make the obvious comment. He hadn't expected her to.

"My father was one of those individuals who could function perfectly well on the job. As far as I could tell, he didn't drink during the day, at least not until the last year. No martini lunches or hip flasks. But when the workday ended, he never failed to treat himself to a well-deserved reward for his endeavors. It didn't stop at one, of course. By the time he got home several hours later, he was mad at the world, mad at my mother and mad at me, in that order."

For a moment, Kerry hesitated, as if she knew the answer to the question she was about to ask but didn't want to hear it. "Was he physically abusive?"

"Not initially. He'd rant and rave about some perceived stupidity, some incompetence on the part of the lamebrains he had to deal with, namely his boss. With time, he saw stupidity and malevolence everywhere, especially at home. If my mother didn't save supper for him, he got angry. If she did and it was over-cooked, he complained. If she waited to prepare it until he came home, he carped that it took too long. She couldn't win, though God knows, she tried.''

Kerry seemed curiously unmoved as he spilled his guts out, until she lowered her head, set her fork aside and said in what could only be described as a little-girl voice, ''Tough way to live.''

She'd finished her food, and Craig motioned to a hovering waiter. ''I think I'll try a piece of the amaretto cheesecake. How about you?'' he asked Kerry.

''Crème caramel, please. Why didn't your mother leave him?'' she asked when the server had delivered their orders.

Craig cut into his dessert with the side of his fork. ''All sorts of reasons—or rather excuses. Your friend Charlene hit them very well on Leslie's show. Mom had married my father for better or worse. She couldn't break a vow. It was a wife's duty to stick by her husband. It was her fault. He was under a lot of pressure. She didn't have any work skills, or she didn't have any that were good enough to earn her own living. It was better for me to have a father than not to have one. The litany went on.''

''So that's why you were inquiring about contributing to my fund to support the home for abused women and children.''

''Like Charlene—'' he almost said like you ''—I know what it's like firsthand,'' he admitted. ''The violence. The remorse. The recriminations followed by more violence.''

''An endless cycle.'' Her eyes were more violet than blue in this muted light. And sad.

''Unless someone steps in and offers a way out,'' he said. ''You're supporting a good cause, Kerry. Something you can be truly proud of.''

''It's still too little,'' she said unhappily, and concentrated on the delicate custard.

''You can't save them all,'' he reminded her sympathetically. ''In fact, you can't save any of them unless they want to be saved. That's the hell of it. So many women accept their lot, blame themselves for it and go back for more. I don't have to tell you most victims of domestic violence refuse to press charges against their abusers. 'He didn't mean it, Officer. He promised me it won't happen again.''' Craig shook his head. ''They rationalize, justify and become enablers for their tormentors.''

He was preaching to the choir and knew it. Would she tell him what had happened the evening before? He hoped so. He also knew that until she asked for help, acknowledged her inability to handle the situation by herself, she would remain a victim.

''You speak of your father in the past tense,'' she observed over a spoon filled with the creamy confection.

''He's dead,'' Craig answered evenly, and replenished his fork with another piece of almond-flavored cheesecake.

Condolences were in order, but as she watched him slip the rich dessert into his mouth, she detected no regret that his father had died. "How did it happen? When?"

"A car accident right after I graduated from high school," Craig said. She thought he spoke with the indifference one would associate with delivering a weather report on the other side of the world.

Kerry wondered if he was really as reconciled to the loss as he appeared, or if under the cool facade of detachment a burning hatred raged. She'd never had any idea this straight-A student and skilled athlete had had such an unhappy home life. He'd been something of a loner, but she couldn't recall his ever being unfriendly or moody. "Was anyone else hurt?"

"No, thank God. He was drunk, of course, and speeding. Lost control on a curve and rolled his car. Naturally, he wasn't wearing his seat belt. Sustained massive head injuries and died two days later without regaining consciousness."

"I'm very sorry, Craig." Kerry had an urge to reach across the table and place her hand on his, but something in his eyes dissuaded her. He wasn't ready for physical contact, and she wasn't sure she was, either. "It must have been terribly difficult for you and your mother."

Craig held her gaze across the table. She saw pain in his eyes, and it made her wonder if he had, like so many victims of abuse, loved his tormentor more than he was willing to admit.

"Mom herself was in the hospital at the time." He pushed his plate aside and leaned back against the upholstered booth. "I'd been outside mowing our lawn when he finally got up that Sunday morning. I thought she'd be safe as long as I was nearby. The old man and I had had confrontations before. I was old enough and big enough by then to fight back, so he knew I wouldn't stand by passively. But when I came in the house…I found her bloody and unconscious on the kitchen floor. He was standing over her, bewildered, as if he didn't know how she'd gotten there. I shoved him aside and threatened to kill him. That's when he ran out of the house and drove off.''

A cold shiver slithered down Kerry's spine. She tried to imagine what it had been like for Craig, constantly mediating between adults who should have been nurturing, only to find his battered mother in one hospital bed, his father dying in another. The victim and the victimizer. Except maybe their son had been the greatest victim of all.

''Did your mother fully recover?''

''They had to remove her spleen, but otherwise she's fine.''

''I'm sure it was a great consolation for her to know you were safely by her side.''

His sole response was the blankness that came into his eyes. ''Right after the funeral, she moved to Mesquite to live with her sister, and I went off to college.''

Kerry was puzzled. It sounded as if mother and son were at odds. Why? Perhaps he still blamed her for not being strong enough to leave his father. Or maybe she blamed her son for not doing a better job of protecting her against her vicious husband. The scars of abuse always went far beneath the skin. Some wounds never healed.

Maybe his father was the reason Craig never married. Abusive behavior tended to be passed from one generation to another, not genetically but as learned response. She noted his equanimity and marveled at it. Was he one of those people who held his temper until it exploded into uncontrollable violence? Had he recognized that and determined never to subject a wife or children to a repeat of what he had experienced? If so, she admired his continence; at the same time, she pitied him for his loneliness.

She knew something about the feeling of not being able to connect—except with her son, Brian, and now even he was slipping away from her. She also recognized that years before she, too, had contributed to Craig's unhappiness, to his feeling of helplessness. He'd invited her to the high school prom at a time in his life that was clearly difficult, then she'd abandoned him for a lowlife. Her avoiding him afterward had been out of her own shame. She'd been blithely unaware she was also sending him the message that her choice was his fault—that he hadn't lived up to her expectations.

"Craig, I need to say something I should have said a long time ago. I hope you'll accept my apology for the night of the prom, for the way I treated you. You were kind and considerate, and I abused your courtesy. I know this is late in coming, but…please, forgive me."

His face softened into a sweet smile, and he reached across the table. Without hesitation, she placed her hand in his. His palm was warm, his fingers strong. "Apology accepted," he said easily. "Now let's put it completely behind us, where it belongs."

The sounds around them faded. She gazed at his mouth, at the full lips that seemed poised to speak but through which no words came. The dimples that sent little shivers of delight through her were lost in the hollows of his slack jaw. As their eyes met, she was transported beyond mere gladness to something strangely erotic. He wanted her, and she wanted him.

The waiter appeared to pour more coffee, but the bass fiddle vibrations of Craig's touch emboldened her even after he removed his hand. They sipped in silence as the romantic strains of a Grieg melody wafted through the crowded room. Kerry bucked up her courage and took the next step.

Confession was supposed to be good for the soul. It was certainly a new experience for her. She'd always regarded admission of wrongdoing as a weakness, not a strength, but this apology had liberated her of at least one of her old transgressions. She couldn't undo the mistakes of the past, but maybe she could correct a more recent one.

"I screwed up when we met at the TV station, Craig. I was surprised to see you, and remembering the last time we'd met, I was feeling very defensive."

"I wasn't exactly Mr. Tactful," he admitted.

"You had every right to ask your questions, and your observations were valid."

The dimples returned, making her pulse jump. The humor in his hazel eyes dripped into his soft, mellow voice. "Does that mean you're willing to let me contribute to your foundation?"

She leaned back against the back cushion of the

booth, withdrawing physically as well as emotionally. "This isn't about money, Craig."

He reached forward, but the separation between them was too far to bridge. "I know that, Kerry, and I appreciate your candor. But I would also like to help you with your shelter. You know now I have a personal interest. In fact, if you're willing, I'd like to match your financial commitment."

Stunned by the generosity of his offer, she felt the heat of her anger quickly dissipate. "Are you serious?"

Reluctantly, he withdrew his hand. "There are some subjects I don't joke about, Kerry. Abuse and alcoholism are at the top of the list." He watched her eyes flicker with uncertainty. "It'll still be your foundation."

"I meant what I told Leslie Fischer. This isn't about me."

"I know that." Pride was inexorably wrapped up in all achievement. But what he perceived as her driving motivation was compassion. She understood the despair of needing help and the strength it took to accept it.

For several minutes they ate and drank in silence. Finally, she licked the last of the caramelized sugar off her spoon and straightened. "I've been thinking over your comment about the foundation's title. You're probably right." She smiled thinly. "The First-Robe Foundation certainly doesn't solve the problem."

"Can I make another suggestion?" At her questioning nod, he said, "How about the Family First

Foundation? Your name is still in it, but the emphasis is on family.''

Her eyes lit up. ''Craig, that's brilliant. Why didn't I think of that?''

He gave her a proud-little-boy shrug and a smile. ''You would have.''

This time it was her hand that reached across the table. ''Are you sure you wouldn't like to have your name in the title, too?'' At his shake of the head, she added, ''Thank you.''

He turned his palm up so his fingers could encase hers. A low-voltage hum came once more with his gentle touch. ''You're welcome, Kerry.'' He locked eyes with her and murmured, ''Anytime.''

ON THE DRIVE back to her condominium, Craig wondered if he wasn't making a mistake in offering to join—even as a silent partner—in Kerry's foundation. The two of them had made progress. He'd let out the skeleton in his closet—that he had at least contributed to his father's death. In exchange, she'd apologized for embarrassing him at the dance. But she still hadn't told him her deep, dark secret. She hadn't even acknowledged her drinking problem. Then there was the question of who was abusing her and why. She wasn't by nature passive or docile, so a more important question was why was she allowing it to happen.

Cosponsorship would mean working together, coordinating policies and programs, plans and expenditures. That wasn't completely true. He could palm off most of those decisions on his staff, just as he did with other business details, but in this case, he didn't want to. Whatever it was that had drawn him to Kerry First twenty years ago was still drawing him to Kerry Durgan now. He was courting disaster—again.

When he was a teenager, he could explain his attraction to the prettiest girl in the school as raging hormones and probably little more. He'd spoken to her so rarely he could hardly claim to have known her as a friend. And now? He couldn't deny the hormones. They were still wreaking havoc with his body. But he was older, more mature, better able to put things in perspective—or he should be.

The pretty girl had grown into a beautiful woman. Ironically, while she'd been obviously aware of her allure in high school, she seemed oblivious to it now, when it was even more powerful. The lack of vanity was part of her charm, but it was also clear she was troubled.

He pulled up in front of her condominium and looked across the seat. She was lost in thought, making him wonder if she was debating about asking him up. Maybe he could persuade her. With the engine still running, he swiveled to face her.

"I've enjoyed being with you, Kerry."

She turned toward him uncertainly. "Thank you for brunch. It was delicious. Thank you for…everything."

He extended his arm across the back of the seat and curled his hand around the base of her slender neck. Her skin was cool to his touch, though he could feel the heat pulsing beneath it. He wanted to touch so much more of her, to experience her warmth pressed against him. He remembered the night of the prom. He'd delayed taking her out on the balcony, postponed satisfying his want for her. He'd never received a second chance—until now.

He inched closer and at the same time coaxed her toward him. The floral perfume of her hair, the feminine scent of her body threatened to override his forbearance. Eyes wide open, he brought his lips to hers. In the split second before they made contact, her lashes fluttered and closed. Their lips met.

She didn't resist. The delicate moan that vibrated against him said she wasn't displeased. He probed with his tongue. Not forcefully, though it took restraint to hold back. When her hand groped his chest, he knew there was no escape, and he thrust forward for a better taste. Hot coffee and crème caramel. Woman and sex. Heat and desire. They all assailed him. He didn't remember shutting his eyes. It didn't matter. His world had only two senses, feel and taste. The feel of her skin, the taste of her mouth. The sensations welling in him would soon have him out of control.

His right hand snaked down from her shoulder, finally circling her left forearm on its way to her breast.

She made a sudden mewing sound, squirmed and pulled back, averting her head.

"Kerry?" Was she angry? Surely his kissing her hadn't come as a surprise. They'd been dueling with words and teasing each other with their eyes all morning.

"Thank you for a delicious brunch," she blurted between short breaths. Her right hand gripped the door handle.

"I'll come up with you," he offered.

"No," she snapped, then lightened her tone. "Thanks anyway, Craig, but it really isn't necessary."

Necessary? This moment, what he felt, wasn't about obligations. He wasn't talking about helping a little old lady across the street. Blinking slowly, he took a deep, silent breath. "I thought we might discuss the foundation," he lied, "consider the extent of services we can offer. Maybe even set up a schedule for expansion."

Her breath was ragged. "I know we have a lot of details to work out," she said, then tried to laugh. It sounded false and pretentious. "But can we do it another time?"

He was trying to figure out what had made her bolt. It was more than the kiss. In fact, he had the feeling the kiss had nothing to do with it.

"It's getting late." She lifted her wrist to check her watch before she realized she wasn't wearing one.

Baffled by her behavior, he nodded to the dashboard clock. "Late? It's only a little after one."

The doorman opened her car door. She seemed suddenly relieved. "Thanks again for brunch, Craig. I really enjoyed it." She accepted the doorman's gloved hand and climbed out of the vehicle, then leaned over and poked her head into the car's open window. "Be sure to call me during the week so we can get together and discuss...things."

He watched her walk into the lobby of her building without a backward glance.

What had spooked her? Then it came to him. There was someone else. Someone waiting. The person who'd hit her.

CHAPTER SIX

KERRY ENTERED her penthouse with a heavy heart. The day had started off uncertainly. She'd debated spending time with Craig, aware he had the power to bring her laughter and hope. He had a way of touching her that kindled the primitive emotions of a woman adored and treasured. When he'd kissed her, he'd set loose a chain of awareness and desire that threatened to consume her.

Craig's hands on her body had been gentle and stimulating, the sweet caress of a man finding pleasure in the feel of her and imparting bliss in its tracks. Persuasive enough, too, to make her imagine the next step, to conjure them together, alone, in bed, making long, slow, volcanic love, the kind where heat rose until it could do nothing but explode.

Then he rubbed her bruised arm. Not to hurt. Craig didn't hurt women. It was a loving, caring stroke, but it touched tender, damaged nerves that yanked her out of the ecstasy of shared indulgence to a different level of reality. With her whimper of pain had also come terrible sorrow. She'd waited almost twenty years for a man to kiss her the way Craig had, waited and dreamed of it without even knowing she was doing so—until it came. The way his mouth fit hers, the sensitive way he probed and gratified, had been everything she'd conjured up in her fantasies, and more.

But the pain of Rafe's hold on her had produced a dilemma. If she invited Craig upstairs, if he removed her clothes, he would see the bruise. When her makeup wore off, the mark of Rafe's hand on her cheek would be exposed. No honorable man could respect a woman who allowed herself to be abused, victimized. Least of all Craig Robeson.

Morning sunlight no longer angled through the windows. The spacious living room was bright and airy, but it didn't glow with the fresh-day sparkle it had when Craig had occupied it only hours before.

She couldn't allow herself to get involved with him, so she'd pulled away. Her life was complicated enough without losing what remnant of respect he had for her. The pure delight of Craig's hands on her body, the warmth of his breath, the taste of his kiss, the burning desire she could feel welling in both of them had distracted her. At least she could say she came to her senses and did the right thing—for once in her life.

Before settling on the couch, Kerry gathered several college course catalogues from the drawer of an end table. If she was serious about going back to school, she'd have to major in something, but she didn't have a clue what. The thought of English lit or history bored her to tears. The sciences scared her, especially since, as Craig had noted, mathematics was a key factor and definitely not one of her favorite subjects. Absentmindedly, she paged through the sections on philosophy and psychology.

She wished she'd handled the situation with Craig better, that she hadn't appeared so cold and indifferent at their parting, especially since it was exactly the opposite of how she felt. With her record of rejecting him, what could he think of her now, except that she was fickle, cruel, unbalanced? The possibility that she had completely lost him this time made her heart ache, but maybe it was better for him to go away mad than to stay. She was no good for him.

On Monday morning, she visited her accountant to review her portfolio. She wanted to see if she could withdraw a large enough sum of money from her cash reserves to buy Rafe off, at least for the time being, until she could come up with a more permanent remedy. Unfortunately—or fortunately—she was so heavily invested and scrupulously accounted for that any substantial change in spending patterns would send up a red flag to her accountant and raise questions. She had the right to spend her money any way she chose, of course, but...

Maybe this wasn't a bad thing. If cash had been accessible, she might have been tempted to go along with Rafe's blackmail, and she knew very well there would never be an end to it. She had to resolve this problem once and for all. But how?

Craig might be able to come up with a solution if she told him about Rafe's return. If he even believed her. Maybe when he called to talk about the Family First Foundation, she could put out feelers to see whether he'd be receptive to helping with her personal problem. Or rather, *if* he called.

During the week, she immersed herself in paperwork and research. She directed her lawyer to legally change the name of the foundation, then had him arrange to get copies of the charters of other nonprofit charitable foundations for her to review. She spent hours studying regulations and procedures, trying to decipher what she could and couldn't do. Poring over the mounds of fine print, plodding her way through legal jargon, was tedious work. She bugged her attorney from time to time, making him explain arcane terminology. He seemed a little annoyed that she didn't simply leave it all in his hands, and perhaps she should have, but it had become a personal adventure, a quest to learn.

By Friday night, Craig hadn't called, and she knew she'd lost him—again. It didn't take a college degree to figure out he didn't want to have anything to do with her professionally or personally. She couldn't blame him. A man would have to be a glutton for punishment to keep coming back to Kerry First...or Kerry Durgan.

For the past several months, she'd spent her Sundays at one of the soup kitchens in the Metroplex, getting to know the routine, the people who worked there and the clients they served. It wasn't a happy place, but she did her best to be upbeat. She donned faded jeans and a worn shirt, wore no makeup, tied her hair back with a pair of plastic barrettes, left her Ferrari at a mall and took a bus the rest of the way to the soup kitchen. The clothes were comfortable, and she loved people watching on the bus ride.

She'd been there about an hour when Craig arrived. He didn't look any more prosperous than she did. With the shadow of yesterday's beard and his conservatively cut hair uncombed, he almost fit in. Even disheveled clothes, though, couldn't disguise his powerful build or the intelligence glittering in his hazel eyes.

"Sorry I didn't get in touch with you during the week," he told her breezily, "but other business kept me tied up."

Kerry wasn't sure she believed him. Was he making excuses? Not that he had to. He owed her nothing, not even the courtesy of an explanation. "But what...what are you doing here?"

"I heard you spent your Sundays here so I thought I'd join you."

He'd been spying on her, after all.

"A new volunteer?" Mrs. Putnam asked. She was a tall, skinny woman with a mass of wrinkles that attested to her seventy-plus years.

"Just for the day, if that's all right," Craig told her.

The man radiated energy the way a radar broadcasts electrical waves. Getting too close to a radar was dangerous, Kerry told herself. Somehow she managed to keep her voice steady as she introduced the shelter director. Since Craig hadn't told her he was coming, she didn't know if he wanted to use his real name. She and several other people here didn't. Only Mrs. P. was aware of her true identity. He spared her the embarrassment of fumbling an introduction by shaking the director's hand. "Call me Craig. Pleased to meet you." He slanted Kerry a grin that would have toppled dishes if she'd been carrying any.

"My, a big man like you," the director said. "I have several jobs I bet you can tackle."

And put him to work she did. He moved cases of canned goods, assembled metal shelves that had been donated without instructions, and repaired an overhead door that had come off its track and couldn't be opened. At every opportunity, he watched Kerry. She stood on the serving line ladling out beans and rice during the height of the rush, but once it was over, she went among the tables talking to people.

She amazed him. Several of the clients were so grubby that he would have given them a wide berth, but she spent a minute or two with them, as well, exchanging pleasantries. When Mrs. P. suggested he take a break, he poured himself a cup of black coffee from a twenty-five-gallon urn. Kerry had moved over to sit with a scrawny, birdlike woman who was obviously very old.

"Who's that Kerry's with?" he asked Mrs. P. The frail old lady reminded him uncomfortably of what his mother might look like in twenty years. The very thought of her coming to a place like this sent a chill down his spine.

The director smiled sadly and poured herself a cup of the acrid brew. "Mrs. Gillian. Her husband died last year of a heart attack. Three days after his funeral she found out he'd lost their entire life savings in one of those scams that target old people." She motioned Craig to a nearby table. "Left her without a penny after nearly sixty-five years of marriage. Has lunch here a couple of times a week. She ought to do so more often, but she's too proud."

Craig was appalled. "Doesn't she have any children to take care of her?"

"They had a son, but he was killed in Southeast Asia almost forty years ago."

"What does she live on?"

"Social Security. But she was a housewife who never worked outside the home, so it isn't much. Rents a tiny little room around the corner. All by herself now, poor dear."

Kerry pressed something into the hand of the octogenarian. Money, probably. Mrs. Gillian shook her head, refusing the gift. Kerry leaned over and whispered something in her ear. This time, teary-eyed, the old woman accepted it and gave Kerry a kiss on the cheek.

"If you still have energy, Craig," Mrs. Putnam said, "I have a couple of packing crates in the warehouse that need to be moved out to the loading dock."

"Be glad to." He caught Kerry's eye and winked as he followed the director to the back door.

"What do you suppose Kerry said to Mrs. Gillian to make her take the money?"

Mrs. P. gave him a rueful smile. "Probably that Donny, her son, would want her to have it."

Craig merely nodded.

The packing crates proved to be clumsy rather than heavy. It was when he was about to return inside that he caught sight of a man leaning against a rusty pickup across the street. It took a moment for the features to register. When they did, Craig withdrew into the shadows and studied the figure to make sure his eyes weren't deceiving him. For there, cleaning his fingernails with a pocketknife, a smug grin on his face, was Rafael Durgan.

KERRY COULDN'T understand why Craig gave her an ill-tempered scowl when he came back into the vast, dimly lit dining room. The intensity of his glare caught her breath. Completely confused by the sudden change in attitude, she watched him politely talk to Mrs. Putnam, then pivot with his jaw set, eyes narrowed, and walk out the front door.

She finished her shift, thanked the woman running the place for the opportunity to help and went home. As she approached her condo, she saw what promised to really make her day. On the side street, not far from the entrance, was an unoccupied pickup that didn't fit the upscale neighborhood. The old truck could have been a delivery vehicle, except this was Sunday afternoon. What really caught her eye, though, was the pair of fuzzy dice dangling behind the windshield from the rearview mirror. The good luck charm sent a cold chill down her spine.

Kerry's heart was racing as she strode through the lobby. There was no sign of Rafe, and the doorman wouldn't allow him upstairs without permission, but she had to ask. "Any calls or visitors?"

"No, ma'am. Nary a one," Earl said pleasantly. "Been real quiet."

Kerry removed a key card from her purse as she marched to the elevator, which was standing open. She stepped inside, inserted the plastic in the penthouse slot and withdrew it. The doors closed and the car ascended, leaving her stomach down around her ankles. She was still clutching the card when she alighted a minute later. Hands trembling, she inserted it into the lock of her door. She knew what she'd find inside—or rather who.

He wasn't in the living room, but she could hear sounds coming from her bedroom down the hall. He was sprawled on her bed, scuffed boots crossed on the shiny satin bedspread, a drink in his hand. The television in the corner was emitting moaning sounds. She caught only a glimpse of a scantily clad female. He'd been into porn when they were married, said it turned him on—like foreplay. She often wondered if he realized how insulting that was. Or maybe he did and it was part of his game. She wanted to dismiss the memories, but awareness that Rafe was here with sex on his mind was frightening.

He smiled at her. "I wondered how long you were going to be with your new boyfriend. Or should I say your old one?" So he knew about Craig. Obviously, he'd been watching her. Probably because he was afraid she'd go to the police. Judging from his mocking tone, he didn't know Craig Robeson was a billionaire. It also explained why Craig had left the soup kitchen without saying goodbye. He'd seen Rafe.

Her ex-husband lifted his glass and toasted her. "Welcome back, babe." He took a hearty swig of his drink. "By the way, you're out of tequila." He picked up the bottle of bourbon from the bedside table. "So I have to drink your whiskey. You really ought to keep the bar better stocked for your guests."

Hot fury whipped through her. Her chest was pounding, her whole body shaking. Worse, she could tell by the smirk on his face that he knew she was at least as scared as she was angry. He'd always been good at reading her.

"I figured you'd be surprised to see me," he replied smugly. "I brought one of my new videos. Thought we might get it on like old times."

She wanted to scream, to cry, to throw things at him. The sights and sounds on the screen left nothing to the imagination. She strode to the television and switched it off. "How did you get in here?"

He frowned at the blank screen for a moment, but then his disappointment dissolved into a chuckle. "Don't bother changing the locks again, babe. They don't make one I can't pick, even the new electronic jobs. I've kept up with technology, you see."

"What do you want?"

He sneered. "I think you know."

She turned toward the door. The bed squeaked but she didn't dare look back. Expecting, dreading a tug on her shoulder, she strode to the living room, grateful when the hand didn't come.

There had been a time when this kind of tension between them would have led to nearly violent sex, the kind of all-consuming physical encounter that left her breathless and spent. Now it only produced a feeling of revulsion, repugnance for him and loathing for herself that she'd ever been willing to let him touch her.

Carrying the whiskey bottle in one hand and his empty glass in the other, he sauntered to the wet bar, replenished his ice and splashed more bourbon over it. The bottle was already more than half gone. He'd always been able to consume huge quantities of booze.

She suspected he was even more practiced now than he had been when he'd disappeared. How had his body withstood so much abuse? Based on the calluses on his hands and the weathered roughness of his skin, his life since he'd fled West Texas hadn't been easy. How ironic, she thought. He used to balk when her father insisted he work with the ranch hands. From all appearances, he'd put in harder manual labor than her father had ever demanded on the Number One.

What would Rafe say if she told him he was an alcoholic? He'd laugh, she decided, and say, "So what? Just keep the liquor flowing."

He asked over his shoulder, "Have you got my money?" He swiveled, his expression intimidating. When he didn't get a response, his dark eyes narrowed. "Don't screw around with me, Kerry. I want what I came for, and I intend to get it."

The ominous statement tightened the painful knot already formed in her stomach, but showing fear in dealing with Rafe had always been a mistake. In a way, she had to thank him for making her strong, for teaching her not to flinch in the face of opposition.

She worked up the courage to go over to the bar and nudge him aside so she could get to the small under-the-counter refrigerator. Doing her best to ignore him and willing her hands to remain steady, she put ice in a tall glass and filled it with Perrier. The heat of his body so close to her and the stale stench of inebriation made her skin crawl. She reestablished distance between them, physically and symbolically, by returning to the middle of the room.

"We're not talking about chump change, Rafe. I

can't just go to the post office and buy a money order. It takes time to raise that kind of dough.''

"You've got it," he insisted.

"Not in cash, you idiot." Anger flared.

Watch your tone. Don't provoke him, she cautioned as she'd done so often in the past. She saw his jaw tighten and decided it probably wasn't bad advice under the circumstances. He hated being called names, especially when they brought his intelligence into question. She rushed on before he could get worked up.

"My funds are all tied up in investments, Rafe. I've been to see my accountant. We're exploring which stocks and bonds to sell. I don't imagine you want me to tell him why, so I have to be discreet. It isn't easy giving away that kind of money."

"Just do it," he said impatiently. "And don't give me any excuses or try cute delaying tactics. I want my money."

It's not your money, she wanted to shout. She'd like to punch his lights out, too, but she knew she was no match for him in physical strength.

"I'll get it as soon as I can," she lied, "but it takes time. Be patient. You've waited this long. A few more days or even a week won't hurt."

Again, he narrowed his eyes at her, this time menacingly. She fought the instinct to cut and run. Doing her best to sound sincere, she said, "You'll get it, Rafe. I promise."

He studied her a moment, not quite sure he believed her, but he had little choice. "I better." He strolled around the room, scrutinizing things the way he had the last time.

What did he really want? He was leading up to something. She didn't have long to wait. Rafe stopped at the piano and picked up the silver-framed portrait of Brian. Kerry's heart lurched and her mouth went dry.

"Maybe it's time I went and visited my kid, let him know his daddy's here for him. You know, show him the ropes. How to pick the best booze, the best broads. Make up for lost time. I know some chicks who can teach him real good."

"Leave him alone."

Rafe raised his head and tilted it to one side. "He has a right to know his papa's alive and well," he said softly. "Think of all the things we could do together. Durgan and son. Has a ring to it, doesn't it? I'll see that he gets a good education, babe, make sure he grows into a well-rounded man of experience."

"Stay away from him," she warned, but there was desperation in the plea. She was playing into his hands and felt helpless to resist. He was threatening the one good thing he'd ever given her, the one person she would willingly sacrifice her life for. She'd taken more than one beating to protect her infant son. Rafe knew that, of course, and the knowledge gave him power over her still.

He knit his bushy black eyebrows and stared at her from under them. "Or what, Kerry?" he asked with quiet intensity. "There's nothing you can do to keep me from seeing my son." He set the picture on the closed top of the piano, but kept his fingertips poised on the frame. "You can't even get me for back child support. Your daddy insisted I didn't need to pay any, remember? He couldn't wait to get me completely out of your lives. Well, the money he sent me ran out years ago."

"What money?" She hadn't realized her father had paid him off. It was just like Adam First, the manipulative son of a bitch.

His eyes sparkled. "You didn't know?" Rafe took a slow swallow of his drink, all the time grinning over the top of the glass, thoroughly enjoying her misery. "Two grand a month as long as I stayed away from you and the kid. Reverse alimony, I guess you could call it. I had to give it up, of course, when I disappeared. That was the tough part. Still, a man of imagination can live pretty well in Mexico if he puts his mind to it."

She couldn't hide her shock, which made him sneer with delight. He picked up the portrait again and once more studied it. "I used to wonder, you know, if he really was mine. Used to wonder who else's handlebar you might have been riding."

When Kerry let loose with a stream of profanity, her ex-husband became highly amused. "No question now, though," he said. "Kid looks just like me. Lucky," he concluded proudly.

"You go anywhere near him—" Kerry warned.

He lifted his brows. "Yes?"

"You go anywhere near him—" she was tempted to say she'd kill him, but he knew the threat would be hollow "—and the deal's off, Rafe. I mean it. You do anything to disrupt his life and you won't get a penny from me, not one bloody cent.''

This time when he put down the picture, he walked away from it. As he moved toward her, she instinctively backed up, which only added to Rafe's delight.

Chuckling, he said, ''I thought you were going to say you'd kill me.'' His grin was complacent and sadistic. ''It would've been very dramatic, Kerry, but we both also know it would've been an empty threat. Kill me? Your precious baby's daddy?'' He glared at her. ''You haven't got the guts.'' When she didn't flinch, he held up his glass in tribute. ''No, this is much better.''

Her heart was pumping so hard she was amazed it didn't explode. Her fingers tingled under the high blood pressure, and she could feel herself becoming light-headed.

Rafe replenished his drink but left it on the counter. ''My beloved son or twenty-five million dollars.'' He flipped an imaginary coin, caught it and slapped it on his tattooed forearm, then peeked under his hand. Smiling, he glanced at her. ''What do you know, the money wins.'' He dropped his pose, then stuck the tips of his fingers into the pockets of his worn jeans. ''A little advice, babe. Don't mess with me. I know where Brian lives. Cross me, and he finds out all about his daddy—and what his mommy's really like.''

Tears were so close to the surface she didn't trust her voice to protest. Wordlessly, she stood, her breath caught in her throat, and watched him saunter to the kitchen. A moment later, the service door closed and the lock softly clicked shut. He was gone. For now.

Biting her lips, she wrapped her arms around her, bent nearly double and hugged herself against the trembling that was racking her body. Tears blinded her, and total despair gripped her heart.

CRAIG WAS more than halfway home when he glanced in the rearview mirror, saw a clear lane and shot across to an exit off the interstate. He was caving in, just as he'd done after she'd betrayed him on the lawn of the Coyote Springs Country Club nineteen years earlier. He'd refused to confront her then, and he was running away this time, too.

He knew where the bruises had come from the week before. Realization that Rafael Durgan was alive made his blood run cold. The notion that the son of a bitch had touched Kerry made it boil with fury. Schneider had gotten it from official records that Durgan was dead. Somehow, Rafe had managed to fool the authorities all these years. Was Kerry an active conspirator in her ex-husband's deception? And if so, why?

The situation didn't make sense. Kerry may have been a victim of circumstances once—circumstances, he reminded himself, of her own making—but that was a long time ago. The grown woman he'd spent time with didn't strike him as a willing participant in the kind of sadomasochistic games Rafe Durgan seemed to enjoy. Kerry Durgan wasn't the timid, insecure and compliant weakling Craig's mother had been. She was strong, independent, determined. She certainly wasn't disposed to playing the willing victim.

Which meant she was an *unwilling* victim.

She hadn't asked for his help, but that didn't mean

she didn't need it. He remembered the chivalric bow he'd given her on the train. "Don Quixote, at your service." Was he tilting at windmills? He'd convinced himself he didn't want to get involved with an alcoholic, yet here he was going to her rescue.

He exited the interstate and took the road toward his home, then detoured to a quiet park and stopped the car, leaving the engine running for the air-conditioning. Kids, mostly toddlers, were engrossed in carefree games, while adults looked on. He envied them. Parents sharing the day with their children. Boys and girls lucky enough to have parents who took time to be with them. He'd never experienced that. His father hadn't gone to a single one of his basketball games. His mother, forever too tired to do things with him or too worried her husband would come home and not find her there, never attended a parent-teacher meeting.

He'd sworn on his father's grave he'd never have children. It was one reason he'd never married. The women he'd been most attracted to all insisted children were essential to a happy home life. Not in his experience. There were times, though, when he missed the family he'd never known. He wasn't an alcoholic like his father. He'd never struck a woman and couldn't imagine a situation in which he would. Still, he couldn't take a chance that that defective gene was there, waiting to be triggered. He was his father's son, but he would never be his father.

Damn it, that didn't mean he had to roll over and play dead. Kerry had made a fool of him with Rafe Durgan once. He wasn't going to let her do it to him again. Not without an explanation and, if necessary, a confrontation. Resolved, Craig slipped the gearshift into reverse, turned and proceeded to Kerry's house.

KERRY WAS NOT a crybaby. Weeping was a luxury she'd learned to do without. No matter how cruel Rafe had been to her, she'd refused to shed tears, knowing they would give him satisfaction and encourage him. So she'd learned to suppress them, substituting biting words or silence.

She was close to crying now. When would this horror end?

The smell of fine bourbon whiskey had her salivating for the taste of it, her nerve ends begging for its tranquilizing respite. She closed her eyes and prayed for the strength to go on.

There was a phone in the corner by the bar. She lifted the receiver, poked in a preset number and waited. "Hi, this is Charlene Higgins. I can't come to the phone right now, but if you'll—"

Kerry slammed down the handset. Char was supposed to be available. Where was she? Out gallivanting, doing her high-powered consultant thing?

Teeth clenched, Kerry went to the bathroom and washed the grime of the soup kitchen from her face. Gripping the edge of the sink, she took several deep breaths and stared at herself in the mirror. She'd get through this. For Brian's sake. She'd get through it.

If only Charlene were here. "You are not tempted beyond your power to resist—with His help," her friend would say.

Yeah, right. And suppose I don't want to resist?

Suppose I'm just tired of the fight? The battle never ends. The only rewards are more battles.

"Do it because you're a better person for fighting than for fleeing. Drinking is an escape, the coward's way. You don't win battles by running away."

I'm tired of the fight. Tired of knowing sober is as good as it's going to get.

What would Charlene say to that? "Do it for Brian."

That's hitting below the belt, Char.

Wearily, Kerry made her way to the bedroom. The light on the VCR was flashing, telling her there was a tape still loaded. She picked up the remote, rewound the tape and ejected it. After grabbing it out of the machine, she stared at the obscene title, marched to the kitchen and tossed the cassette into the trash compactor.

Tears of frustration struggled for release. She pictured the man she'd married and hated herself for her choices. She pictured the man she'd rejected and mourned what they had both lost. He was lonely, too. She hadn't missed the desolation in his eyes when he talked about his youth. Craig Robeson was a good man who'd deserved better from his parents. From her. A good man, she told herself, whose virtue hadn't brought him happiness.

She returned to the living room.

What was the point of self-discipline when it didn't bring relief, solace?

What was the point of resisting temptation when there was no reward for success?

She plopped into a chair, feeling lonely and bereft.

There was no one in her life who mattered. Rafe, the bastard, had never been a soul mate.

Brian was grown and on his own. He wasn't even going to visit her on his break. She represented the past in his life—a past he'd probably just as soon forget. He didn't need her anymore—if he ever did. *My father was a better parent to him than I was.*

Craig? He'd been willing to support her foundation—until she pushed him away. Not once, but twice.

Her life was a waste, she decided as she rose and approached the bar. Might as well clean up this mess, get the smell of good bourbon whiskey out of her nostrils.

There wasn't much left. A few shots at best. Her mouth watered, forcing her to swallow. Her hands shook as she reached for the bottle and the cork. Her nerves were a-jangle, raw, exposed. She closed her eyes, but that made the room swirl. *Calm down,* she ordered herself. But even tightening her lips couldn't keep them from quivering.

"I can't take any more of this. I need help." She knew even as she whispered the words that the only comfort she was going to get was in her hands. Alcohol was a depressant, and she needed something to dull the pain, to take away the sharp edges of despair.

The neck of the bottle clattered against crystal as she poured a perfect shot. She lifted the glass and closed her eyes and inhaled the oaken scent. The first contact burned her lips and tongue, then smoothed into a familiarly pleasant, reassuring tang. She let it roll around her mouth before swallowing the rest of it.

God, it tasted good.

CHAPTER SEVEN

CRAIG PULLED UP in front of Kerry's building, left his keys in the ignition and stepped into the well-appointed lobby.

"I don't know if you remember me, Earl," he said to the doorman with a big smile and extended hand. "I'm a friend of Mrs. Durgan. I came by to see her last week."

"Yes, sir, Mr. Robeson. Recognize your car, too."

"We had an unfortunate incident at the soup kitchen where Mrs. Durgan and I were serving today. I'm afraid she's a bit upset," Craig said. "I thought I'd stop by and see if I could cheer her up."

Kerry would be furious if she found out he'd portrayed her as a flighty female who became disconcerted because some homeless person might have called her a name, but it was the best excuse he could conjure up under the circumstances.

"Sorry to hear that. She's such a generous lady. Now that you mention it, she did seem a bit... preoccupied when she came in."

Craig pushed a folded bill into the man's palm. "How about letting me go up and surprise her?" Had he been thinking clearly, he would have stopped off and bought flowers or candy for show.

The doorman glanced at the folded money and almost did a double take when he realized there was a zero after the five. It was so large a denomination he should have been suspicious. If he was, greed won out. Casually he slipped the bill into his pocket. "Of course, sir. Right this way."

He led Craig to the open door of the elevator, motioned him into it, inserted a card in the penthouse slot and stepped back with an ingratiating smile as the shiny brass door slid closed.

Lousy security, Craig noted as the car began its rapid ascent. The elevator opened onto the tastefully appointed foyer. He went to the door on the left and knocked.

No response. He rapped on it again, louder this time.

"Go away. I won't let you in. Go away or I'll call the police."

Even through the closed door, he could hear Kerry's anger. No, not anger—fear. Was Durgan with her? Had he beat her again?

"Kerry, it's me, Craig. Open up. Please."

Silence, but he could see a change in the light coming through the little peephole. A moment later the door flew open and Kerry threw herself into Craig's arms, nearly bowling him over. Reflexively he wrapped his arms around her and felt her entire body trembling against him. He also smelled whiskey.

She held on to him for a minute, then separated herself. "I'm…sorry," she muttered, her head down.

He coaxed her inside and closed the door behind them. Her fingers shook as she frantically put on the chain. In the living room, she paced. At least she didn't make a beeline to the bar.

"I'm sorry, Craig," she repeated, but didn't seem to know where to go from there.

He had the impulse to pull her into his arms, but she was halfway across the bright, open room, and he was afraid pursuing her would add to her skittishness. "Why don't you take a seat and tell me what's going on."

Heaving a tremulous sigh, she plopped down on the couch and waved him to the matching chair across from her. When she remained silent, Craig said, "I saw Rafe Durgan outside the shelter."

She closed her eyes and leaned against the soft leather, her face a mask of agony.

"Kerry, what's going on? You told me he was dead. The police think he is. I believe an explanation is in order."

Indecision glittered in her violet blue eyes. Craig knew her well enough to realize she hated having to explain her actions, but she seemed to understand she had little choice. Or perhaps desperation made her want to talk.

"He showed up last week. I hadn't seen him since our divorce. I thought…"

"He was dead," Craig finished for her.

She nodded mutely.

"Why isn't he?"

Taking a deep breath, Kerry repeated Rafe's account of how he'd faked his own demise.

"So he's back. What does he want?" Though Craig was confident he knew the answer.

''Money, of course.''

He studied her. Money alone didn't frighten people. They fought over it, were inspired by it, got angry and bitter about it, even killed for it. But it didn't terrify. There was more to this than a demand for money, but that was as good a place to start as any. ''Are you going to give it to him?''

''If I thought it would keep him away, I would,'' she declared, then paused. ''But I know him. He won't be satisfied. He'll just want more.''

''Have you called the police?''

''What for?'' She shook her head despondently. ''He hasn't committed any crime, at least none that I can prove.''

''How about assault and battery?'' he asked.

Her eyes shot open. ''You know?''

''Did you really think I wouldn't notice?'' He couldn't hide his temper at being taken for a fool. ''There was a reason I told you about my parents, Kerry. I recognized the telltale signs of abuse. I was hoping you'd be honest with me.''

She closed her eyes again. ''I had a feeling you did,'' she muttered.

He walked to a side table and reached for the phone. ''The first thing we need to do is call the police.''

Kerry shot up and put her hand firmly on his. ''No.''

He stared at her quizzically. ''Why not?''

''It won't do any good.'' She steered him to the sofa. ''The police won't be able to do anything.''

''Kerry, he's a fugitive.''

''Not anymore.'' She pushed him down on the seat.

"He was very careful to point out that the statute of limitations ran out a long time ago on his outstanding warrants." She began once more to pace. "He's clean, Craig, at least as far as the law is concerned."

Craig was no expert on the law, but what she said did make sense. The only crimes he was aware of for which there were no statutes of limitation were capital offenses, like murder and kidnapping, and Rafe Durgan, scum though he was, had never been accused of either.

"There's another problem," she went on. "When the newspapers get hold of this—and they will—Rafe will know I betrayed him. That'll make him more mad and vicious."

"Betrayed him?" Craig nearly exploded as he jumped to his feet. "You sound as if you owe him some sort of allegiance." His hands were clenched, and his voice rose. "You don't owe him a damn thing, Kerry."

"Listen to me," she demanded. "Betrayal is how *he'll* see it, and he'll take it out on Brian."

"He threatened your son? That's another good reason to go to the police," he argued. "They can protect him."

Frustration swelled inside her. "You just don't get it, do you? He won't physically attack Brian, because if he does he loses all leverage over me. Despite what you may think of Rafe, he's not stupid. He knows if he harmed either of us he'll have my father and brothers to contend with. No, Rafe might kidnap him, even hold him for ransom, but he'll stop short of physically hurting him. Besides, he doesn't have to kidnap Brian to turn his life into hell. Do you understand the kind of psychological damage he can do by simply showing up at Brian's school, making himself visible, tormenting the boy with his presence? There won't be a damn thing anyone can do about it, either. He's the boy's father, after all.''

''We'll get a restraining order against him. He won't be allowed to go anywhere near Brian.''

Kerry laughed almost hysterically. ''You really think that'll stop him?'' She shook her head at Craig's naïveté. ''Even if I did get a court order, Rafe can still do a lot of damage from a distance. Letters. Rumors. Proxies. Brian thinks his father's dead. I want it to stay that way.''

''Don't be stupid.'' Craig's anger flared. ''Your son's going to find out. You can't keep this from him forever.''

She flinched at his outburst. So he did have a temper. Strangely, it made her feel better, maybe because she sensed no physical threat in it. He was concerned—for her and her son. She took a deep breath. ''Someday he'll have to be informed,'' she said almost calmly, ''but I don't want it to be now. He's barely eighteen. Give him time to find himself before he has to deal with this.''

''You can't just do nothing,'' Craig observed, thwarted. Procrastination was a loser's strategy. ''You can't pretend Rafe isn't here. You have to tell Brian, warn him.''

''He's safe for the moment,'' she countered, unmoved by Craig's appeal. ''Spring break starts tomorrow. He's going away with some friends. Rafe won't be able to find him. There's time, but you have to promise me you won't go to the police.''

They faced each other across the coffee table. An eternity seemed to tick by. This was her problem, not his. She was familiar with the principles involved. He wasn't. But delaying tactics smacked of cowardice.

''I won't go to them now,'' Craig finally conceded, ''but I can't say for how long. This problem isn't going to go away from benign neglect, Kerry. Rafael Durgan is dangerous and has to be dealt with.''

She turned, took a step and spun around, her eyes blazing with anger. ''Don't you think I realize that? I lived with the bastard for three years. I know exactly what he's capable of. I also know his hot buttons, and getting the police involved is one of them.'' She sagged. ''Maybe I ought to just give him the money.''

Craig understood the feeling of helplessness, the urge to run. ''You said yourself it wouldn't work, that he'd only come back for more.''

''It'll take even him a long time to go through twenty-five million dollars,'' she murmured.

''Don't be so sure. If he's a gambler, he could lose it virtually overnight in Vegas.''

She walked to the large window and gazed past her roof garden to the looming skyline. A small plane was climbing high into the sky. It seemed so graceful, so placid and proud of itself with its nose in the air.

She paced the room like the proverbial caged animal, her fingers entwined and fidgeting, her head bowed, and she seemed to get more worked up with every step. Finally she came to the picture of her son, picked it up, studied it, put it facedown on the piano and walked to the bar.

Craig had an urge to run over and pull her away, but in her present frame of mind, that would probably make her more defiant.

Her hands spanned the edge of the bar, her attention riveted to the bottles lined up in front of her. His eyes were glued to her hands. Why wasn't she stepping back? She picked up the bottle of bourbon and poured two fingers' worth. His heart began to pound.

"Please don't drink that, Kerry." He was pleading. He cared for her too much to let her destroy herself and he hated her for making him care.

"I need to calm my nerves," she explained. "You don't understand what this has been like."

He swore over his father's grave that he'd never again let another person make him feel weak and vulnerable.

"I know you're hurting. I know you need help." He moved beside her and started to put his arm around her, but instead of leaning into him as she'd done earlier, she shrugged him off. "Who's your counselor?" he asked sympathetically. Every recovering alcoholic who went through Alcoholics Anonymous or any of the programs like it had a buddy, someone he or she could call when the urge reached dangerous levels— a friend who would stay with the tempted drinker, in person or on the phone, to talk him or her out of taking that first drink. The system was often successful—if the recovering alcoholic would make the call. But there were no guarantees, and Kerry had already taken the first drink.

"It doesn't matter," she murmured.

"Is it Charlene?" She was Kerry's best friend. "What's her number? I'll call her for you."

"She's away somewhere." Kerry's tone was flat, mournful, defeated.

"Then let me be her stand-in. We'll talk. Go somewhere, if you like. Together we'll get you through this crisis."

"There is no crisis." She stepped away from the bar as if to prove it. "Thanks, anyway."

"There's nothing wrong with asking for help," he reassured her sympathetically. "You're under a lot of pressure right now, and you're tempted. You've already had at least one drink, but that was a while ago. I'll stay with you as long as you like."

"I'm fine," she insisted. "I'm not some alkie who requires coddling all the time. I'm fine," she repeated. But she wasn't fine, and they both knew it.

"Being tempted doesn't make you bad, Kerry. You've had a shock. Under the circumstances, anyone would try to find someone or something to guide them through this tough passage. But you know in your mind and in your heart you're not going to find the answer to your problems in a bottle. You've been there, Kerry. You know this isn't a solution. Please, let me help you or put you in touch with someone who can."

For a moment he thought she was going to give in and furnish him a name and number. But pride was a mysterious factor. It could make people better or it could block them from asking for the kind of assistance they desperately needed and wanted.

"I don't want your help or anybody else's," she snarled, and stamped her foot.

That was when he saw the situation was lost. He'd pushed too hard. He should have—

He stopped. A long time ago, he'd blamed himself for what his father was. Several years in Al Anon— counseling for the families of alcoholics—had taught him otherwise. He wasn't going to fall into that trap again.

"Don't play so damn high and mighty with me, Craig," she shouted. "Yeah, I had a drinking problem for a while, but I'm past all that. I've been on the wagon for a year now. I'm over it."

"Listen to what you're saying." The entreaty was gone from his voice. "You know what they call this kind of rationalization—"

"I never was an alcoholic anyway," she countered petulantly, refusing to listen to him. "Not really. Being dry as long as I have been proves it."

"Stinking thinking, Kerry. That's what they call it." The steel was back. Not sharp, but hard, firm and uncompromising. "Don't try to fool yourself or me. You're an alcoholic, and you always will be, whether you want to admit it to me or not. Isn't one of the first things you learned at Betty Ford's that you have to be honest with yourself? That you have to admit you need help?"

"Get out of my face, Craig," she yelled. "This is none of your business."

He was handling this badly, but he had to get her away from the bottle. He stifled an urge to bellow at her—to pull her into his arms and beg her not to take another drink. The decision had to be made *by* her, not *for* her. He could snatch the drink from her hand, empty every damned one of the bottles down the drain. It would just delay her getting the drink she craved. She had to quit because she wanted to, not because someone forced her to.

"Kerry, it's not too late," he said gently, compassionately. "You've had a drink, but you're still in control. Leave it alone."

"To calm my nerves," she implored in a hopeless attempt to convince herself.

His heart ached. "It won't calm your nerves, Kerry. It'll kill them. Is that what you want? To go back to the zombie state you were in before you got help?"

"I want you to stop badgering me," she screamed.

He felt powerless, deflated. "I will," he said sadly, "if you don't take that drink. It isn't necessary. You don't need it. You're stronger than it is. All you have to do is prove it."

"Oh, I can prove it," she said flippantly. "I'll take just one."

Don Quixote had tried once more to come to the rescue, but the windmill was bigger and mightier. "One is too many, Kerry, and a thousand isn't enough. I'll stay with you," he told her again, "for as long as you need me, as long as you don't take another drink."

She fingered the glass.

"But if you take it," he warned, "I'm out of here. I won't be an enabler. I won't stand by and watch you do this to yourself." *I won't let you do this to me.*

She glared at him smugly, and he saw she didn't really believe him—or didn't want to.

"Take that drink and I'm leaving, and I won't be back. You'll be on your own."

He saw doubt in her troubled concentration as she studied him. Indecision. An urge to withdraw. Until defiance hardened her resolve. She smirked, lifted the glass in a toast and tossed the contents down in one gulp, her gaze never leaving his.

He took a deep breath and closed his eyes. He'd failed. Squaring his shoulders, he mounted the three steps to the entryway. After releasing the chain and opening the door, he turned to her one last time.

"God help you, Kerry," he said, and walked out. He heard the glass shatter against the door as he closed it behind him.

As much as Craig knew he'd done the right thing in leaving Kerry—or as she would probably put it, abandoning her—it tormented him. He felt like a quitter, a deserter, and it revived all the contradictory emotions he'd suffered with his father. A longing for love and affection. Fear of the man who could give or withdraw them. Guilt that he must be in some way responsible for what Harry Robeson had become. Self-loathing that he should need approval from someone he didn't respect. And a crushing sense of impotent shame that he could do nothing about any of it.

How many times had he told himself he wouldn't get involved with a drinker? Yet he'd gone back to Kerry Durgan in spite of knowing who and what she was. She had a disease. What was his excuse? Testosterone? It not only sparked his libido, it short-circuited a man's power to think straight.

But staying and arguing with Kerry after she'd started drinking again would have validated her behavior and made him a facilitator. He couldn't do that. He wouldn't. Sobriety alone could put her back on track. Had she poured herself another drink after smashing her glass against the door? Probably. Was she capable of stopping at this point? Probably not.

In the lobby, Craig wrote a telephone number on a piece of paper he took from his pocket notebook, folded a hundred-dollar bill under it and handed it to the doorman.

"I need your help, Earl. Here's my cell phone number. I'd very much appreciate it if you'd call me if Mrs. Durgan goes out. It's important. I will, of course, make it worth your while, especially if you can find out where she's going. You understand, this is between you and me."

"Of course, sir," the doorman responded in a confidential tone. "Be glad to help in any way I can."

Craig drove downtown and parked in the lot across from the central police station. He could have gone inside and asked for Detective Dawson, but there was a good chance Craig would be recognized, and he didn't want to raise speculation or take a chance on someone from the press being around, sniffing out a story.

Not wanting to tie up his cell phone, he used the mobile in his car to call inside. Several minutes later a man emerged from the building, walked to a car in the designated parking zone and drove off. Craig followed to a coffee shop a few blocks away.

"Thanks for seeing me, Hank," Craig said after they shook hands. They found seats at a yellow Formica-topped table. "How's Lucille?"

"Doing great." Hank wasn't a particularly tall man, which made him suited for gymnastics in high school and college. He didn't claim to be able to do a double reverse somersault from the parallel bars anymore, but he was still trim. His physical speed and strength served him well both on his job and at home, and he always gave Craig a workout on the handball court. "She's decided, though, that she doesn't want any more kids."

Craig raised an eyebrow. "Seven's enough, huh?"

"One for every day of the week." Hank grinned. "I suggested we try for one for every day of the month, but she nixed the idea."

Craig laughed. "Smart lady."

Hank and his wife had had one child who had been born with a severe genetic birth defect. They'd loved the infant unconditionally. A year later the boy died. Advised by their doctor that there was a strong likelihood another pregnancy could result in the same congenital deformity, Hank had had a vasectomy and they'd elected to adopt. Three of their seven children were physically handicapped, but as far as Craig was concerned, they were the luckiest kids in the world to have such loving parents.

The charity train he and Kerry had ridden to Fort Worth had been to support the rehabilitation center Hank and Lucille took their kids to, but even they didn't know he was the one who'd endowed the trust that supported it.

A waitress came to the table carrying a glass carafe of coffee in one hand and two cups in the other. She poured Hank's without asking but quirked an inquiring eyebrow at Craig.

"Thanks," he said with a nod. Wordlessly, she filled his cup and left.

"Haven't seen you in a while," said the plain-clothes detective.

"Been busy." Craig had sold them their first house almost fifteen years earlier when Hank was still a rookie and they were starting out as newlyweds. Craig wasn't sure why they'd become fast friends, but they had, and he knew he could count on Hank.

"Ah, the exciting world of high finance. By the way, Lucille will be all over me if I don't invite you to dinner."

"Thanks, I'd like that, but not tonight. Give me a rain check."

"You know where to find us." Remarkably, Hank and his wife had stayed in that first home. It was well built and in a good neighborhood, and Hank had added on to it over the years. It was the biggest house on the block now, and by far the most attractive. "So what's up?"

Craig told him about Kerry's husband reappearing after so many years, about his attempt at extortion and his capacity for physical violence.

Hank listened thoughtfully. "She's right about a couple of things. At this point, there probably isn't much we can do. Any warrants that might have been out on him at the time would have expired long ago, so technically he's no longer a fugitive from the law. If she wants to press assault-and-battery charges against him, we can nab him on that. Unfortunately, there were no witnesses, the bruises have faded by now and a good lawyer would make sure the court didn't hear about his old record. Even if he was convicted, he probably wouldn't receive more than a slap on the wrist and an admonishment to sin no more. You know what that's worth.'' He sipped his coffee, as displeased with what he was saying as Craig was at hearing it.

''A restraining order is an option, but she's right about that, too. It'll probably just make this guy, Durgan, more incensed and dangerous,'' Hank added.

Craig huffed. ''I know, but I thought it important to inform you of what's going on.''

Hank nodded. ''I'd strongly advise her to come down to the station house and fill out a report. At least it'll be on file if there's a repeat performance. But as I said, at this point there isn't much we can do. You didn't see Durgan hit her. You didn't even see them meet.''

''How else would she know he's still alive?''

The detective considered the question. ''You're not going to like what I have to tell you, my friend, but I'll say it anyway. She told you she wasn't aware Durgan was alive until recently, but you can't be sure that's true, either. You say she's got a drinking problem. I don't think I have to remind you what convincing liars boozers can be.''

He was right. Craig didn't like it, but he had to

acknowledge it was a valid point, objectively speaking.

"I think you're wrong," he told his friend. "At least, I hope you are. She'll file charges against Durgan once she's satisfied she can make them stick. At the moment, though, there's another problem. Kerry's been on the wagon for over a year as far as I know, but this episode has thrown her for a loop. She started drinking today. Whether she'll continue or stop on her own, I can't predict. I've asked the doorman to call me if she goes out."

Hank nodded in instant understanding. "And you want me to pick her up for DWI if she does."

"It's dirty pool, but—"

Hank regarded his friend sympathetically. "I'm amazed you'd get involved with an alcoholic, Craig. I've known you to drop women because they got tipsy at a party. You hate drunks, but obviously, this woman has something that appeals to a different part of your brain." His smile was man to man. "You realize she won't thank you for this."

Craig was uncomfortably aware of that. When— rather than if—she found out he'd gone to the police about her, old charges of spying would be moot. He'd be persona non grata at her house, in her charity work and in her life.

"At least she'll be safe, and so will other people on the road," he said, feeling like a traitor salving his conscience.

The silent waitress returned and refilled their cups.

"Cat got your tongue today, Erma?" Hank asked.

"Dentisht," the woman slurred.

"Ugh. Sorry 'bout that. Hang in there. Time cures everything."

The woman shrugged—*no choice*—and returned to the lunch counter.

A few minutes later, Hank was talking about the progress one of his kids was making in physical therapy when Craig's cell phone buzzed.

"She just went out, Mr. Robeson. Only a minute ago. Took her car. I asked her where she was going, like you said, but all she would tell me was that she needed to do some shopping."

"Thanks, Earl. I appreciate your help."

Craig disconnected and put the instrument in his pocket. "She's gone shopping. My guess is it'll be at the Galleria, since it's close and has all the upscale boutiques."

Hank had already unbuckled the cell phone from his belt. "What kind of car does she drive?"

"A Ferrari. Bright red. You can't miss it. She's got a personalized license plate—Kerry D."

Hank passed on the information and hung up. "A patrol will check out the parking lot and surrounding area. If she's there, we'll keep an eye on her."

"Call me when you pick her up."

CHAPTER EIGHT

KERRY FUMED at Craig's high-handed attitude. As if she didn't comprehend what she was doing! She could handle this. Hadn't she proved that over the past year? Her friends were so damn free with their advice. They thought they knew her better than she knew herself. Well, they didn't. They hadn't endured what she had. How could they possibly understand?

Poor Brian. He'd grown up thinking his daddy was dead when all the time the louse had been living it up in Mexico. Not that she cared. She was well rid of the son of a bitch. In fact, she wished he were dead. It was going to be rough on Brian when he found out.

Craig didn't have a clue. He didn't realize how she'd been treated. It hadn't been easy with Rafe forever on her case about her old man wanting him to work like an animal. And her father hadn't fooled her with his pretending to be so nice when she knew damn well he thought she was nothing but a tramp. To top it off, he was always buying Brian things, trying to bribe the kid away from her. He thought she hadn't figured it out, but she had. She wasn't stupid.

Well, she'd shown him. Shown them all. She'd show Craig, too.

He said she couldn't take one drink, but he'd been

wrong. She'd had just one, and it wasn't affecting her at all. Of course, he hadn't hung around to see. Now to do some shopping. What did she need? A silky negligee would be nice. But what the hell for? There certainly weren't any men in her life. Not that she'd mind bouncing a few mattress springs with Craig. What color would turn him on? Black lace was a perennial favorite. Or maybe red. She'd have to think about it.

The parking lot was jammed with Sunday shoppers, but she was in luck. She managed to zip into a spot near the main entrance just as someone was pulling out. The jerk in the big Cadillac who'd been waiting for it wasn't very happy, but tough luck.

She locked up and strolled inside. There was a casual bar and grill near the entrance. It smelled of charcoal-broiled beef fajitas and fried onion rings.

"Can I get you something to drink?" the waitress asked as she seated her and handed over a menu. "We have frozen margaritas on special. A dollar apiece, if you're having nachos."

The aroma of cumin, oregano and refried beans was inviting. "That sounds good."

One margarita wouldn't hurt. The bourbon hadn't even produced a mild buzz, and having a margarita with food wouldn't be a problem, either. There was music coming over the PA system. Reba MacIntyre.

Kerry had entertained notions of becoming a country singer once. Everybody said she was good, but then she'd had to get married and, of course, Brian was born. So the career was forgotten. Forgotten by everyone but her. She used to listen to the radio when

Rafe was out mending fences or whatever the hell it was her father had him doing in the hot sun. She'd sing along, harmonize with the lead vocalist and try to hear what it sounded like. She hadn't done that in a long time, though. Like so many other things.

When Brian had been about two, a country group in Coyote Springs had asked her if she'd be interested in joining them. It would have been a good way to find out if she could make it as a singer, but Rafe had blown his top. Her place was home taking care of him and his kid, not getting up on a stage with clinging pants and a tight shirt so other guys could drool over her. He tried to make it sound like he wanted her all to himself, but she knew he was really afraid some guy would make a pass and she'd flirt right back. It might have been fun.

Her drink arrived in a long-stemmed bowl glass rimmed with salt. Rafe always drank tequila. She'd never much cared for it except in a mixed drink like this. Of course, this one was a little weak, but what could you expect for a buck? As soon as the food arrived, she'd have to order another. Nothing cooled the tongue after eating spicy jalapeños like a nice salty margarita.

"Your food will be here shortly," the waitress said a few minutes later. "Can I get you another drink?"

Service was pretty slow. Good crowd. And the drinks were watered. "Sure. Might as well."

Her third one arrived with her platter of nachos. Not that it made any difference. She wasn't very hungry. The chili peppers only made her more thirsty.

The lounge was beginning to fill up by the time she

pushed aside the nearly untouched plate of cold tortillas, beans and guacamole. She glanced at her watch. If she was going to do any shopping, she better get to it.

At Victoria's Secret she dallied over lingerie, then on an impulse bought a deep purple negligee. Passionate purple. She giggled to herself. *I wonder if he likes purple and if he's very passionate.* He was always so reserved and gentlemanly. Was he like that in bed, too? *Excuse me, ma'am, but would it be all right if I...* The clerk looked at her funny when she tittered. *Is your name Victoria?* she wanted to ask. *Well, I've got a secret, too.*

She snickered as she left the shop and walked toward the entrance where she'd parked her car. Maybe she'd stop at the lounge and have another margarita. Shopping was thirsty work, and there sure wasn't anyone to go home to.

"I don't know what Craig was so upset about," she muttered as she sipped another drink. "These things aren't doing a thing for me. I told him I could handle this stuff." Just like every man she'd ever met, he thought he knew best. First her father orders her to marry Rafe, then Rafe takes over as the male-in-charge. Now Craig seemed to think he should be her keeper.

A George Strait song came on, and she began to hum along with it. Not bad, she decided, then noticed a guy at the end of the bar staring at her. What the hell was that creep gawking at? Probably time to get home, anyway.

She almost lost her balance when she slid off the

barstool. Someone must have spilled a drink on the floor and made it slippery. They ought to clean things like that up before someone got hurt and sued them. She stepped into the waning sunlight. Golly, it was still hot out. Now, where had she left her car? Oh, yes, right by the entrance. But where? She couldn't see it. Must be behind that city bus.

She walked around the bus, and sure enough, there it was. She unlocked the door and climbed in. Sweat was trickling between her breasts. Too damned hot. And quiet. Need some beat. She started the engine, opened the electric windows, set the air-conditioning on full blast and punched on the radio. She found a country station and upped the volume. Much better.

Giving the rearview mirror a cursory glance, she backed out of the space and rammed the transmission into forward gear. At least, she thought she put it in forward. When she took her foot off the brake and stomped on the gas pedal, the car lurched violently backward and jolted to a stop, to the combined sound of crunching metal and tinkling glass.

She looked in the mirror. A boy of maybe ten or eleven was sitting on the hood of the car behind her, his eyes wide, his knees drawn up to his chin. *Doesn't he know he shouldn't sit on people's cars? I bet the rivets in his jeans scratch the finish. The owner is going to be really ticked when he finds out.*

A man wearing tan pants, boots and a big silver belt buckle was standing beside her car door, saying something, but she couldn't make out what it was. He leaned down, reached through the window, scowled in her face and turned off the ignition. The music stopped.

"What are you doing? What's going on?" she demanded. *Who does this big lug think he is?*

"Just shut up, lady, and stay where you are."

"How dare you talk to me that way? Let me out of this car." She tried to open the door but he had his knee firmly pressed against it. "You have no right—"

Somewhere close by, the wailing sound of a police siren was winding down and the reflection of red lights was flashing around her. So many people had gathered, and they were making her nervous. What were they after? Her car?

"What happened?" a male voice inquired.

"She pulled out of this spot without looking and damn near hit the kid there. If he hadn't been quick enough to jump on the hood of that car, she would have kneecapped him."

That can't be me they're talking about, Kerry thought. *They must be talking about someone else. I'm always a very careful driver.*

An overweight man in a police uniform came up to her and opened the car door for her. She was about to thank him when he ordered, "Step out, ma'am."

Pretty cheeky. Didn't even have the courtesy to say please. "What's the problem, Officer?"

"Step out of the vehicle, ma'am."

"I—"

"Now."

I don't know what he's so upset about.

She worked her legs from under the wheel. The

small car was always difficult getting into and out of, but it hugged the road beautifully.

"Have you been drinking, ma'am?"

"I..." She hesitated and then decided honesty was the best policy. "I had one watery margarita a little while ago...well, seems like hours ago."

More people had gathered. Some were snickering, others frowning and shaking their heads. *This is all a terrible mix-up. Back home in Coyote Springs the cops know who I am and take care of me. Sure, they stop me once in a while, but it's always to make sure I'm all right, then they escort me home. My name may be Durgan, but people there recognize me as Adam First's daughter, and they respect me. Obviously these city slickers don't realize who I am. Well, my lawyer will see to it they find out.*

CRAIG ARRIVED at the police station before Kerry was brought in. It wasn't a happy place under any circumstances. People didn't go there because they were in a festive mood or because they wanted to socialize. That realization made Craig wonder, not for the first time, what attracted men and women to an occupation that constantly dealt with humanity's flaws.

The challenge, some said. The possibility of righting a wrong. The chance to put bad guys away. Whatever the reason, Craig was grateful there were people willing to devote themselves to the profession, for it definitely was. Nobody ever referred to it as a job.

The bad guy in this case wasn't a man but a woman.

He heard Kerry before he saw her. She was yelling and snarling, telling her captors in very colorful language that they didn't know what they were doing or who she was or what a big mistake this was. She seemed to take great pleasure in explaining to them that they were going to be sorry.

Then he saw her, and the scene grew even uglier. She was being led in handcuffs by two heavyset uniformed policemen, each holding an arm to keep her from bolting. Where she thought she could go under the circumstances was anybody's guess.

Her beautiful, off-the-shoulder black hair was disheveled enough to be described as a rat's nest. Her pistachio-green cotton shirt was askew, the top button undone, revealing creamy bra and straps against alabaster skin. One tail of the shirt was hanging out of her khaki pants. Her mascara and eye shadow had run, streaking her cheeks black and blue. Fury and liquor made her eyes red and raw-looking.

She kept up the contortions until she saw Craig, then she drew herself up and stared at him. Her initial reaction was one of unvarnished pleasure. Hope. Salvation. Her knight had arrived. Don Quixote to the rescue. Then bewilderment set in and she growled, "What are you doing here?"

He stood straight and faced her. In a calm voice, he said, "A friend of mine called me a little while ago. Said they were bringing you in."

The answer appeared to mollify her. Questions like how the friend knew Craig would be interested didn't seem to dawn on her.

"Good. Now, get me out of here. I don't know what this is all about, but I'm sure you can work it out with them. First, tell them to take these damn cuffs off me.''

''I can't do that, Kerry.''

She gaped. ''What do you mean you can't do that? Of course you can. You've got to. Tell them to take their hands off me and let me go.'' When he didn't comply, she added. ''Oh, all right. I'll pay whatever fine they want me to, though I don't understand why I should, but—'' she screwed up her mouth in disgust ''—get me out of here. I want to go home, Craig.'' The last came out as a whine.

''You're going to have to stay here tonight, Kerry.''

''What? Stay here?'' she screamed. ''In the police station?''

''In jail,'' he told her.

Her eyes grew wide. Apparently, the idea had never entered her head. ''That's ridiculous,'' she shouted. ''Look, pay them whatever they want and I'll reimburse you. I have the money. You know that.''

Quietly, patiently, he said, ''It's not a matter of money. You've been arrested for drunk driving. You have to spend the night in jail. That's the law.''

''I am not drunk,'' she announced.

If she could smell herself, she wouldn't say that, Craig thought. ''Maybe you don't realize it, but you are. You're drunk, and you were driving. You almost hit a little boy. You could have killed him, Kerry, or crippled him for life.''

She threw her shoulders back. ''I did no such thing. Who told you that? It's a lie.''

''There are witnesses.''

''They're all lying,'' she insisted.

Craig shook his head. It was useless trying to discuss this with her in her current state. Maybe in the morning after she'd sobered up.

A policeman behind a desk said, "We have to take her now, Mr. Robeson."

"Take me? Take me where?" Kerry cried in panic. "What's going on? What are they going to do to me? Craig, help me," she begged. "Please. I'll do anything. Please. Don't let them do this. I'll do whatever you want. Please." She was trying to pull away from her guards, sinking onto the floor in an attempt to keep them from moving her.

Craig's throat was so tight it was a struggle to get the words out. "There's nothing I can do for you now, Kerry. I'll see you in the morning."

As the cops started to drag her away by the arms, she dug in her heels. Then the foul language and curses began, accompanied by vows of hatred.

Craig watched in silence as she was carted through a set of double doors. Her imprecations echoed along the walls for a minute before they were lost in the distant maelstrom of noises.

Detective Hank Dawson had stood in the background during the melee. He moved to his friend's side and rested a hand on his shoulder. "You all right?"

How could he be? "Fine."

"There's one consolation," Hank informed him.

"What's that?"

"At least your head won't hurt in the morning."

It's not my head that's hurting now, he wanted to say, but from Hank's tone and touch, he knew his friend understood that. Why had he ever gotten involved with Kerry First Durgan? Why hadn't he left her alone? She didn't want him in her life. Why did he even consider having her in his?

"What time will she be released in the morning?" he asked.

"Around eight."

"I'll get here early."

CRAIG WAS waiting for Kerry when the jailer brought her out. She glowered at him, angry, ashamed, humiliated, exhausted and very sober—more sober perhaps than she had ever been in her life.

"You did this to me, didn't you?" she asked, but it was a statement rather than an accusation.

Sometime during the night, when the moans and curses had subsided and she'd coiled herself up defensively in a corner, she'd realized Craig's being at the police station hadn't been as simple as a friend calling him about her arrest.

"Yes," Craig said simply.

No elaboration. No excuses. No apology. He'd had her thrown in jail and kept there. It had been the worse nightmare of her life. Even Rafe's violence hadn't affected her as deeply. She wanted to hate this man standing in front of her. She should be cursing him, slapping him across the face for what he'd done, but she was powerless to do any of those things. She'd always admired strength, and sometime after the liquor had worn off and logic fought for dominance in her pounding head, she'd realized that Craig Robeson was very strong, too strong for her to fight.

"I'll take you home," he said, and waited for her to respond.

Without uttering a word or giving any signal, she walked past him to the exit.

The air seemed fresher than she ever remembered the outdoors being. Still, she wondered if the clawing stench of pine disinfectant would ever leave her nostrils. Instead of cleansing, it made her feel dirtier than she was. Underneath it she could still smell the sickening odor of unwashed bodies, of clogged plumbing, of vomit and blood.

The sounds of women cursing, throwing up, wailing and crying had been straight from Dante's *Inferno*. The food was unpalatable. Thank God, she hadn't been hungry. She didn't even bother to fight when another woman, probably in her fifties but looking decades older, snatched the tray from her and starting wolfing down the congealed stew or whatever it was supposed to be.

Craig held the door to his Saab for her. She got in silently.

"I'll have someone pick up your car later," he said after he slid behind the wheel and started the engine.

She didn't say thank-you. She didn't say anything.

"There's a makeup case in the back seat if you want to use it. And I brought a raincoat you can put on over your clothes. Sorry it's not raining."

"Very considerate of you," she managed to say. It was, for the moment, the closest she was willing to come to thank-you.

He seemed untouched by her brooding hostility as he drove conservatively through city traffic, then finally swung into her circular driveway. He shut off the engine, left the keys in the ignition and got out. The doorman was there to open her door. Not batting an eye at the sight of her raincoat in the sunny spring weather, he greeted her. "Good morning, Mrs. Durgan."

"Good morning, Earl." She marched to the main entrance.

Craig caught up with her and escorted her inside. She said nothing when he stepped into the elevator with her. She merely took out her key card and inserted it into the penthouse slot.

No words were spoken as they ascended the thirty stories. He waited to see if she would invite him in. She didn't specifically do so, but she didn't object when he followed.

Dropping her handbag and the makeup case on the hall table, she turned to him and looked him straight in the eyes. He stood inside the doorway, impassive, prepared, it would seem, for a tirade or a slap.

She wasn't a crier. The last time she'd allowed herself to cry in front of anyone had been at her mother's funeral. Now she was powerless to hold back the tears. He narrowed the space separating them and gathered her in his arms. Without saying a word, he held her against him, stroking her hair and uttering a soothing, "Shh."

"I should hate you," she moaned into his chest. "That place—"

"It's over," he murmured, and planted a kiss on the top of her head. "It's over." He rocked her. "I'm sorry," he said softly. "But there was no other way."

She sobbed for several minutes before pulling back enough to look at him with red-rimmed eyes. "It worked. You got my attention." She had to touch him again, had to feel his warmth and strength. She pressed herself closer and heard the drumming of his heart. "You did the right thing."

Suddenly frightened by the need curling through her body, she arched back once more. "I...I have to shower, get cleaned up. I smell like the drunk tank." She extricated herself from his embrace though he made no attempt to hold her against her will. Boldly, she smiled at him. "Thanks to you."

"Go shower, then." He withdrew, giving her space. "I'll have breakfast ready when you get out."

She would have preferred an offer to wash her back or any other part of her he might be interested in touching, but her mind and body were rushing things. There was time.

The kitchen smelled of frying bacon, fresh-brewed coffee and warm buttered toast when Kerry entered it a half hour later. Her hair was still damp, but it was gloriously clean. She'd shampooed it three times, letting the rich lather also cleanse the rest of her body. She couldn't say she felt good, exactly. The worst of her hangover had passed an hour or so before she was released, leaving her weary and drained, yet she was experiencing a sort of elation. Maybe it was from not having slept all night. Maybe it was because Craig had been there for her and was still there for her now.

"What time does your maid arrive?" The clock on the wall said almost nine-thirty.

"Usually around nine, but I called her from the bedroom and told her to take the day off—with pay."

"She'll love you forever. How do you like your eggs?"

"Poached, and just one, please."

She chuckled when he didn't even bat an eye but smiled. After adjusting the gas under a pot already in place, he carefully cracked three eggs and lowered them into the simmering water.

"I learned a lot yesterday," she said as she poured herself a cup of steaming coffee and sat at the table by the window. It was already set for two.

"Like what?" He set a plate in front of her—egg, bacon, buttered toast—deposited his larger portion on the table opposite her and slid into the seat.

"Like I never want to see the inside of a jail cell again as long as I live." She was scarfing down the food before her, unaware till then how hungry she was. She gulped coffee, then put down her cup and faced him squarely.

"I'm well aware that what you did wasn't easy, Craig. That it wasn't done out of malice or anger, though God knows you have the right to feel those emotions toward me."

"No, I don't." He rested the hand holding the fork on the edge of the table. "You're not bad, Kerry."

The warmth of his words and the kindness in his voice made her smile. "Just a fool." She laughed at his embarrassment. "But that's not what I want to talk about."

She picked up her fork and began to eat again. He did the same and waited for her to continue.

"I had my last drink yesterday," she announced proudly between bites of toast. "You probably don't believe me, but it's true. You made me see where I was headed, what I was doing to myself." She took another sip of coffee.

"I hope so." He reached across the table and placed his hand over hers.

"I realize it won't be easy," she admitted.

"It'll get easier with time." He tried to assure her, and prayed what he was saying was true.

"I managed it for a year."

"One day at a time, and I'll be here whenever you want me, whenever you need me."

"I thought you'd abandoned me last night," she said plaintively.

He started to say something, but she shook her head to stop him. "That's when I realized how much I want your respect." It had come as a real shock—the sudden awareness that what he'd done had been out of love. Somehow, through the fog of inebriation, she'd recorded the torment on his face when he'd seen her at the police station, handcuffed and ranting. What he'd done, calling the police and having her arrested, hadn't been painless for him.

Another picture had also crept across her consciousness. The boy sitting wide-eyed on the hood of a car, his knees pulled up to his chin. She could live with being an alcoholic, with fighting the urge for liquor every day of her life, but she couldn't live with herself if she'd hurt a child. Even if the pit of insanity they called the drunk tank hadn't convinced her to reform, the lasting image of that terrified boy did.

"You mean a great deal to me, Kerry. I don't know where all this is going, but I'm willing to find out if you are."

There was a noise at the front door, and suddenly it slammed. Kerry's eyes went wide, and Craig could see fear drain her face of color. Durgan?

CHAPTER NINE

"Mom? Where are you?"

Kerry's color returned with a vengeance, and the fear Craig saw in her was of a different sort.

"Oh, my God, it's Brian." She jumped up from the table. "What's he doing here? He was supposed to go to Florida on break. What if Rafe shows up? If he finds him here—"

"Calm down." Craig had also risen from the table. He reached out and took her hand. "If you don't want him to know something's wrong, you're going to have to stay cool."

"We've got to get rid of him," she said in a hushed voice.

He framed her shoulders and kissed her on the forehead. "We will."

"Mom?" Brian called again.

Kerry took a deep breath and strolled into the hallway.

"Brian, honey, what a surprise!" She put a broad smile on her face. Craig came up behind her. "I thought you were going away on your spring break." She swept over to her son and gave him a big hug and kiss.

"Change in plans," he said, stepping back and eyeing the stranger suspiciously. "Stan had to come here to Dallas to see his father. They think he may have had a heart attack or something. Mitch totaled his car—"

"Was he hurt?"

"Nah. Not a scratch, but his mother says she's not going to give him another one for the rest of the year. And Carl met this girl who has a place in Malibu. She offered to teach him to surf, so he took off with her."

"What about your other friends?" Kerry asked.

"They'd already made their own plans."

Craig observed Kerry's son. He was more mature than in the photo on the piano, a little under six feet, lean and trim. A runner's build, or maybe a swimmer's.

"Who are you?" Brian inquired.

Craig stepped forward, his hand outstretched. "Craig Robeson. Your mother and I are old friends."

"We went to high school together," Kerry added cheerfully.

"Pleased to meet you." Brian shook Craig's hand, but he was more wary than friendly.

"Too bad your plans fell through," Craig said casually. "What did you have lined up?"

"Scuba diving off the Florida Keys, but the weather's turning sour, anyway."

Craig nodded. "This is hurricane season, after all. How about the mountains? Do you snow ski?"

"Yeah, but we checked Colorado and Utah, and the only resorts we could get reservations at on such short notice have lousy conditions."

Craig chuckled. "Figures."

"How about New England? Or even Europe, honey? You really enjoyed your trip to St. Moritz with Uncle Gideon last fall."

"Too late. Everything's booked. Where's Evelyn? I'm hungry." Brian strode to the kitchen, followed by his mother and Craig.

"She has the day off."

Brian stopped when he saw the two unfinished breakfasts on the table by the window. He turned sharply to his mother. "Did I interrupt something?"

"Honey," Kerry muttered defensively.

"We were having breakfast," Craig said. "Can I fix you something? Our eggs were poached, but I can fry you some if you prefer. There's plenty of bacon."

Brian stared at his mother. "Your hair's wet." He assessed Craig for signs that he might be wet behind the ears, too.

Craig went to the counter, retrieved the coffeepot and filled their cups. He held up the pot. "Want some?" He took the lack of response to be a no.

"What the hell's going on here?" Brian asked.

Craig returned the carafe to its place. "I got here about an hour ago," he explained casually.

"He's contributing to my foundation," Kerry told her son. "Isn't that wonderful? You've heard of Robeco. Craig owns the corporation."

"You spent the night here, didn't you?" Brian challenged him.

An explosive "No!" came from Kerry and Craig simultaneously, which instantly made it sound like a lie. Judging from Brian's face, that was exactly how he interpreted it.

Kerry panicked. Hearing a question like that from her son... She'd had a few men in her life after her divorce from Rafe, but she'd never brought them to the house on the ranch. Brian might have heard rumors—she hoped he hadn't—but she could always point out that she hadn't violated their house, their home.

She also hadn't considered how her son might react to a man in her life. She'd assumed he'd be happy for her, and under different circumstances, he probably would have been. Finding her like this... She could see how it must appear. She had the option of asking Craig to leave, of course, then convincing Brian he was misinterpreting what he'd seen. But Brian was in danger if he stayed here. Rafe would do anything to get his hands on money—including use his own son. Better for Brian to leave here angry than get caught in the crossfire between his mother and his *dead* father. Suppose he wanted to meet his dad. And what if Rafe turned him against her? No use taking chances.

She sidled up to Craig and wound her arm around his. "I told you we're old friends, Brian. I'm a single woman. I have a right to see men if I want to."

Brian's deep tan took on a nearly maroon hue. "Seeing men...but sleeping with them..." he sputtered. "Well, I'll just leave the two of you alone, then," he snarled, and stomped from the room.

"Brian, please, wait. Let me explain," Kerry called as she followed.

Her son whirled to face her, his expression one of

outrage and disappointment. "I can't imagine what else there is to say, Mom. You'll be pleased to know Uncle Mike went over the facts of life with me some time ago. So, you see, there really isn't anything to explain." He turned to Craig. "You do anything to hurt my mother, and I'll kill you."

"Brian!" Kerry exclaimed in horror.

He gave her a cold stare, spun around and stormed to the hall, where he picked up his tote bag and strode out of the apartment, slamming the door behind him.

Kerry pressed her hands to her lips, her shoulders hunched. Craig came up behind her and wrapped his arms across her middle.

"Brian'll be all right when he calms down," he assured her. "It's always a shock when kids find out their parents are normal humans with normal urges."

She turned in the circle of his arms and cried on his shoulder. She never cried, and here she was doing it twice in one day, in the same man's arms.

"He hates me," she muttered against Craig's chest.

"Not by a long shot." He held her hips and smiled into her tear-filled eyes. "I'd say just the opposite. He loves you very much. Otherwise he wouldn't have threatened to kill me."

She disengaged herself. "How can you treat this so lightly?"

"Not lightly, Kerry." He dropped his hands to his sides. "I don't treat anything that affects you lightly."

She'd always wanted someone to cherish her. Her father had tried and failed. Rafe never even made the effort. In a sense, she'd lost her self-respect, too, and now this man, who should have nothing but contempt for her, said he cared. It gave her a warm feeling, but it frightened her, as well. After so many failures, how could she be sure of her emotions or be worthy of this man?

"I have to go after him," Kerry insisted, but made no move to do so.

He lifted her hand and placed it on his chest, letting her feel the beat of his heart. "Not yet. Give him time to cool off."

"But—"

"Brian'll be all right." He gave her a reassuring smile. "Let him be. Besides, you said yourself you didn't want him hanging around here."

With the merest adjustment, she molded herself under his arm. "I wish I could go back and start all over." She raised her head. "What am I going to do about Rafe? What if he saw Brian?"

Craig tightened his hold on her. "Not likely. He's probably sleeping off his own hangover this time of day."

Kerry laughed but stopped when she realized she was dangerously close to tears again.

"Do you want any more breakfast?" he asked.

She nestled against him. "I just want you to hold me, Craig. It's been so long since I've been held. You're good for me. Better than I deserve. Better than I have any right to ask for."

"Kerry," he whispered in protest.

"I don't deserve you," she went on as if he hadn't spoken her name. "But I need you." Her eyes were dewy. "Make love to me, Craig," she said in a soft voice. "Take me to my bed and make love to me."

His response was to lower his head and capture her lips with his. If she thought this was going to be a mild-mannered mating, she was quickly convinced otherwise. He plunged into her mouth with a passion that took her breath away, yet there was a gentleness in his aggression, a seeking rather than a taking in the way his tongue curled against hers.

When finally he broke off, he cradled her face between his hands and smiled at her. ''You said something about a bed.''

She laughed, delighted, intrigued by the coming adventure. Happy. At least, that was the only word she could think of for the strange, wild emotion going through her—if she had been thinking about words at all. She took him by the hand and led him down the hall.

The bedroom was large, light and feminine, the bed big, silky and inviting. He turned her toward him, held her hand at his side, touched his lips to her brow and murmured, ''Perfect.'' They both knew he wasn't referring to the room or the bed.

She began to unbutton his shirt. He fumbled with the snaps on her blouse. She tugged his shirt off his shoulders. He removed hers. She yanked his T-shirt out of his trousers and pulled it over his head. He released the clasp on her bra and let it fall away. She ran her hands across the hair-dusted muscles of his chest. He cupped her breasts and shivered at the sensation of her nipples peaking in his palms.

The momentum of their grappling increased. Tension built. Touch evolved to taste. Fondling advanced toward union.

"Protection," he mumbled in sheer, breathtaking torment as he nuzzled her neck.

"I'm on the pill." She was equally breathless, writhing at the sensations his hands and tongue were conjuring within her.

"I haven't been with—"

"I trust you." She closed her eyes, the more to soak in the sensation of his touch.

Naked, his breath ragged, he lay beside her on the bed. She treasured his patience, his slow, progressive assault on her senses, the sweet intoxication of his touch. She closed her eyes and sighed when his hand covered her mound and ventured beyond. Boneless, limp with need, she was consumed with unbearable want for more of him.

He lavished her with kisses, her cheek, her eyes, her ears, her mouth until neither of them could bear the tension any longer. He rose above her. She guided him inside. As her warmth surrounded him, he was sure he couldn't last. He strained against release.

She smiled at him. "It's all right." Her eyes gleamed with pleasure.

"I'm not going anywhere without you," he assured her, the words caught between mischief and torture.

She laughed then and threw her arms around his neck. "Are you sure?" she asked as she arched her hips.

He groaned and pushed deeper. The rhythm lasted but seconds before she heaved against him with an ecstatic cry. A moment later, he joined her in the rolling, pounding thunder of orgasm.

WHEN THEY were spent, she cuddled against him, her hand resting on his belly, her cheek against his chest. She listened to his heart beat in time with hers.

"I wish we could stay like this forever," she said.

"You'd get bored."

She couldn't resist running a finger along his clean-shaven chin and full mouth. "I don't think so."

They lay entwined in each other's arms for some time. Finally, Craig asked, "Why did you ever get involved with Rafe, Kerry? Couldn't you see he was no good?"

Her body stiffened, and for a moment he thought she was going to erupt at him, but the emotion seemed to pass.

"It's a long story," she muttered.

"I've got time." When she didn't immediately respond, he suggested, "How about I make us some fresh coffee and you tell me all about it?"

She studied him through wide-open eyes. "I'll make it." She shifted out of his embrace, climbed off the bed, snagged a robe from the back of the bathroom door and left the room. Craig pulled on his jeans and T-shirt and followed her to the kitchen.

"My mother died when I was between sophomore and junior year in high school," she explained as she removed a bag of gourmet beans from the refrigerator and poured a measure of them into an electric grinder. "I'd just turned fifteen."

Craig slid the stainless steel basket from under the top of the coffeemaker and put in a clean filter. "I'm sorry. Losing a parent is always difficult, especially when you're young and trying to figure so many things out.''

She said nothing until the grinder stopped. ''The day Mom died, after we came home from the hospital, Dad went into his office and poured himself a drink.'' She dumped the aromatic contents into the lined basket and pushed it in. ''I'd seen him take a beer once in a while with the ranch hands and at parties, and maybe a glass of wine at a holiday dinner.'' She unplugged the grinder. ''But I'd never seen him drink hard liquor before. If it helped him get over the pain, I decided, maybe it would help me, too.''

Craig leaned against the counter and rested his hands on its edge. ''And that's when you started secretly drinking.''

''I had to be discreet.'' She kept her head lowered. ''There was plenty of liquor in the house, but Dad never touched it, so it wasn't hard for me to take a little bit from each bottle. Eventually they'd all be empty, of course, but I wasn't thinking that far ahead.''

She poured water into the machine and flipped on the switch. The coffeemaker started to gurgle, and they returned to the living room. She sprawled on the couch, her legs extended across the cushions in a way that clearly didn't invite him to join her. ''I became pretty rebellious after that.''

He sat in the chair opposite her. ''It couldn't have been easy watching your mother die, knowing there was nothing you could do about it.''

''Maybe if she'd gone to a doctor sooner...but Dad was always busy on the ranch.''

"You're not saying he refused to get her medical attention, are you?" He couldn't believe Adam First was the kind of man who was too busy to deal with his wife's health.

Kerry wanted to say he was; Craig could see it in her eyes. "No, he did everything he could, but it was already too late. He hired a housekeeper to take care of the house, cook, clean and do the laundry. After Mom died, he went back to running the ranch like nothing had happened."

Craig didn't accept it. The man he met wasn't cold and uncaring, but Craig could imagine him burying himself in his work, exhausting himself as a way of dealing with the pain of his loss. Craig had done that in college after his father's death. He'd also been alone, and a nearly manic level of activity and drive for perfection had been his coping mechanisms. Had Adam focused outward to the neglect of his children, or had he simply failed to see that one of them needed extra loving?

"Were you the eldest?"

"The oldest girl. Michael's two years my senior."

"What happened then?"

"Rafe came to the school. He was exciting, different, bold, a maverick—"

"And he knew how to get booze," Craig conjectured.

She smiled wanly. "Yeah. He would get it as long as I had the money, and getting money from Dad wasn't hard. I could always come up with an excuse for needing a few extra bucks. School supplies, a new dress or pair of jeans. Gas money after I got my driver's license.''

"I remember you always had a roll of peppermint candies and offered them around.''

She smiled, almost nostalgically. "Especially when I couldn't get vodka.''

It amazed him that, as attuned as he was to his father's drinking habits, he'd completely missed Kerry's telltale behavior. He hadn't been through counseling yet, hadn't learned the quirks and behavior patterns of secret drinkers, and in his rapture over the stunning coed, he'd fantasized that the candies were to keep her breath kissing sweet. Besides, who would ever have suspected an apparently well-adjusted sixteen-year-old girl of being a closet lush? "So you were drinking the night of the prom,'' he observed.

"I'd had a couple of drinks before you picked me up, but the little purse I used that night was too small for a flask. I was relieved when I found out some of the punch was spiked. You always gave me the wimpy stuff,'' she continued with a smile. "A couple of friends traded cups with me when you weren't looking. By the time Rafe showed up I was already half lit, but I was also worried one of the chaperons would discover the spiked punch and remove it. Then I'd be stuck without a drink.''

Typical alcoholic paranoia, Craig reminded himself—the fear of liquor not being available. "So the real reason you ran off with Rafe was for booze.''

She softened her voice and her expression. "It wasn't to get away from you, Craig. I liked you, enjoyed being with you. You were clean and wholesome, and a part of me wanted to be like that, too, but I knew I wasn't.''

Low self-esteem. It went hand in glove with paranoia. He couldn't help but speculate what he would have done if he'd known she was a boozer. He certainly wouldn't have asked her for a date. And if he'd known she was drinking that night? He probably would have tried to sober her up before taking her home.

''What happened?'' He wasn't sure why he asked the question. He knew damn well what had happened—if not that night, on some other.

''Rafe drove me out by the spillway. We could be alone there. He had plenty of liquor. It didn't take too much more for me to get sloshed.''

''And you had sex with him,'' he concluded, unable to disguise the disgust in his voice.

Her lips tightened and her eyes blazed with anger, then suddenly she flushed in an expression of guilt. ''It wasn't like that, Craig. Have you ever heard of date rape?''

He raised his brows.

''They didn't use that term back then, but that's what it was. Rafe wanted to have sex and I didn't. He said I owed him. I said I'd get him money. But that wasn't what he wanted. 'I'll take it out in trade,' he said, and that's what he did.''

Craig's jaw clenched. ''You're telling me you didn't have consensual sex with him? You were raped?''

She nodded.

He closed his eyes and breathed deeply through his

nose. Ugly images whirled around his brain—of her struggling, scratching, crying while that animal forced himself on her.

"Then why the hell did you marry him? How could you when he did that to you?" He was furious, and it showed in the brittle, accusing edge of his words. "Kerry, how could you?"

She jumped up, equally upset. "Because my father made me, that's why. The honorable Adam First—" she spat the words out "—said no grandkid of his was going to be a bastard."

Craig stood and followed her with his eyes. What he was hearing was unconscionable. "I don't understand, Kerry. Your father forced you to marry the man who raped you?"

She spun away from him, strode to the bar, stopped and mumbled, "I didn't tell him."

Craig's head was reeling. No one in the family seemed to notice that the sixteen-year-old girl in their midst had a drinking problem. Now he was hearing that date rape had resulted in a shotgun wedding.

"Kerry—" he wanted to understand "—why the hell not? I can't imagine him making you marry Rafe if he'd known."

She demurred. "It wasn't all Rafe's fault. It was mine, too."

Craig's heart froze. She sounded like his mother when Harry wasn't around.

"Rafe never had a chance at happiness," Kerry insisted. "His mother was a tramp who didn't care about him, and his father was in prison."

Craig's mother hadn't been a loose woman, but she

had been weak. As for his father, it might have been better if he had been in jail. At least then he wouldn't have been around swinging his fists.

"They weren't the only people in his life. He had teachers, as I recall, who tried very hard to help him. He chose to be what he was."

"That's easy for you to say," she snarled. "You became successful."

Craig was incensed at the twist this conversation had taken. Not too long ago, she'd thrown herself into his arms, terrified by the return of Rafael Durgan, and now she was defending him.

Even more insulting was her comparing Craig with a rapist and wife beater. Had she heard nothing he'd told her last week over brunch? Did he have to show her his scars to prove he'd served his time in hell?

"Am I supposed to apologize for my achievements?" he asked. She wouldn't be the first. There were plenty of people who felt every successful person prospered at the expense of others. Never mind that he played strictly by the rules and employed tens of thousands of workers at wages far above scale.

"No, of course not. It's just that—"

"I gained my success through hard work, Kerry. Nobody gave me any special breaks. I had to make it on my own. As for being rich, there are three ways to get there. Inherit the money. Steal it. Or work for it."

"Actually," she said conversationally, "Rafe was a good worker. Even Dad, who didn't like him, admitted he worked hard on the ranch."

"So why didn't he stay? As the boss's son-in-law,

it sounds like he had it made." Craig checked himself and asked less harshly, "Tell me, did you love him?"

The question seemed to deflate her. "Maybe... sometimes," she admitted quietly. "Being with him was exciting." She fell into a thoughtful silence. "That's one reason I went with him that night, Craig. The booze was part of it, sure, but it was also the adventure of not knowing what was going to happen next." She hesitated. "Maybe I wanted him to rape me that night."

Craig barely kept his voice level. "No, Kerry, you didn't." To her lowered head, he said, "Look at me."

Shyly, she lifted her gaze to him.

"You might have wanted to have sex with him that night," Craig conceded patiently, "but you didn't ask to be raped. By definition, rape is against your will. It's impossible to want something involuntarily. So if you're suffering some sort of guilt complex because you think you asked to be raped that night, forget it. He forced you to do something you didn't want to do. You were foolish to go with him, but that doesn't make you an accomplice."

"It only makes me a fool. Gee, thanks, Craig. That's a great consolation."

He ignored the sarcasm. "Don't you think it was wrong not to tell your father?"

She jutted her chin defiantly. "He wasn't interested in excuses. All he cares about is his precious ranch and the family's reputation."

"I find that hard to believe. Wanting his grandchild to have a legitimate last name doesn't sound sinister to me."

"So you're on his side, too." Kerry had expected him to understand and console her, and all he was doing was throwing more guilt at her. She'd sold her share of the ranch to get away. The Number One was stifling her. She needed her independence. She wasn't cut out to be a rancher's wife, or a rancher's daughter, for that matter. Of course, she knew selling her interest in the family ranch would hurt the old man, but that hadn't been her primary intent. At least, that was what she kept telling herself.

"I really am on your side," Craig assured her, "but you've put yourself on the horns of a dilemma. You expected your father to protect you, yet you didn't give him the information he needed to do it right. So he went with what he had. He did try to guard you, your reputation and the heritage of his unborn grandchild. Later he defended you and your son against a violent husband, and you blamed him for that, too. Seems like he couldn't win."

"Seems like I can't, either," she retorted. "You called me a fool a couple of minutes ago, and now you make it sound like what Rafe did was my fault."

Craig's deep voice took on an impatient edge. "What Rafe did was *his* fault, Kerry," he said slowly. "But lying to your father was *your* choice. You can't keep blaming other people for your mistakes."

"I don't believe this." She exploded. "Who the hell do you think you are, judging me?"

He closed his eyes and took a deep breath. "Sweetheart, I'm someone who's been there. That's why I'm supporting your shelter for battered women and children."

Again, he was preaching to the choir. Besides, this wasn't about other people. It was about her.

"You know the steps necessary for staying sober, Kerry," he went on after a minute. "You have to face up to what you've done to your family and ask for their forgiveness."

"Leave my soul to me, Craig."

"You've come so far, sweetheart. Now it's time to mend fences."

She did not want to discuss her family—not yet. "I talk to my brothers and sister periodically. We're not close, but—"

"And what about your father?"

"Leave him out of this," she snapped, as if he'd pinched a sensitive part of her. In fact, he had.

Craig wanted so much to drop the subject. Holding a person's feet to the fire wasn't something he enjoyed, but doing the difficult and often the unpleasant was part of his makeup. Perseverance had made him the successful businessman he was. The stakes here were far more important than land or money. Kerry had to heal herself, which meant coming to terms with how she'd hurt other people.

"Why are you so hung up on my father, anyway?"

He thought it was obvious, but apparently it wasn't. "It could be that I'm jealous," he admitted. "You have a father who cares about you, a father you can talk to. I only met him once—well, twice actually, but it was the same night—and I liked him. He could have raked me over the coals when I didn't bring you home from the prom, but he didn't. He treated me like an adult even though I wasn't. I never had a father like that, Kerry. You can't imagine how much I envied you.''

Her eyes softened at the reminder of what his life had been like.

''You've hurt him.'' Craig rested a hip on the arm of a chair. ''You've robbed him of something that was very precious to him.''

She turned away. ''I said I don't want to talk about it.''

He walked over to her, placed his hands on her shoulders and gently tugged her to face him. ''I've seen how generous you are with your emotions when you're talking with homeless people. Let that spill over into your personal life.''

''It's none of your business.'' Her voice was beginning to show temper.

Undaunted, he said, ''It became my business when we made love, Kerry. I don't fall into bed with every woman I meet.''

''Just the ones who turn you on,'' she mumbled.

She was looking for a fight. He understood why. Both his friends and his enemies said he was like a bulldog when he thought he was right. Persistence might be admirable, but inflexibility and self-righteousness weren't exactly endearing qualities.

''I don't make love to every woman who turns me on, either. I have sex with some of them, but that's a different matter. You and I didn't just have sex, Kerry. It went beyond that—for you and for me.''

She pulled away and walked to the wall of windows that gave a stunning view of the city of Dallas. ''And so, because we made love, you think you own me, you can dictate what I do.''

''No,'' he responded simply. ''It means that I have a vested interest in your happiness.'' He propped himself against the side of the baby grand piano. ''You're never going to be happy until you own up to what you've done.''

''Go to hell, Craig Robeson. My relationship with my father is my concern, not yours. It will never be yours. And neither will I.'' She spun around, her hands bunched in fists. ''I think you'd better leave.'' She stormed out of the living room. A minute later, he could hear her slamming pots and dishes around in the kitchen.

He returned to the bedroom and finished dressing. Having the doorman see him coming from her penthouse in wrinkled clothes wouldn't help her reputation or his mood.

When he emerged, he found her in the living room sitting on the couch, her back to him, sipping from a cup of coffee and reading a magazine.

''Kerry—'' he started.

''Goodbye, Craig. Thanks for everything.''

He almost sighed as he let air out of his lungs. Stepping behind her, he bent and placed a gentle kiss on the top of her head and wondered if it would be the last time he'd be able to inhale her scent. ''Goodbye, Kerry.''

CHAPTER TEN

KERRY WAS totally baffled about how things could have gone so completely wrong. Their lovemaking had been...well, *spectacular* was the word that came close. It was more than a confirmation of her sexuality; it was an assurance of her worth as a woman, as a person. Then suddenly, with the exchange of a few sentences, the world seemed to reverse course. Consigning the dregs of her cold coffee to the kitchen sink, she put the thought aside. She needed to find Brian.

Then what? Tell him that his father was still alive and was out to make his life miserable? Certainly not over the phone or in the mood he was in. For now she'd settle for knowing he was safe.

She'd met Brian's buddy, Stan Tang, Jr., and his parents the previous fall. The Tangs owned a restaurant on the east side of town. It was prominently listed in the yellow pages. Kerry had intended to go there for lunch but had never gotten around to it. She checked the white pages for a home number. Several Tangs were listed, but only one Stanford.

His wife, Giselle, answered the phone on the second ring. Kerry identified herself and reminded the weary-sounding woman that they'd met at a homecoming game at Tech.

"They're still running tests," Giselle said in response to Kerry's question about Stan, Sr.'s condition. "They're calling it a cardiac incident now rather than an actual heart attack."

"That's good news," Kerry noted, "isn't it?"

"All I know," the woman on the other end said with a sigh, "is that it scared the daylights out of both of us."

Kerry asked a few more questions and sympathized over the torment of uncertainty in a potentially fatal situation. Unwanted, maybe because of her last conversation with Craig, her father sprang to her mind. Adam had been the picture of health the last time she'd seen him, at his birthday party, before he broke his leg in the tornado that destroyed the ranch headquarters, before Kerry had gone into Betty Ford's to dry out. Suppose something like this happened to him. Suppose he died. She'd never see him again. A cold wave of panic rushed through her.

"And he might come home tomorrow," she heard Giselle say.

"I'm glad to hear it. By the way, has Brian been by to see y'all?"

"He brought flowers." There was a smile in the other woman's voice. "It was very sweet of him."

Where had he learned that kind of thoughtfulness? Kerry wondered. Most likely from his uncle Mike or his aunt.

"You wouldn't happen to know where he is right now, would you?"

Giselle paused to consider. "He mentioned something about stopping over at the restaurant. Stan, Jr., is filling in this week while his dad's recovering."

A few minutes later, Kerry called the family restaurant and spoke to the young Tang.

"He was here a couple of hours ago, Mrs. D., but he left."

"Did he happen to mention where he was going?"

"No," Stan replied. "I assumed home, but he might have gone over to see the Hardings."

Kerry didn't recognize the name.

"Gib Harding's on the track team with us at Tech."

Brian's interest in running came as a complete surprise, since he hadn't been on the track team in high school. His doing well at it was even more astonishing.

She asked for the Hardings' number and ended the conversation with a word of encouragement and a request to have Brian get in touch with her if he showed up again. "Yes, it is important," she replied to the boy's question.

An inquiry at the Hardings' yielded no help. He hadn't called or stopped by there.

Kerry had just hung up when the phone rang. Startled, she jerked her hand away, then laughed at herself and snatched up the instrument. "Brian?"

"Not me," announced a jovial female voice. "I go by the name of Charlene."

"Char?" This wasn't the voice she wanted most to hear, but it was very welcome anyway. "Where are you?" she asked anxiously. "Where've you been?"

"Fishing. The kids are on spring break, so we spent a few days out at the lake. Now we're right here in Big D." She exaggerated her mild Texas drawl so that it came out sounding like *Ware rot cheer 'n Big D.* The last syllable rose, making it almost a question. ''Tomorrow it's Six Flags.''

''Fishing. I tried to call you—''

''Did you leave a message? I checked my answering machine twice a day.''

''No. I didn't bother.''

''Couldn't have been too important, then. Hey—'' her voice softened into concern ''—Craig phoned me a little while ago. Said he had to go out of town for a couple of days and suggested you might need a friend. What's up?''

He called Charlene. Did that mean he was afraid she'd dive into another bottle of bourbon? Damn conceited of him, thinking she'd break her vow merely because they'd disagreed. Or maybe he was honestly concerned about her. He hadn't mentioned going out of town, but then, they hadn't really talked about him once they got to the bedroom.

''Do you have a couple of hours?'' Kerry jested.

''I have all the time you need,'' Charlene answered seriously. ''The kids are spending the night with some friends.''

It would help to talk, to let her hair down. ''How about dinner tonight?''

''Great. I'm filling in at the hotel. Why don't you come over here. They've hired a new chef. We can sample his delicacies.''

''Mmm. Sounds intriguing.''

Charlene chuckled. ''It better be appetizing. They're paying the dude a bundle.'' They agreed on a time.

Kerry received a call a few minutes later from a

towing service. Mr. Robeson had asked them to pick up her car at the police impoundment yard. Where did she want it delivered?

"Back here, I guess," she answered without thinking.

"Okay," the male voice on the other end said, "but I thought you might want to get it repaired first."

"Repaired?" Only then did she remember she'd done damage to the Ferrari and would probably be hearing from the owner of the other vehicle, too. She didn't even know what kind of car she'd hit. "I haven't seen it. Is it pretty bad?"

"The whole back end is smashed in, lady."

She'd envisioned a broken taillight. Apparently, she'd struck the front of the other automobile with more impact than she'd realized. The young boy on the hood came to mind again, and her whole body went cold at the thought of what she'd almost done.

She gave the tow service the name of the dealership where she'd purchased the foreign sports car, then telephoned to let them know it was being delivered for whatever repairs were necessary. One advantage of being a multimillionaire, she reminded herself, was that she didn't have to worry about the cost—which would undoubtedly be astronomical.

At a quarter to seven that evening she had Earl call a cab for her. Half an hour later, wearing a lilac sunburst pleated skirt with a matching lace-up double-breasted blouse, she breezed with apparent nonchalance into the sumptuous lobby of the Dallas Hawthorne Hotel.

Charlene said she'd be in the catering office on the

mezzanine. Rather than take the elevator, Kerry climbed the sweeping staircase, feeling grand and very feminine. Inside the glass doors of the business suite, her friend was standing over the receptionist's desk, thrashing through a clipboard holding various colors of paper.

"Hey, nice outfit." Charlene grinned. Her mauve designer business suit of wide-lapelled formfitting jacket and straight-line skirt perfectly complemented Kerry's less formal dress. "Give me five minutes. How about a cup of coffee or a Coke?"

"Go on with what you're doing. I'll be fine." Kerry took a seat beside an end table with a Chinese ginger jar lamp on it and picked up a magazine. She was more interested, however, in observing the busy consultant bustle between the catering manager's office and the receptionist's desk, giving opinions and recommendations. Charlene moved and spoke with the unmistakable confidence of someone completely in command of her life. Maybe one day they could go on Leslie Fischer's show again and give Charlene's success story. It would help women know it was possible to regain dignity and be productive.

Twenty minutes later, her friend stood in front of her, arms akimbo, and released a heavy sigh that would have signaled exhaustion were it not for the broad smile on her face. "Sorry to take so long, but—"

Kerry put the unread magazine aside. "I love work," she commented as she got up. "I could sit and watch it all day long."

Charlene laughed, linked her arm in Kerry's and

ushered her downstairs to a quiet alcove in the main dining room.

A round table that could have served four comfortably was set for two. As soon as they were seated by the headwaiter, the chef came out to greet them.

He was younger than Kerry had expected, still in his twenties, tall and rather thin. His bonhomie seemed a little affected, but Kerry realized after a few seconds it was more a matter of nervous inexperience than insincerity.

He proposed a sampling of several new dishes, which they both approved. He seemed mildly disappointed when they declined his wine suggestions, opting instead for water. Apparently, no one had bothered to tell him the consultant didn't imbibe.

"So what's been going on?" Charlene asked after the chef had retreated to his kitchen.

"A little setback," Kerry announced.

"So I gathered." Charlene relaxed against the back of her chair, elbows on its arms. "Want to tell me about it?"

"I imagine Craig already has."

Charlene cocked an eyebrow. "He didn't tell me anything, Kerry. He only said you might need a friend."

The first course arrived. Mushroom turnovers in a cream cheese pastry with a delicate tarragon sauce.

"Very discreet of him." When Charlene offered no response to her sarcasm, Kerry went on. "I got picked up for DWI yesterday."

"Go on." That was all the other woman said. No

shake of the finger or lecture. No frown or sigh of disappointment.

Kerry related every gory detail. Rafe coming back. His attempted extortion. His threats. Her taking a drink. Craig walking out when she took the second one. Her being picked up in the mall parking lot after almost hitting a kid.

At that Charlene's eyes went wide. "Anybody hurt?"

"If he hadn't been quick, I might have crippled him, Char. Had he been a toddler, I probably would have killed him."

"God."

"Yeah." Kerry bowed her head, again miserable at the recollection of what she'd done, what she might have done.

They sipped water while the second course was served. Green salad with pine nuts and roasted garlic.

"I assume Craig knows about all this."

"A friend of his on the police force called him. He was at the station house waiting for me when I was brought in." Kerry bit her lip. "In handcuffs."

"Standard procedure," Charlene assured her, as if that lessened the humiliation. "So that's why he said you could use a friend."

"He admitted later that he'd alerted the cops. They were on the lookout for me."

"I can see why you're a little miffed at him, then."

Kerry speared a piece of endive while she fumbled for words. "He did the right thing."

Charlene's brows rose at the admission. She apparently hadn't expected her friend to be so generous or understanding. "It couldn't have been easy for him—" she reached out and covered Kerry's hand "—but it was what needed to be done."

Kerry swallowed. "I know."

Charlene smiled encouragingly. "I'm glad you're able to see it that way."

The third course arrived. Crab-stuffed sole amandine.

"Sounds like you found someone you can count on," Charlene observed. "Someone you can trust."

There was that word again. *Trust.* The word she'd used when they were making love. A sacred word. One that had been missing from her life for so many years. But she did trust Craig. He was tough and unrelenting. Still, he made her believe there was good in the world and that she could share in it.

"He's more than that," she said, "and yet that's everything, isn't it?"

"So if it's not about your arrest or his role in it, what's the problem between you two?"

"We had a little disagreement."

Charlene slanted her an expression that said, *Obviously,* then she asked, "About Rafe? Brian?"

Kerry broke off a piece of tender fish. "About Dad."

Clearly confused, Charlene inquired, "What does your father have to do with any of this?"

"Not a darned thing, but Craig seems to think I should apologize to him."

Charlene frowned. "For what? You told me your father already forgave you for selling your share of the ranch."

Kerry was beginning to realize that half-truths were more complicated than outright lies. It was true that her father had forgiven her for selling her share of the ranch to the bank that had then taken control away from him. What she hadn't revealed to Charlene or Craig was that she hadn't asked for his pardon. Adam First had granted it, unsolicited and unconditionally.

Of course, it wasn't the matter of the ranch that Craig had been so upset about. It was deceiving her father about the circumstances of her becoming pregnant, something she'd never told anyone else about, not even Charlene. Owning up to a lie to her best friend was one thing. Confessing to her father was another matter entirely. This time, she feared, there might be no forgiveness.

She was conscious of the woman sitting across from her studying her with concern. "There's more to it than that."

Charlene waited before saying, "I'm available whenever you want to talk about it."

Reaching across the table, Kerry touched her friend's hand. "Thanks. That means a lot."

"I hope you work it out." Charlene smiled sympathetically. "There's something about you and Craig that feels right."

Kerry's face grew warm as she contemplated Craig's touch, not just physically but emotionally. He was bringing a new dimension to her life, awakening passions and hopes she'd buried so long ago and so deeply she thought she'd never find them again. She had a lot to think over, things she had to figure out on her own. "So how was the fishing?" she asked, changing the subject.

Two DAYS went by with no word from Craig. Kerry had half expected him to send flowers as a peace offering. He was the kind of guy who would do something like that. When had anyone last sent her flowers? She didn't want to count the ones she'd received at the hospital in Coyote Springs, where she'd ended up after the big tornado had ripped through the Number One Ranch. It was while she'd been there that her father had put Brian up to talking her into going into treatment. She'd agreed, but with the condition that Adam First leave her alone, never try to see her, stay the hell out of her life. She knew he wouldn't like it, but he went along with it to get her help for her drinking problem. That was what they all called it then—a drinking problem. A temporary case of overindulgence. She was also confident that once her father gave his word, he'd keep it. Adam First's word was his bond.

On the third day, Kerry finally broke down and called Craig. "Robeson residence. Jacobs speaking."

"Jacobs, this is Kerry Durgan."

"Yes, Mrs. Durgan. How may I help you?" He addressed her as Mrs., not Ms., which meant he knew who she was. How much had Craig told him?

"Is Mr. Robeson available?"

"I'm sorry, madam, but he's out of town."

"When do you expect him back?"

"It's hard to say, Mrs. Durgan. Within a day or two. May I tell him you called?"

"Please, and would you ask him to call me at his convenience?"

"Certainly, madam. As soon as he returns, I'll give him the message."

Kerry hung up the phone and went into the living room. Automatically, she glanced at the bar. She'd considered getting rid of the bottles, but she couldn't avoid all the booze in the world. She'd had Evelyn replenish the bourbon but not the tequila. As a hostess it behooved her to offer spirits to guests when appropriate. No sense penalizing them for her weakness. As she perused the sparkling crystal and well-known labels, she recalled the night she'd spent in jail; she remembered the smells and the sounds of the drunk tank and the sight of wretched people wasting their lives. She wouldn't become one of them. Not ever again.

She veered in the direction of the kitchen and stopped dead. Her heart jumped, then pounded painfully.

Rafe was standing not more than ten feet away, smiling at her in a manner that made her skin crawl. *He is one of them,* she thought, *one of those derelict human beings.*

"Hello, Kerry." His voice was unctuous, smug.

Reflex had her crossing her arms protectively against her chest.

"I told you I'd be back."

A combination of fear and outrage set her on the attack. "How the hell did you get in here?" She pivoted stiffly and descended the three steps into the living room. Her knees were weak. What scared her more than the shock of his presence was the fact that she hadn't heard him enter her apartment—through the kitchen service entrance, no doubt. She'd had the locks changed, and there was supposed to be a guard on duty.

"Aren't you glad to see me?" he inquired in a hurt tone. Even with her back to him, she could visualize the arrogant sneer on his face.

She whipped around to confront him. "Like a tornado in a rainstorm."

His chuckle devolved into a leering grin. "You always did like it rough."

Did she? It was the only way she'd ever experienced sex—until Craig came into her life. He'd been vigorous, even dominant, but not rough. She hadn't been afraid of him. Lovemaking hadn't been surrender to him so much as collaborating with him. A mutual alliance for mutual gratification.

"Don't confuse what I accepted with what I liked or wanted."

He stepped to the phone, unplugged the handset and laid it on the table. It wouldn't ring. Anyone calling would get a busy signal. Satisfied they wouldn't be disturbed, he came down the steps and crossed the room to the bar. "Are you saying we didn't have a good time, babe? Gee, you could have fooled me."

She stifled the urge to tell him Craig was ten times, a hundred times the lover he'd ever been. Attacking his manhood or masculine pride wouldn't be smart, though. "What are you doing here?"

He frowned when he didn't find any tequila, then gave a tiny shrug and poured a generous quantity of rye whiskey. His tastes, it seemed, had become eclectic. He took a moderate sip, smacked his lips and, with a very pleased smile, said, "I saw my kid."

Kerry's heart froze. Her breathing stopped. Had he talked to their son?

"He's tall, taller than me. Not as strong, though. Needs to put on some muscle so he'll look like a man and not a boy—or a girl."

"Did he see you? Did you talk to him?" She hated the tremor in her voice and could only hope Rafe didn't pick up on it.

He shook his head. "I just happened to be sitting in the parking lot the other day when he drove up. Nice wheels he's got." Rafe raised his glass in a salute. "I thought about coming up here with him for a nice family reunion—"

"Leave him alone," she growled, unable to keep from raising her voice. Her knees were shaking, but she was afraid if she sat down she wouldn't be able to get up again.

Rafe lifted his eyebrows and shot her a smug grin, then moved to within a foot of her. He extended a forefinger and placed it under her chin. She was repulsed by his touch but knew better than to back away. Fear was always a turn-on for Rafe.

"I'll leave him alone," he said very quietly, very confidently, "if you cooperate."

What did that mean? The thoughts that went through her mind filled her with alarm and disgust. She could taste bile in her throat.

"Cooperate? How?" This man had once been her husband, the only man in her life, in her bed. Would she let him have her if that was the price for her son's safety?

Fortunately, he backed off and settled his butt against the arm of the couch. His arrogant posture said he was aware of what she was thinking, knew she was apprehensive—no, downright scared—and she saw that the realization sweetened his pleasure.

"I'll make a deal with you," he said complacently. "I thought over what you said about not letting people know what's going on, so I've decided to let you off the hook easy. Instead of the full twenty-five mil, give me five, babe, and you'll never hear from or see me again."

She didn't believe him. Five million would be a down payment. He'd be back for more when that ran out, as it inevitably would, unless he killed himself spending it first. She suspected he realized it, too, but it didn't make any difference. He was in the position of power, exactly where he liked to be.

She strayed to the wing chair and sat, ridiculously relieved at the distance and perspective the chair afforded her. "Five million dollars," she repeated thoughtfully, as if she were contemplating the offer. "That's still a lot of money."

Rafe moseyed over to the piano and took the picture of their son. "A mere tenth of what you got for selling out your old man."

She didn't appreciate his choice of words. He, of all people, was hardly in a position to throw stones, but considering his other offenses, hypocrisy seemed a minor affront. Rafe had never shown anything but contempt for the big rancher who represented everything Rafe wasn't and never would be. But this wasn't the time to debate the issue.

She had to do something, stall him—though what that would accomplish, she wasn't entirely sure. Delaying tactics might give her a chance to think of some way of foiling him.

"I've been liquidating assets," she lied. "I've transferred that much into an account. I can write a check and you can be on your way to Mexico or wherever you want to go."

He slammed the picture flat on the top of the baby grand hard enough to make the strings vibrate. Somehow, she managed to keep from jumping, though her heart leaped.

"You really think I'm stupid, don't you?" He skirted the instrument and took a menacing step toward her. "You'll write me a check that'll probably be worthless. Or you'll put a stop payment on it the minute I walk out the door." When his intimidating tactics failed to elicit a reaction, he plopped casually onto the sofa and put his feet on the coffee table, none too gently. "Besides, it would be traceable." He took a swallow from the glass of rye. "No, you're going to do it my way."

"How…how's that?"

"Just shut up and listen." He reached into his scruffy jeans pocket and pulled out a piece of lined paper, which he tossed on the low table separating them. "This is the number of an account in Honduras. I want you to transfer the money, five million, into that account. Got it? It's a lot safer than walking around with a check in my pocket, and nobody can trace it once it's deposited.''

''It's too late today,'' she reminded him.

''Tomorrow, first thing.''

She nodded. She had no intention of meeting his demand, but at least this gave her time to figure out how to thwart him. Would Craig be back tonight? Would he help her? She reached forward, picked up the scrap of paper, gave it a cursory glance—saw a series of numbers—and stood up.

''You'll stay away from Brian?'' She'd intended it to be a statement, but her underlying fear turned it into a question. ''You have to promise to leave him alone.'' She knew she was pleading, but she couldn't help it. ''You won't see him—ever.''

''Worried about our little boy. Ah, that's touching. Maybe I ought to make sure he knows what a man's supposed to do.''

''You go near him and the deal's off.''

He sprang to his feet, and without thinking, she retreated. It was only a small step, but she bumped against an end table. She stumbled and had to catch herself from falling. Her nervousness brought a smile to his lips, but his eyes remained as hard as ever. ''You don't want to renege on our arrangement, babe, because then you'll get me real upset, and you remember how I am when I'm unhappy.''

''I want you to keep away from Brian.'' Why was she telling him this? He already knew it. All her begging accomplished was to reinforce his awareness of how desperate she was—a stronger tool for him to use against her.

He moved still closer. Soon he would have her against the wall. "He's my son, too, Kerry. My little boy," he said with mock affection. "A kid shouldn't be without a daddy to guide him on the exciting journey to being a real man."

She stood up straight and put as much force into her voice as she could muster. "Rafe, I mean it. If you don't stay away from him—"

He grabbed her by the wrist and pulled her against him. "Or what, babe? Your daddy isn't here now. You can't run to him. Not that there's anything he could do even if you wanted him to. And you don't, do you?" He fixed his eyes on hers and laughed. "No, I didn't think so."

She tried to twist her arm out of his grasp, but he was too strong for her.

"What's the matter, sweetheart, don't you like being with your Rafe?"

"Let me go." Panic had her struggling, though logic told her it was counterproductive. She needed to be calm, passive.

He tightened his grip. "Not yet, sweet thing. It's been a long time. A real long time. You were pretty good years ago. Let's see if you still are."

Terror rioted through Kerry's veins. If only she could get away from him, lock herself in her bedroom. He might break down the door, but not before she was able to dial 911. Would help get here in time? Or would he... Then she remembered he'd disconnected the phone.

"You were always so skinny. I like my women with a little more meat on their bones, but—"

She marshaled a commanding voice. "Rafe, stop."
For a moment he paused, though he didn't loosen his
grip. Then she added, "This isn't right." She realized
instantly it had been the wrong thing to say.

His face broke into a glowing smile. "For who,
querida? It's absolutely right for me. Just what I need,
in fact. I bet you need it, too."

He placed his hand on her blouse and began rubbing
her breast. Not gently. She tried to push his hand
away. He slapped her across her face. Her cheek stung,
then burned.

"Now it's your turn," he whispered in her ear.
"You want to hit me back? Go on."

Kerry knew then that she was doomed. If she fought
him, it excited him more. If she didn't, he got what
he wanted without a fight. Either way, he was going
to rape her.

CHAPTER ELEVEN

CRAIG WAS in a foul mood when he arrived home. His business trip to Mexico had been less than successful. Government officials there were putting up obstacles to the development he was advocating, demanding a bigger cut in the profits for the necessary permits. He'd negotiated his way around similar juggernauts before, but he had neither the heart nor the patience to haggle this time. In the end, he'd placed his final offer on the table and walked out.

The distraction, of course, was Kerry. He kept thinking about the progress they'd made in their relationship and how it had all slipped away when he brought up her father and the subject of forgiveness. He was a fool—not just for picking a fight with her but in thinking there could ever be a permanent bond between them. He admired people with strong wills, but Kerry had a chip on her shoulder that advanced the term *willful* a step beyond stubborn. Besides, she was an alcoholic. Okay, he conceded, a recovering alcoholic.

He'd shunned drinkers his entire life, and now he'd gotten involved with one. Forget that she was beautiful—as if he could—that the very thought of touching her sent his hormones into heated turmoil, that making love to her had carried him to a height he'd never reached before—then catapulted him over the top into a free fall that went beyond imagination.

In spite of her self-doubts and sometimes misguided actions, she'd demonstrated steel-mindedness in protecting her son when she and Rafe had lived together and bravery in dealing with Rafe since his reappearance. Craig sensed she felt unlovable, yet he knew she was capable of tremendous devotion, for she was a woman who never did anything halfway.

She'd slipped off the wagon in a crisis. What was to say she wouldn't do the same thing at the next one? The promises of alcoholics were untrustworthy no matter how sincerely they were made. Hadn't his father promised on numerous occasions to stop drinking? But there had always been another stressful moment that one drink would alleviate.

Be her friend, Craig counseled himself. *Be a shoulder for her to cry on from time to time. Sympathize and encourage, but don't make her a part of your life. All she'll do is disappoint and hurt you. Yeah, right,* he scoffed at his own naïveté. *Play with fire but don't get burned.*

The limousine pulled into his driveway in Flower Mound. Before the chauffeur stopped under the colonnaded entrance, his majordomo opened the massive front door of the mansion.

"Good afternoon, sir," Jacobs said in greeting as the uniformed driver held the rear door of the stretch limousine.

Craig returned the papers he'd been working on to his open attaché case, acknowledged the greeting with a nod and asked if there were any messages. He half expected a call from the negotiator he'd been dealing with in Mexico. Sometimes ultimatums paid off.

He'd given Kerry an ultimatum, too—reconcile with her father or lose a friend, a lover. Why was apologizing to a man Craig hardly knew so important to him? The question had haunted him for days.

"Yes, sir. Mrs. Durgan phoned."

So she was making the first move. It sounded encouraging, yet he refused to get his hopes up. There was still a lot they had to work through. A lot of soul-searching on both sides. "When?"

"Only a few minutes ago," Jacobs told him. "She requested that you return her call at your convenience."

While the chauffeur and butler busied themselves with his luggage, Craig marched to his office and stood over the desk, where correspondence was piled in neat stacks. He quickly thumbed through the mail. Still on his feet, he dialed Kerry's number. It rang several times and was then replaced by a busy signal. Call waiting, he deduced, but she'd chosen not to respond to it. Apparently, the conversation she was having was too important to interrupt.

He settled into his chair and scanned the routine letters. After a few minutes, he hit the redial button. Still busy. Strange, since she was supposed to be waiting for his call.

Should he go to her penthouse? Whatever they had to discuss would probably be better said face-to-face. He tried her number again. Still busy. He hit the intercom button and asked Jacobs to have his Saab brought around. While he waited, he dialed her number one more time—again without success. Who was she talking to?

This time of day, it was only about a twenty-minute drive from his place to hers. On the way over, he used his car phone, but her line continued to be busy. Strange that she would ask him to return her call and would then tie up the phone so long—unless she was talking to Brian. Would she break the news of Rafe's resurrection from the dead over the phone? Maybe, if the boy was too far away for them to get together, or because she was afraid her ex-husband might follow her and find out where Brian was.

Craig struggled to suppress the nagging feeling that something was seriously wrong, but it persisted and increased as he drew nearer her residence.

The doorman greeted him affably.

"Is Mrs. Durgan in?" Craig asked.

"Yes, sir. Shall I announce you?"

Craig considered. A tip would get him onto the elevator to her suite. Should he simply appear at her door, giving her no option whether she wanted to see him or not? He decided against it. Their meeting should be her choice. "Please," he instructed the doorman.

Earl poked in her number. "I'm sorry, sir, she's not responding."

"Busy signal?"

The other man nodded. If Craig's calculations were correct, she'd been on the phone for at least half an hour. Not a long time for casual conversation, he reckoned. Maybe she was talking to Charlene. Women talk. That might take hours. He almost smiled. But why wouldn't she respond to her call waiting? Unless her friend was helping her through another crisis. It explained why she didn't want to be interrupted. There was another possibility—that she was talking to her father, but somehow, he didn't believe that was the case.

"Could Mrs. Durgan have gone out without you knowing it?" he asked the doorman.

"If she went through the garage, sir, but there's a guard on duty who would have notified me. Besides, her car isn't here."

Craig frowned, then remembered he'd had his secretary check with the towing service to make sure the Ferrari had been picked up from the impoundment yard. They'd reported delivering it to a dealership for repairs.

"Yes, of course," he said pensively. "She's having some work done on it."

"Maybe she left the phone off the hook," Earl offered helpfully.

"Doesn't that result in an irritating beep telling you that?" Craig countered.

The doorman nodded. "Let me try again."

The same nonresponse.

Craig's discomfort level was rising. "Has she had any visitors today?"

"No, sir. No one."

He was overreacting. Just because she called him earlier didn't mean she would be sitting by the telephone waiting for him to call her back, especially when she didn't know for sure when he'd be returning home.

He thanked the doorman for his time and walked to his car. Besides the front door and the garage, there was only one way out of—or into—the building. The service entrance in back. But what would be the point of sneaking out of the building, especially since she didn't have any transportation? Even if she rented a car, it would be dropped off at the front of the condo.

Craig pulled around the side of the high-rise and scanned the parking lot. Then he saw it. A scarred pickup with fuzzy dice dangling from the rearview mirror. He drove by it and saw the Mexico license plate. Durgan.

Dread coiled in Craig's stomach. Ignoring the neat lines on the pavement, he parked the Saab haphazardly out of the traffic lane and bolted to the back door of the building. Locked, of course. He supposed he could go to the lobby and bribe the doorman to let him upstairs, but when he got there he would be faced with the solid door to her penthouse. The doorman might have an emergency access key. But Craig didn't want to take the time to persuade him to use it.

A call box was set in the wall beside the service door. He pressed Kerry's button. No response. That wasn't a surprise.

From his days selling real estate and managing properties, Craig knew every building had a weak point. He examined the snap lock on the steel-paneled door. Old, of good quality but not particularly sophisticated. The space between the door and the frame was unguarded. Using a credit card, he quickly opened the latch.

He stepped to the delivery elevator. A special card was needed to go to the penthouse from the front door. Here, he had only to press the top button. Craig's breathing slowed and deepened as he ascended. Exiting into a small vestibule, he found a door on the right, another on the left. He advanced to the one on the right. The lock was obviously new, but it was hardly sophisticated. Surely there was a manual dead bolt on the inside. If Durgan had entered this way and shot the bolt behind him, getting in without a battering ram would be difficult. Unlike the movies, in real life, charging against closed doors with one's shoulder tended to break the shoulder rather than the door.

The light was barely adequate. Craig listened for sounds coming from within but detected nothing at first. Then he thought he heard the muffled scream of a woman.

A surge of adrenaline had his hands shaking. Forcing them to be still, he diddled with this lock as he had the one downstairs. It seemed to take forever, then miraculously there was a click and the door opened.

He listened. Maybe his imagination was working overtime. The commotion could be coming from a TV. If Kerry was in the bedroom by herself watching an old movie, he'd have a lot of explaining to do.

Quietly, he moved through the kitchen into the hallway. The apartment's front door was straight ahead. To the right was the archway and the three steps leading down to the living room. Everything was quiet. He headed left, down the short hall that led to the bedrooms. The door to the master suite was closed. He crept toward it, grateful for the thick carpet that smothered his footsteps.

Suppose he opened the door and found them in bed together. He dismissed the idea. Kerry would never have sex with Rafael Durgan voluntarily.

Then he heard her cry, and his blood ran cold.

"That's it. Fight." Durgan's gruff voice. "I like it when you struggle."

With no weapon, Craig burst into the room. The double doors slammed against the walls. His mind had only a second to register what his eyes were seeing— Kerry flat on her back on the bed in a pool of torn clothing. Durgan on top of her, his belt unbuckled but his pants still up.

Craig leaped and caught Durgan around the neck. They tumbled off the side of the bed. Unfortunately, Craig was pinned chest up beneath his adversary's back. Durgan arched his spine, clamping Craig more solidly to the floor. Instead of twisting and letting his fists fly as Craig expected, he stuffed his hand into his loose jeans pocket.

At first, Craig thought he was trying to secure his pants. But when Durgan, still on top of him, squirmed none too gently and scrambled to his feet, Craig found himself looking at the barrel of a snub-nosed .38 revolver.

"Move," Durgan growled, "and I'll blow you away. Piece by piece."

Craig glowered but had little choice. Was Kerry still on the bed? What condition was she in? If this piece of scum hurt her... Without thinking, Craig started to rise, only to find the gun pointed at his private parts and his assailant grinning. "We can start here. Want to sing soprano?"

Craig froze in a half-crouched position. At least he could see Kerry. She was on the far side of the king-size bed, her arms scissored across her naked breasts, her knees drawn up. Her lips were thin, her eyes wide. She was in shock but apparently unharmed.

With what might have been practiced dexterity, Durgan secured his belt with one hand. As if realizing his attacker was gauging the situation, he took a small step backward, establishing greater distance to make sure Craig couldn't easily trip him.

"You came at a bad time," Durgan told Craig. "I was just beginning to enjoy myself. Maybe I ought to let you watch." He cast an amused glance at Kerry, whose dazed stare was already fading. "What do you think, babe?"

"I think you're sick," she managed to say.

He chuckled. "You disappoint me, *querida*. Where's your sense of adventure?"

"Get out of here, Rafe. Just go," she ordered.

"Oh, I'm going, all right. For now." He tucked in his shirt. "But I'll be back. I want that money, honey." He chuckled at his rhyme. "And I'm going to get it, babe. Either that or Brian gets to know how his papa and mama made him."

Craig again started to get up.

"Stay right where you are, pretty boy—" Durgan pointed the gun at Kerry "—or my son will be sharing his inheritance with his resurrected daddy."

Laughing, Rafe backed out of the room, pulling the doors shut behind him.

Craig leaped to Kerry's side and put an arm around her naked shoulders. "Are you all right?"

She threw her arms around his waist. Barely stifling a groan, she couldn't keep the tears from streaming down her face. "I am now. Thanks to you."

He stroked her head. Softly he began to ask, "He didn't—"

"No, no," she muttered against him. "He didn't get that far."

Taking in a huge fortifying breath, he unclasped her arms from around him. "I'll be right back."

"No," she cried, but he was already at the door. She pressed the tips of her fingers to her mouth in anxiety.

Craig charged into the hall. A glance to the left confirmed the chain was still on the front door. Durgan hadn't run out that way. But the phone's handset was unplugged, the wire hanging loose. Craig slipped into the kitchen, not sure Durgan wasn't hiding in there, waiting for him. The would-be rapist was gone. He checked the service hallway. The elevator door was closed, and with no floor indicator above it, it was impossible to say if he'd already reached the bottom. Craig tore back into the kitchen and picked up the wall phone. He got only a buzzing sound. Of course—the broken connection in the hallway. He raced to it and plugged in the receiver. A quick-dial button was marked Doorman. He stabbed it. Earl answered on the second ring. Too damn long.

"A man is coming down in the service elevator,"

Craig told him in a rush. "He's armed, so be careful, but if there's any way you can stop him—"

"The service elevator? Hang on a minute."

Craig drummed his fingers on the narrow table. He should be with Kerry, not talking on the phone. She said she was all right, but how could he be sure?

"Mr. Robeson—" the doorman's winded voice rushed back on a minute later, "—I'm sorry, sir. He was already gone by the time I reached the service area." He gulped for breath. "A truck was peeling rubber...out of the parking lot. Mexican license plate. I managed to get the number."

"Good work. I'm calling the police, Earl. When they arrive, send them up immediately."

"Of course, sir. Mrs. Durgan...is she all right?"

"I think so." *I hope so.* Maybe he should call an ambulance for her. She'd said Durgan hadn't raped her, but what other damage had he imposed? Probably the kind that no medical doctor could find or fix.

Closing his eyes in a silent prayer, he hung up, then immediately dialed 911. With forced calm, he identified himself, his location, the nature of the emergency and asked for Detective Dawson to come if he was available.

When Craig returned to the bedroom a few seconds later, Kerry was sitting on the side of the bed, still in a semidaze. She'd pulled her torn shirt across her breasts and was clutching it with both hands. She was shivering yet hadn't made any effort to put on her pants, which lay on the floor in front of her. Craig reached into the bathroom and snagged a pair of large fluffy sage-colored bath towels. He draped one across her lap and cloaked the other across her shoulders. Sitting next to her, he wrapped an arm around her. Gradually she leaned into his side, rigid at first, then she slumped against his chest and sobbed.

He stroked her back and ached at the misery he felt racking her. Outrage slammed through him as he thanked God they were alone. After a minute, she pulled herself away from him and attempted to dry her eyes with a corner of the towel.

"It's all right now, sweetheart. He's gone. The police are on their way. Will you be able to talk to them?" he asked gently. She was still in mild shock. Understandable after almost being raped.

She nodded. "Just give me a minute. I'll be fine."

"Do you want to lie down? A glass of water?"

"I want to shower, to get the feel of his skin off me."

She threw herself into Craig's arms and wept.

After a few more minutes of holding her, he said, "Let me get your robe. The police will be here any second now. They'll want you to tell them what happened."

She dipped her head, then raised it. "Okay."

Craig was helping her slip into the silk dressing gown when they heard the heavy knock on the front door. Reluctantly, he left her to answer it.

Hank Dawson stood in front of him, hard-faced and determined. At his side was a much younger uniformed policeman.

"Thanks for coming, Hank. I didn't know if you'd be available."

Hank introduced Officer Stevens, then asked, "What's going on?"

They stepped into the hallway, and Craig closed the door behind them. "I told you about Durgan. He showed up here and damn near raped Kerry."

Hank scanned the room, apparently looking for signs of a struggle. "Damn near?"

"I arrived in time to stop him."

"Is he still here?"

"No." Craig shook his head. "He pulled a gun and got away."

"Where's Mrs. Durgan?" Hank asked.

Craig led the two policemen to the master bedroom. Kerry was standing in the middle of the room when they entered. The defeated expression that had been on her face only minutes earlier was banished. She greeted her new visitors politely, sat at her dressing table facing them and recounted her story concisely and unemotionally.

"Do you have a photo of Durgan?"

She rose and went into her closet. They heard things being shuffled around. A few seconds later she emerged, carrying a framed portrait.

"This is the best I can do," she said. "It was taken about fifteen years ago, a few months before our divorce. He's put on weight since then and added wrinkles...and a mustache."

"We have a computer artist who can take this image and age it. If you would be available to help him—"

"Absolutely," she said. "Tell me where you want me and when, and I'll be there."

"I know this is very difficult for you, Mrs. Durgan—"

"What is difficult, Detective, is knowing he's still out there and that he might approach my son. I want him caught before he does any more harm."

"So do we," Hank affirmed.

He stayed another hour, asking questions, taking notes while they drank coffee in the kitchen. A technician arrived and lifted fingerprints. Hank made an appointment for her to go to police headquarters to work with their graphic artist on the photo.

"We've issued an all-points bulletin," Dawson told her as he was getting ready to leave. "I hope, before too long, we'll have him in custody. Can I count on you to testify against him?"

"I'll testify," she assured him. "You can depend on it. But I wouldn't be too confident about picking him up soon. He stayed hidden for over twelve years. He was tough then. He's tougher now and even more ruthless. He's not going to be easy to catch. If he goes back to Mexico, you'll never find him."

It occurred to her that she hadn't even had the presence of mind when he reappeared from the dead to ask where in Mexico he'd been.

"We'll do our best to make sure he doesn't," Hank promised.

Craig escorted his friend to the door and saw him out. When he returned to the living room, Kerry was standing by the bar, a bottle of bourbon in her hand.

Craig froze. This was the moment of truth he'd been dreading. With anyone else, under circumstances like these, he'd probably approve, maybe even recommend a drink to quell the tension. But this was Kerry. It wouldn't be one drink, and instead of dulling anxiety, it would begin a new cycle of manic behavior.

He went quietly to the bar and leaned against it, his head canted to face her. He suppressed the impulse to cross his arms and hover over her like an avenging angel. She didn't need a judge, but a friend. He propped his hands casually on the counter behind him and watched her holding the bottle.

"Thinking about having a drink to calm your frazzled nerves?" He'd wanted the words to be neutral, nonaccusatory, but the question itself implied censure.

She gazed at him, studied the bottle in her hand, looked at him again and put the bottle on the bar. Placing her hands flat on the countertop, she leaned forward, head lowered. "I want it, Craig. I want it badly." She raised her chin. There were tears in her eyes. "I want it, but I don't need it. I'll never need it again, as long as I have you."

He wrapped her in his arms. "You're so much stronger than you've given yourself credit for," he said softly. Seeing the doubt in her eyes, he understood the question she harbored—did he still want her? There was only one possible answer. He brought his mouth to hers and kissed her.

Kerry caved against his chest and listened to the smooth, steady beat of his heart. He tipped her chin up with the edge of his finger, met her eyes and kissed her again, more deeply this time.

"I really do need to shower," she told him when they finally broke off and she was resting her head against his chest. "Rafe always left me feeling dirty, soiled."

"Would you like someone to wash your back?" Craig asked eagerly.

She lifted her head and smiled at the playful sparkle in his eyes. "Thank you for asking. That means a lot right now." She released her grip on him. "But not this time."

"Rain check, then. Whenever you're ready."

She raised on tiptoe and kissed him tenderly on the lips, then went into the bathroom and closed the door.

Craig wasn't surprised when she lingered an inordinate amount of time in the shower. He used the interval to call a local restaurant and order pizza to be delivered. She might not eat it, but at least it would be available.

Half an hour later she emerged from her bedroom wearing loose-fitting jeans and a baggy sweatshirt. Her still damp, shiny black hair was pulled into a ponytail. Casual, yet sexy as hell.

"I need to talk to Brian," she insisted. "I have to know he's all right. Rafe said he saw him."

"They met?"

She shook her head. "Rafe said he only saw him. He didn't talk to him."

"So Brian still doesn't know about his father," Craig concluded with certainty.

"How can you be so sure?"

"If Brian discovered his father was still alive, he would have called you."

She screwed up her mouth. "He's mad at me. Remember?"

Craig shook his head and offered her a sympathetic smile. "Not to the degree that he wouldn't call about something like this."

"I hope you're right." But the statement lacked conviction.

Craig understood her desire to protect her son from the ugly truth, but sometimes hiding from truth did more harm than good. "I know you'd rather he never learned about what's been going on, Kerry, but it can't be avoided. When Rafe's picked up, the news will be in the papers. It'll be a lot easier on your son if he's forewarned. Besides, if Rafe does go after him, he needs to be prepared so he can protect himself."

She wore a hangdog expression. "I've already called all his friends. None of them has seen him."

"Call them again," Craig urged. "Tell them you have to get hold of him. It's a matter of life and death."

Her head jerked up at his choice of words. Craig would have liked to think he was using scare tactics, but the truth was, it could be a matter of life or death.

CHAPTER TWELVE

"WHERE ELSE could he be?" Craig asked when Kerry's second round of telephone calls failed to locate Brian.

"There's one other place he would go," she declared with sudden enlightenment. "I should have thought of it sooner." Or maybe she had and had suppressed it. "The Number One. That's where he grew up. For him, it's home."

"Well, call there and see."

She could hear the impatience in his voice. He didn't know how difficult it was for her to talk to her family. She'd embarrassed herself and them more than once with her drunken behavior. They barely tolerated her now that she'd sobered up. She supposed they wished her well, but her brother Michael was the only one she felt comfortable with. He'd been every girl's dream of a big brother—protective, respectful and infinitely caring. The kind of man you could count on. Reluctantly, she picked up the phone and dialed his number. She was relieved when he answered the phone.

"Michael? It's Kerry."

"Hey, Sis. Haven't heard from you in a while. How are things going? Big D. treating you all right? Saw you on TV a while back. You looked great. Meant to call and tell you. How's the foundation going?''

All thought of her charity efforts had slipped from her mind. "Real fine. Say, is Brian there?''

"Sure is. Arrived a couple of days ago. Said his spring break plans had fallen through. Didn't you know?''

"Yeah, he stopped by here first. He wanted to go scuba diving in Florida, but the father of the guy he was supposed to go with got sick.''

"That's what he said. So what's been going on in your life?''

She wasn't about to mention her stint in the drunk tank. She'd have to tell him about Rafe's return, though, and how her life was in turmoil in so many ways.

"Do you remember Craig Robeson?'' she asked.

"Craig Robeson? Name sounds familiar. Oh, yeah. Big guy. Basketball player, right? Wasn't he your date for the high school prom?''

Michael could still be kind. Everyone else in the family would probably have referred to him as the guy she ditched at the prom. "He lives in Dallas now. We ran into each other a few weeks ago. He's a big developer. You may have heard of his company, Robeco.''

Michael chuckled. "I'll be damned.''

"He's agreed to help finance the Family First Foundation.''

"Family First. You changed the name.''

"His idea.''

"I like it.''

"Yeah, me, too."

Telling her brother about it reminded her how remarkable it was that Craig was supporting her. It was a good feeling, to know he was at her side as a friend and...

"The other morning when Brian showed up unannounced," she continued, "Craig happened to be here having breakfast with me."

"I'm glad to hear you're getting along so well."

Kerry almost laughed. From the tone of the comment, it was clear Brian hadn't told him about walking in on what he thought was a love nest. Had her son's anger waned, or had he withheld that detail because he was ashamed his mother might be sleeping with someone? She released an audible sigh.

"I'd just come out of the shower," she said into the receiver. "My hair was still wet, and...well, Brian got the wrong idea."

There was a brief pause at the other end. "I wondered if something was bothering him. He seemed too moody for it to be about missing out on a scuba diving trip." Michael paused again. "I wouldn't worry about it, Sis. He's a big boy now."

"Yeah, well, I wanted to make sure he was there. I need to let him know it wasn't the way it looked."

"I'm sure he's calmed down by now."

"There's something else I need to talk to him about, that you should know, too." There was a small hesitation, during which Kerry bit her lip. "Michael, Rafe isn't dead. He's been hiding out in Mexico all these years."

Her brother was quiet for so long she worried the connection had been cut. "Michael?"

"I don't believe it," he mumbled. "Rafe's really alive?"

"He showed up a little over a week ago." Kerry could practically hear the wheels grinding in her brother's head.

"What does he want?"

"Money, of course."

"Why am I not surprised? Tell him to go to—"

"If only it were that easy," Kerry interrupted, aware of the anger roiling in Michael's terse words. "He's threatening to go to Brian."

"What does he expect to gain by that?"

Kerry's hand tightened on the receiver. "He knows how much Brian means to me. I haven't been a perfect mother, Michael. I realize that, but…I don't want to lose Brian." She hadn't put it into words before, and now that she had, her heart sank. It didn't make any difference if what Rafe told Brian was true; Rafe could destroy her in the eyes of their son. She blinked back the tears and repeated, "I don't want to lose him."

"You won't," Michael said flatly, as if it were an incontrovertible fact. "You've called in the police, of course."

"They're searching for Rafe now."

"Good." There was finality in the one-syllable word. Kerry was tempted to tell Michael it wasn't that simple, that when they did find him, there probably wasn't much they could do to him.

"That's why I've got to talk to Brian," Kerry explained.

''Here's the number you can reach him at.'' Kerry automatically jotted it down on the pad by the telephone. ''He's staying with Dad and Sheila at the Home Place. And if you need anything, Sis—anything—be sure to call me. You know I'll help.''

Encouraging words. She'd always been able to depend on Michael. No matter how torqued he sometimes got at her antics, he never abandoned her. He didn't defend what she did, but he did try to protect her. Even after she'd sold her share of the ranch, the bond hadn't been completely broken. He was still ready to come to her rescue. Awareness of that kind of unconditional love was humbling, especially since she knew she wasn't worthy of it. She wondered if he'd still feel that way when all this was over.

A minute later, she said goodbye.

Craig had been standing to the side, listening. ''Well?''

''Brian's safe.'' She tidied the table, though it didn't need it. ''He's staying with my father and his new wife,'' she replied dismissively.

''That's a relief.''

Kerry walked into the living room and stretched out on one of the soft leather couches.

Craig stayed where he was, his hands dangling at his side. ''Aren't you going to call him?''

''There's no need right now,'' she replied casually. ''Brian's perfectly safe where he is. Rafe would never go to the ranch.'' She picked up a magazine from the coffee table. ''He knows he'd be shot.''

Craig drew back incredulously. ''A little while ago, you were worried sick about your son, and now that

you've found him, you're not going to call him?'' He
read the series of digits she'd written down. ''Whose
number is this?''

''My father's,'' she said as she skimmed pages.
''Brian's staying at the Home Place.''

''Ah. I'm beginning to see the light. You're afraid
your dad'll answer the phone,'' he taunted, ''and
you'll have to talk to him.''

''Don't be silly.'' She wasn't going to get riled.
''We agreed when I went into rehab that it'd be best
if we kept our distance.''

Craig shook his head. ''Kerry, going into rehab was
for your own good. My bet is he would have made a
pact with the devil so you'd get help.''

Absently, she browsed through the periodical.
''What's done is done. We really have nothing to say
to each other.''

Shoving his hands into his pockets, Craig stepped
in front of her. She had to fight the urge to look up.
''On the contrary. I think you have a great deal to say
to each other.''

The shiny paper snapped when she turned a page.
''Keep out of this, Craig.''

His glare told her he wanted to grab the magazine
out of her hands, fling it across the room and shake
her. Yet his voice was restrained when he said, ''I
can't. Not if we're going to have any chance together.''

She still refused to look at him.

''The deal you made with your father—that he stay
away from you—was the stinking thinking of an in-
ebriate. You're sober now. Sober because you can be,

because you want to be. It's a giant leap forward, but it's progress that won't last unless you take the next step. You have to acknowledge what you've done, identify the people you've hurt and make amends to them. It seems to me your father is at the top of that list."

She knew he was right, but she wasn't ready yet. Maybe she never would be. Angry with herself and the man standing in front of her, she said, "Are we talking about my father or yours?"

A grimace tightened his mouth, and she instantly regretted her outburst, but he seemed to take no offense at it. Instead of anger, she saw sadness in the arch of his eyebrows.

"Maybe," he acknowledged. "Maybe I've idealized your father into the dad I so desperately wanted and never had. It's too late for me and Harry Robeson to ever find reconciliation, Kerry. I'll never be able to ask him to forgive me for my failures as his son, but it's not too late for you. Make amends—"

He slumped against the corner of the sofa. "I'm sorry, sweetheart. You don't need a lecture. But you do have to come to terms with the consequences of your actions. If you don't, you'll have lost the most precious thing sobriety can bring you—self-respect." He leaned forward, rested his elbows on his knees and spoke with imploring gentleness. "If you won't let me help you, please find someone who will."

She raised her head and nearly flinched at the plea in his eyes. "And if I refuse?"

"As long as you refuse," he reiterated, "you undermine any chance of finding the peace of mind you need to stay sober.''

She was fully aware that the myth of the happy drunk was essentially that—a myth. People didn't habitually indulge in liquor or drugs because they were happy. They didn't alter their minds to seek some great insight, but to escape what they felt in their hearts—unhappiness, shame and guilt.

But just as intoxication didn't bring release from severe psychological problems, sobriety didn't guarantee their resolution, either. It only allowed the individual to face them squarely and honestly.

''And if I fall off the wagon, you'll leave me.''

He extended an arm on the back of the couch. She knew she was challenging him, forcing him to speak the ugly truth. He met her glare. There would no turning back.

''I told you, Kerry, I will not be a facilitator, an enabler. If you drink, you'll do it alone.''

Her jaw muscles flexed. She closed the magazine and tossed it on the coffee table, her gaze never leaving his. ''So what you're saying is that your love is conditional on me talking to my father.'' She crossed her arms. ''And you're reassessing your love for me,'' she concluded laconically.

He climbed to his feet and stared out the window, carefully choosing his words before responding. ''Not my love.'' Facing her, he said, ''I love you, Kerry. I've never said that to another woman. But I'm saying it to you. I love you. I started to fall in love with you long before the night of the prom, and I think I've been in love with you ever since.''

She'd wanted all her life for a man to say those words, and now that the words were spoken, she found herself rebelling against them. "That's nonsense."

"Nonsense that I could carry a torch for you all these years?" he asked with a mild grin that didn't disguise the seriousness of his question. "Or nonsense that anyone could love you?"

One of Rafe's slaps couldn't have stung more. When she refused to meet Craig's eyes, he continued in the same introspective manner. "Maybe it was adolescent infatuation back then—the animal attraction of a testosterone-crazed boy for a beautiful girl. It's a lot more than hormones now."

When she didn't respond, he went on. "I'm still attracted to you by your beauty, but I love you for your intelligence, your sense of adventure, your spirit and strength in the face of opposition."

She raised an eyebrow. Apparently, *strength* wasn't a word she expected him to use in describing her. He'd come to realize that, despite her bravado, she thought of herself as defiant but weak and unworthy of love.

He grinned at her. "Kerry, you're setting up a foundation to help people. That's generous. But you also sit and listen to people pour their hearts out. You offer them a kind word, a smile of encouragement. The money you give them can't buy that. It requires strength and love. It took courage to endure Rafe's abuse in order to protect your child from a man I suspect you genuinely wanted to love, and then go on to raise your son by yourself. And I know, more than you realize, the enormous amount of willpower you've had to call up to overcome your addiction to alcohol."

He watched her violet blue eyes melt as he recounted her virtues, saw the humble wish that what he was saying was true. Doubts still tormented her, however.

"I haven't won yet," she said with a wry expression. "It's only been two days."

"But you know you can win. One day at a time," he said sincerely. "You've come to grips with where drinking was taking you. You've peeked over the hill, recoiled from what you've seen there."

"But," she prompted.

"But…" He hesitated. "The person from whom you got that strength of character, that inflexible determination to achieve—whether you want to acknowledge it or not—is probably your father. I don't pretend to know him, Kerry. Undoubtedly, he has some flaws." He paused and smiled. "If you're really a chip off the old block, I bet one of them is pigheadedness."

Her lips curled in the beginning of a grin, and he allowed himself to grin back. He came around the coffee table and sat on its corner, taking her hands in his. "I've made love to you, Kerry. I've shared an experience that's been like no other in my life. You've awakened a longing I've never experienced before and that only you can satisfy."

She closed her eyes, swept away by the sensation of his hands holding hers, by the recollection of the time they'd spent together and the way he'd made her feel. She wanted to feel that way again.

"I think family is more important to you than you're willing to admit, sweetheart. No matter how hard you try to push him away, you love your father, just as he loves you.''

''You think I'm a coward,'' She murmured.

He kissed the tips of her fingers. ''I think separation from a family who loves you is far more painful than an act of contrition.'' He smiled at her. ''I think anyone who has the courage to fight off a rapist and the gentleness to hold a lonely and discouraged old woman's hand has more than enough grit to do what has to be done.'' He released her, stood up and once more extended his hand to her. ''Make the call, Kerry. Please.''

She breathed deeply. He saw her fighting with herself. Finally, she nodded. ''You're right.''

She pulled against his firm grip, rose from the couch and went to the phone. Glancing at the number on the pad, she dialed. It rang several times before an answering machine picked up. She hated talking to machines, and after all this time, it seemed grossly inadequate to leave a curt message to return the call. ''Nobody's home.''

Craig watched her hang up. ''What now?''

''I'll call Michael and ask him to break the news to Brian.''

''I don't think he should hear it from his uncle, Kerry. How about this? My sources tell me the Homestead Bank and Trust is planning to offer several thousand acres of the Number One for sale in the next month or two.''

Her brows rose. ''Break up the Number One?'' The idea appalled her, though she herself had tipped over the first domino.

"Seems like a good investment," he continued matter-of-factly. "I'd like to check it out firsthand. Why don't I fly us both to the Number One. You can talk to Brian about his dad while I get with Michael and your father to discuss the land deal."

She considered for a moment. "I can't. I have to appear in court tomorrow on the drunk driving charge, and I want to meet with my lawyer and accountant to set up a scholarship fund for the boy I almost hit."

He recognized delaying tactics when he saw them. "A court appearance is more important than your family? Your lawyer can arrange a continuance."

She hung her head. "Don't be melodramatic, Craig. Buying and selling real estate is what you do. So go do it. In the meantime, Michael can do what he does best—be a family man."

"Your son needs to hear it from you."

She jumped from the couch, took a step, then spun abruptly to face him. "Let's get something straight, Craig. He's my son. I'll take care of making sure he's safe. I've told you before and I'll tell you only one more time. This is none of your business. Now butt out."

CRAIG THOUGHT about Kerry all the way home. He seemed to do a lot of that these days, to the point where she was becoming a major distraction. Did he mean what he'd said—that any chance he and Kerry might have together depended on her reconciling with her dad?

It seemed an unfair condition, but he knew if she was going to stay sober, she would have to find peace of mind, and she couldn't do that unless she faced the man she'd hurt the most and acknowledged her mistakes. Even if her father rebuffed her, she would still have the consolation of knowing she'd made the effort.

Jacobs informed him he had received no urgent calls. The correspondence on his desk held nothing that required immediate attention. He picked up the phone and dialed a number his private investigator, Al Schneider, had furnished him. A couple of rings later the call was answered.

"Michael? This is Craig Robeson."

"Craig." The surprise at the other end was obvious. "Kerry told me you're contributing to her fund. Thanks for helping Sis out."

"My pleasure." In fact, they'd never gotten around to the details of their partnership. "But I'd like to talk to you about something else—in person. If I fly to Coyote Springs this evening, would it be possible for you to meet me there? I know this is very short notice, but—"

"I assume this is about Rafe."

"In part."

"When will you be leaving and what are you flying?" Apparently, the decision was made. A man of action. Craig liked that.

"I have a Learjet. It'll take me about half an hour to get to the airport, then figure a few more minutes to file a flight plan, check out the plane...I'd say within an hour."

"Don't bother going to the Springs," Michael said. "We have a five-thousand-foot improved runway on the ranch that'll accommodate you, and we can put you up here for the night.''

"I don't want to inconvenience you any more than I am already.''

"Actually, this is easier for me and saves us both time. We have plenty of room in the guest house.'' Michael gave Craig the coordinates for the airstrip. "If you leave in an hour, you should be here around six. I'll be waiting at the hangar for you.''

"Thanks, Mike. I know this is an imposition. I appreciate—''

"Friends of the family are never an imposition. See you around six.''

The words *friends of the family* were said mechanically, almost tersely, yet they echoed in Craig's brain during his flight to Coyote Springs. Craig had never invited anyone from school to his home during the two years he'd lived in West Texas. The house, though small, was fastidiously neat and spotlessly clean, but it was impossible to predict what would happen if and when his father made an appearance. The chances of Harry barging in the door drunk and mean discouraged any notion of having casual friends over.

From the air Craig could see the town had grown. Judging from the size and design of the new additions, it had prospered, too. The small city with its friendly people represented the low-water mark in his life— one he'd never had any desire to revisit.

Finding the landing strip on the ranch was no problem. The fields were drier than he remembered, but then he recalled there had been drought conditions for several years.

Michael First, wearing a big West Texas smile under his cowboy hat, was leaning against the side of a maroon pickup when Craig turned off his engines in front of an old wooden hangar. Three or four years older than Craig, he was not quite as tall, but he was very powerfully built. He gave his guest a firm handshake that imparted confidence and acceptance.

"I'm sorry about the short notice," Craig said as he tossed his overnight bag in the truck's bed and climbed into the cab. Cool evening breezes wafted through the open windows.

"Not a problem, really. We enjoy having guests, so please don't think you're imposing."

They drove a few minutes in the waning sunlight. "How's Kerry handling that son of a bitch showing up after all these years?" Michael asked.

They turned onto a dirt road that slowly descended into a narrow canyon.

"She's shaken, but she's coping."

"Coping," Michael repeated quietly.

"What you really want to know is if she's drinking. There was a little setback, but she's over it. She's doing fine, Mike."

The driver nodded.

"Who all knows about Rafe's coming back?" Craig asked a minute later.

"After I talked to Kerry today, I called Dad and told him. By now, he'll have told his wife, Sheila. I told my wife, Clare, as well. My brother and sister, Gideon and Julie, live in town. They'll be coming out tomorrow for the weekend. Dad said he'd wait till then to bring them up to date. Some things are best discussed face-to-face.''

Precisely what Craig had told Kerry, but face-to-face involved looking the other person in the eye, and she wasn't prepared to do that yet.

''Brian doesn't know?''

''Kerry asked me to tell him, but Dad and I agreed to wait until we could all be together. We're not sure how he'll react, but having family around should help.''

The pink-and-purple edge of the horizon was swallowed by a thick growth of massive oak trees as they progressed into the valley. In the waning dusk, Craig could make out the twinkling lights of a house up ahead.

''This is the Home Place.'' Michael pulled up in front of a rustic single-story building. ''Part of the original sixty thousand acres of the family ranch. Dad and my stepmother, Sheila, live here now.''

''I know about Kerry's selling her share of the ranch and your father losing control of the place as a result,'' Craig confided.

''It's not much of a secret. I'd still like to wring her neck. The good part is that Dad seems very content here. He's doing what he loves most, raising horses chiefly, a few cattle, and spending a lot more time with the family.''

The front door of the house opened, and a man stepped onto the wide porch. Behind him a woman's outline appeared.

Michael waited for Craig to come around to his side of the truck, then walked with him toward the older couple. "Dad," Michael said, as they ascended the steps, "you remember Craig Robeson."

Adam shook Craig's hand with a grip that matched Michael's. "I sure do. Good to see you again, son. This is my wife, Sheila."

"I'm very glad to meet you," the slender, blond-haired woman said as she, too, shook his hand. She ushered him into the house.

The room they entered was large and comfortable, with overstuffed furniture that seemed to invite slouching. Brian was standing at the far end of the room, leaning against a doorway. His posture shouted attitude.

CHAPTER THIRTEEN

"HELLO, BRIAN," Craig said.

No response.

"Brian, why don't you get Mr. Robeson's bag from Uncle Mike's truck and put it in the guest house while I fix us all something cold to drink," Sheila prompted in an attempt to break the tension between the two men.

"Your hospitality is very generous, Mrs. First. And please, call me Craig."

She gave him a wide grin. "Only if you call me Sheila. And it's no trouble at all."

"How is she?" Adam asked a minute later when they were standing in the kitchen and his wife was pouring tea from a pitcher into tall glasses filled with ice. Craig noted that Kerry's father tried to make the question sound casual, but the subtext in his voice and the way his deep blue eyes searched for reassurance said otherwise.

"She hit a rough patch after Rafe returned, as you might expect, but she's weathered it. I think she's going to make it this time."

Adam exhaled loudly. "I hope so. She's been through enough."

Remarkable, Craig thought. After all she'd subjected her father to, the man could still worry about what she'd endured.

He was a sharp contrast to Harry Robeson, who always saw himself as the victim of other people's malevolence. Adam First might not be the perfect father, but he was an admirable one.

"I made a lot of mistakes with her, Craig, mistakes I've always regretted."

"Don't assume all the guilt. She wasn't completely honest with you, but I'll let her tell you about that."

"Is she coming here?" The hope in his voice was unmistakable.

Good question, Craig thought. "I can't tell you precisely when, but give her a little more time, and I'm confident she'll do the right thing."

"I told her before she went into rehab that I forgave her. There's no reason for her to stay away."

"How much does Brian know about his old man?" Craig asked.

"That he was a piece of scum. I don't think he has any actual recollection of abuse, but he's aware it happened. Like the rest of us, he believes his father was killed in a car accident a couple of years after the divorce."

"He seems like a good kid."

"He is." There was pride in the statement. "With all her problems, Kerry did her best to be a good mother for him."

The subject himself appeared in the kitchen with Craig's bag. From the expression on his face it was obvious he knew they had been talking about him. Craig wondered how much he'd overheard.

He turned to the young man's grandparents. "Would you mind leaving us alone for a couple of minutes?"

Adam shifted his attention from his guest to his grandson. "Use my office."

"We eat in about half an hour," Sheila called as her husband escorted them from the room.

The den was a squarish room paneled in knotty pine. All the pigeonholes of the rolltop desk overflowed. Papers were strewn beside a blinking computer on a modern table, and a gun cabinet opposite the two casement windows displayed a variety of firearms. A man's room. A comfortable workspace and retreat.

Craig settled into an easy chair and observed Kerry's son for a moment. "I owe you an apology, Brian. The other day when you came to see your mother—"

"You mean you lied when you said you weren't sleeping with her?" he asked sarcastically. He leaned against a windowsill, arms crossed. His brown eyes didn't waver from Craig's.

Trying to stem a surge of anger, Craig answered evenly. "No, I didn't lie." He'd slept with her later, which meant he was equivocating. He'd condemned Kerry for her verbal sleights of hand and now he was doing the same thing.

"That's not the way it looked to me," Brian responded incredulously.

Calmly, Craig replied, "Looks can be deceiving." Getting into a word-slinging contest wasn't going to solve anything. "We intentionally misled you."

Brian pulled back. "You mean you wanted me to think you two were sleeping together? Why the hell would you do that?"

This isn't coming out right. Start all over, he told himself. "Brian, right now you don't have a very good reason to like me—"

"Ah, gee. Now, what would ever make you think that?"

Craig took a deep breath. "Before you condemn, please sit down and hear me out." When Brian didn't move, he went on. "Your mother wanted to get you to leave—"

"So you could go to bed together."

"Damn it, will you shut up a minute and listen?"

The two males stared at each other, tension palpable between them. Finally, Brian moved to the other easy chair and parked a thigh on its arm. "Okay. I'm listening."

It wasn't Craig's place to tell him about his father's return, yet without that information, none of the rest of his explanation made any sense.

"Your mother has gone through a particularly traumatic time these past couple of weeks. She has some problems she had to work out on her own, and she didn't want you to get involved." He was making this explanation sound like rejection and hoped that in a few minutes Brian would understand his mother's motivation was love, not indifference. "To protect you."

Brian's eyebrows drew together. "Protect me? From what? You're not making any sense."

"I know I'm not," Craig agreed. "Not yet. But in a few minutes your grandfather is going to tell you something that I hope will make it clear. All I ask is that you listen with an open mind and remember that your mother loves you very much.''

Totally baffled, Brian shook his head and shrugged.

''But there's something else I have to tell you. Man to man.'' He paused. ''I care about your mother.''

''You mean you want to marry her—or just go to bed with her?''

Marry Kerry. He'd carefully avoided even thinking the notion. He wasn't the marrying kind. His brief affairs had convinced him of that. And Kerry... There were so many obstacles.

''I don't honestly know where our relationship is headed. There's a lot we still have to work out, and I'm not sure we can.''

More confused than ever, the young man asked, ''Are you asking me if it's all right for the two of you to be together?''

Craig considered the question. ''I guess I am. You're the most important person in her life. I don't want to come between you. I also know that if you and I were to compete, only one of us could win.'' He added with a wry grin, ''And I'd lose.''

''I...'' Brian didn't seem to know how to respond.

''All I ask is that you give me a chance. Give us both a chance.''

''I don't want her hurt.''

''Neither do I, and if I ever think my being with her is harmful, I'll leave. You have my promise on that.''

Mutely, the son nodded.

Craig offered his hand. With some reluctance, Brian accepted it.

"Now, let's go see your grandparents." Craig was tempted to put his arm over the young man's shoulder, but they weren't ready for that yet.

He had been vaguely aware of the sound of a car pulling up while they were talking. He stepped into the living room and found a tall woman with medium dark hair, intelligent brown eyes and a sureness in her posture. Michael's wife, Clare, Craig decided, even before they were introduced. Certain people belonged together, and these two were definitely well matched.

"The girls are staying over at Elizabeth's for the night," she explained to the group at large after shaking Craig's hand, "and Dave is working on a project with his pal at Neal's house."

"Let's eat." Adam motioned everyone into the dining room.

"Do you like smoked sausage?" Sheila asked as she hustled through the kitchen door carrying a platter of cut links.

Craig sniffed the air, inhaling the tangy aroma of spice and smoke. "Makarek's?" he asked, wide-eyed.

"You remember it?" Adam broke into a broad smile.

"Best I've ever had. But surely Gus Makarek isn't still making it."

Adam chuckled. "Gus, Sr., finally retired a couple of years ago. His son's taken over and is still using the same old secret recipe."

Craig drank tea. "There are certain things I associate with places. Makarek's sausage is definitely at the top of the list for Coyote Springs."

''Well, in a little while Sheila's potato salad will be at the top of your Home Place list.''

''I'm looking forward to it.''

Conversation during the meal centered on an Irish dance troupe that was coming to Coyote Springs. Kerry's brother Gideon was getting tickets for the whole family through the university. Half an hour later, they were all assembled in the family room at the back of the house. It equaled the living room in size but had a stone fireplace and doors leading to a wooded hillside. Adam motioned his guest to the couch. ''No use beating around the bush,'' he said from his wing chair near the hearth. He studied his grandson. ''We have some news to tell you, son. About your father.''

''My father?'' Brian cocked his head and shot Craig a suspicious glance. ''What's he got to do with anything? He's dead.''

Craig took a long, deep breath. With a nod from Adam, he spoke. ''That's what everyone thought— that he was killed in a car crash some twelve or so years ago. But it wasn't him they found. Your father's alive, Brian.''

The young man bolted from his chair. ''I don't believe you. Mom would have told me….'' He stared at the visitor as understanding began to dawn.

''He reappeared without warning only a couple of weeks ago.''

''Where has he been?'' Then warily Brian asked, ''In prison?''

Craig shook his head. ''Hiding out in Mexico. At the time of his disappearance, there were several warrants for his arrest. The statute of limitations has run out on them now.''

''I don't believe you.'' But he did, and judging by his clenched hands, the news made him angry. He glared at his grandfather. ''Did you know?''

Adam interlaced his fingers. ''I found out just before Mr. Robeson arrived.''

''Your mother called me this afternoon,'' Michael explained. ''She wanted us to be together when you were told.''

Brian focused on Craig. ''That's why she was trying to get rid of me? She didn't have the guts to tell me herself?''

Craig tried to imagine the jumble of thoughts and emotions going through the young man's head. ''She was hoping you wouldn't have to find out.''

''Why shouldn't I? He's my father.''

So the boy still yearned for his dad, even though he knew the man to be a bum. ''He's demanding money.''

From the expression on the teenager's face, Craig had a pretty good idea what Brian was thinking. *He didn't come back to see me. He doesn't care about me. He just wants Mom's money.*

''Did she give him any?''

''No, and he's pretty mad about it.''

''Yeah, I bet.'' He faced the high mantel, then turned to confront Craig. ''So why are you telling me now?''

''Because eventually you'll find out anyway. Your mother's main concern is for your safety. Your father said if she didn't give him what he wanted, he'd come after you.''

Brian's eyes widened, more in shock than fear. ''Why? I can't give him anything.'' Then light dawned. ''You mean he'd kidnap me?''

''That's a possibility,'' Craig admitted.

Sheila raised a hand to her mouth in shock. ''His own son? He'd kidnap his own son for ransom?''

''He'd do it,'' Adam asserted categorically, rage ringing sharply in his voice.

''Let him,'' Brian snapped. ''I'll kill the bastard.''

Sheila reached out to him, but the teenager didn't want gentle sympathy.

''That's exactly why she didn't want to tell you,'' Craig explained. ''She was afraid of your reaction.''

''This is all my fault,'' Brian said earnestly. ''I should have stayed with her instead of going to college. She needs me.''

''No, it's not your fault,'' Michael retorted sharply. ''Don't blame yourself for something you can't control.''

''He's right, son,'' Adam said firmly. ''The person to blame is your son of a bitch of a father.''

''Adam, please,'' Sheila implored.

''Okay, okay.'' He closed his eyes for a minute. ''What's done is done.''

''You're going back tomorrow,'' Brian said to Craig. ''I want to go with you.''

''That's not a good idea,'' Craig argued. ''Your presence will only make your mother more vulnerable. Let me give you the straight skinny about your father, Brian.'' He had the others' undivided attention, as well. "Rafe Durgan is a user. He uses people for as long as it's to his advantage. He manipulated your mother before and after their marriage."

"Because of me," Brian snapped.

"No." Craig was adamant. "You've got it backward. You just happened to be someone he could use, and he did...to make your mother feel incapable of controlling her own life, helpless to protect you. That was one of the reasons she drank. Not because of you, Brian, but because of him. If you leave school to stay with her, your father will have won another victory. She'll feel she can't manage her own life."

"And she'll start drinking. Is that what you're telling me? If I go to help her it'll be my fault when she gets drunk again."

This wasn't going the way he intended. "That's not what I'm saying, Brian. The next drink your mother takes is her choice, not because of anything you did or did not do. But don't rob her of the comfort of knowing you're out of danger and the satisfaction of conquering this demon on her own terms."

"Craig's right," Clare concurred, pitching in for the first time. "Your mother has to fight this battle by herself."

"She's very proud of you," Craig told Brian. "Constantly brags about you studying architecture in college, getting straight As, running track."

"I can study architecture anytime," he countered. "I need to be there. To protect her."

"I've hired private security to make sure she's safe."

"It doesn't make any difference. She's my mother."

"Let's sleep on it," Adam proposed. "We can talk about this again in the morning."

BRIAN WENT OUTSIDE. Saying he needed to stretch his legs, Craig followed him. The young man was sitting on the steps of the guest house.

"I'm sorry about what's happening," Craig said.

Brian shrugged unconvincingly.

"Your mom is going to be all right. I know you're worried about her drinking, but I really think she's conquered it this time."

"What would you know about it?"

Craig sat beside him and rested his elbows on his knees. "My father was an alcoholic." He gave the statement a moment to sink in. "I never brought friends home because I didn't want them to see the way we lived. When he was sober, my parents were always fighting."

"At least you had a father."

Craig snorted. "When he was drunk, if I wasn't home he knocked my mother around. The rest of the time, he used his fists on me."

Brian said nothing.

"At the end of my senior year in high school, my father lost his job because of his drinking. In their last fight, he put my mother in the hospital."

Head down, Brian asked, "What happened to him?"

Craig took a deep breath. "I killed him."

Brian froze and seemed suddenly afraid to turn his head to look at the man sitting next to him.

"It wasn't intentional. I pulled him off my mother and told him if he ever laid a hand on either of us again, I'd kill him."

"Did you mean it?"

Craig lifted his shoulders and let them fall. "It's one of those phrases we use in a moment of anger. Whether I would have, I don't know. At the time, I certainly felt capable of it. Apparently, he thought so, too, because he backed off. He was scared of me. I could see the fear in his eyes, and I remember how good it made me feel—knowing I'd finally conquered him. Things would be different now, I thought. I'd be in control." He inhaled slowly and let it out. "My father ran out of the house, jumped in his car and burned rubber getting away—from me. A mile down the road, he rolled the car." Craig examined his fingernails. "He died in the hospital a couple of days later of massive head injuries."

Brian said nothing for an extended interval as night sounds purred and pulsed in the background. Crickets chirped. Frogs ribbeted. Somewhere off in the distance a coyote wailed for a mate.

"Take me with you tomorrow," Brian finally implored.

Craig let the request hang in the air a moment before responding. "I will, Brian, if, after all your grandparents and I have told you, you're absolutely sure that's what you want to do. But your grandfather's right. Sleep on it and decide what the best thing is for your mother. She loves you more than anyone or anything in this world. I understand your wanting to help and protect her, but putting yourself in harm's way is going to make the situation more difficult for her. If anything were to happen to you, she'd blame herself.''

''But it's *his* fault, my father's. Everybody says so.''

''If something happened to you, do you really think we'd ever be able to convince your mother of that? This is a battle she has to fight for herself, Brian. Without help, no matter how well intended, from you or me.''

THE SNORT of horses woke Craig the following morning, jarring him from a peaceful, dreamless sleep. He climbed out of bed and looked out the window. Brian and several other mounted men were weaving their way single file among the pines that dotted the hillside. Cowpokes, he thought, and envied their carefree lifestyle.

He quickly showered and dressed, then walked the short distance to the main house. His nostrils twitched at the smell of brewing coffee and frying bacon before he got there.

''I hope the boys didn't wake you,'' Adam said, when he opened the back door with a chipper smile. Without waiting for a response, he handed his guest a steaming cup.

Craig took a grateful sip, sighed, thanked his host and entered the warm kitchen.

''Good morning,'' Sheila said from the stove, where she was flipping pancakes. ''Breakfast will be ready in a few minutes.''

Halfway through his first coffee, Craig felt human enough to attempt a conversation. "Was that Brian I saw riding off?"

Sheila deposited a platter of flapjacks and a plate of crisp bacon in the middle of the table.

"Yep. Dig in," Adam answered.

Craig didn't hesitate. The strong brew had his blood pumping, and the smells had his mouth watering. "Does that mean he's not planning to return to Dallas with me?"

"You seem to have convinced him. For now, at least."

"Good." He dotted griddle cakes with butter and poured warm maple syrup over them.

"Are you going back immediately?" Sheila sat between the two men and took a modest portion of food.

"Actually…" Craig hesitated, then decided to plunge in. "I was hoping we might discuss a little business while I'm here." At Adam's quizzical expression, he said, "I understand some Number One land is going to be offered for sale in the next couple of months."

His host snorted. "The vultures are already circling."

"Adam!" Sheila exclaimed, clearly embarrassed.

"Sorry," Adam apologized. "That was unfair."

Craig waved the comment away. "No. You're right. It must be very difficult seeing the ranch broken up. I understand you have first option on any sales. Do you intend to exercise it?"

Adam shook his head and picked up his cup. "They're offering a hundred and fifty sections. I can afford to buy a portion of that, but what would be the point? I'd be tying up money I can use elsewhere. The Number One is a thing of the past. It's time to move on.''

An honest assessment. Craig tried to gauge how the man truly felt. He seemed resigned, but he must hurt like hell.

''By the way, how did you know about it?'' Adam asked. ''The bank has been keeping the decision under tight wraps.''

Craig allowed a small smile. ''Land deals are my business.'' In a grotesque imitation of a sinister foreign accent, he added, ''I have my ways of finding out.''

Adam chuckled good-naturedly. ''If you have the time, I have the helicopter. How about a tour?''

''You don't mind?''

Without waiting for her husband to answer, Sheila asked, ''Will you be back for lunch?''

''We'll stop off at Cordero's place. I'm sure La-Turna will fix us up.''

For the next several hours, they flew over one corner of the eight-hundred-square-mile spread. Its size and diversity impressed Craig, who was used to dealing with large tracts of land. They discussed the drought, livestock and water rights. By the end of the tour, Craig came away convinced he should bid on the package. Its potential was virtually unlimited.

They returned to the Home Place late in the afternoon. Adam's son Gideon and daughter Julie had arrived. Unlike Kerry and Michael, who were dark haired, the younger siblings were blond. Both, how-

ever, had the characteristic First blue eyes. Gideon,
Craig learned, was a kinesiologist working in the athletic department at TUCS, Texas University at Coyote
Springs, and Julie was in graduate school, earning a
master's in education.

That Craig felt so instantly at home with these
strangers amazed him. He wondered how Kerry could
bear to separate herself from them. He'd thought a
good deal about her during the course of the day. As
he'd listened to her father, he'd tried to imagine what
it was like growing up with a man who seemed so
comfortable in his skin. Michael, to whom she claimed
to be the closest, had been the most reserved of the
group, yet even with him, Craig felt at ease. His wife,
Clare, was definitely a supermom with apparently
boundless energy and, Craig suspected, the real dis-
ciplinarian in the household. Their kids were certainly
polite and respectful, yet they were still allowed to be
kids. He envied them all.

"I'm not going back with you," Brian commented
while he added another small log to the mesquite fire
under the baby back ribs that had been slow-cooking
for several hours.

"Your grandfather told me," Craig replied. "I
know it wasn't an easy decision, but I think you've
made the right one."

"I have a question for you."

"I'll answer it if I can."

"You said your father was a drunk. Do you drink?"

Craig remembered the report that Brian had been
picked up for DWI. It was one of those strange phe-
nomena that the children of heavy drinkers, the people

who suffered innocently from the effects of alcohol, often chose it themselves. Brian might or might not become a problem drinker, but the danger was there and no doubt weighed heavily on his mind.

"I have an occasional beer or a glass of wine with a meal," he admitted. "I rarely have two and I never get drunk."

"So why are you interested in my mother? If you don't drink together—"

"We didn't drink together when we knew each other in high school, and I won't drink in front of her now. Your mother is an alcoholic, Brian. She can't drink."

"Do you know what she's like when she's drinking?"

How much should he disclose? That he saw her reeking of alcohol, cursing and screaming as they pulled her away to the drunk tank for the night?

"She fell off the wagon after your father showed up. It wasn't pretty, Brian, but she's over it."

"Yeah. That's what she said last time and the time before that." He was silent for a long minute. "I figured when I saw you that you were after her money, but Gramps says you have more than she does."

"I'm not interested in her money."

"So why are you interested?"

Craig shook his head as much in amusement as sympathy. "If I could answer that, Brian, I'd know the secret of love. The best I can do is tell you that there's something about your mother that resonates in me, that makes me want to be with her, to help and protect her."

"She's a drunk. She'll let you down."

The way she's let you down so many times in the past, Craig thought. *Except,* he wanted to remind Brian, *you still love her.* "Maybe she will, but right now I'm willing to take that chance."

CHAPTER FOURTEEN

CRAIG HAD MENTIONED where his mother lived.

Kerry couldn't say exactly why she wanted to see Mrs. Robeson, except that Craig's mother was an important person in his life, and through her Kerry might be able to get a better handle on the man she was falling in love with.

She checked the telephone book. There was only one Robeson—Gina—listed with an address in Mesquite. Kerry considered calling ahead to make sure the older woman was there and the time was convenient, but she decided against it. Dropping by unannounced would make it more difficult for Craig's mother to turn her away.

The Ferrari was still in the shop and probably would be for some time, so she rented a new Lexus and drove to Mesquite, situated on the eastern edge of greater Dallas. The address turned out to be a small, attached town house in a well-kept, upscale retirement village. The landscaping appeared professionally designed and meticulously maintained. It was pleasant, unimaginative and had a slightly institutional feel about it.

A woman of medium stature with well-coiffed graying hair answered the door. Her initial expression, the kind reserved for a welcome guest, quickly disappeared when she realized she didn't know her caller. "If you're selling something," she said with obvious annoyance, "you can go away. No solicitors allowed."

"I'm not selling anything, Mrs. Robeson. I'm a friend of Craig's and I'd like to talk to you for a few minutes if you have the time."

The invocation of her son's name didn't seem to take the chill from her features. Gina Robeson surveyed her visitor with a critical eye. "Who are you?"

"My name is Kerry Durgan. You may remember me by my maiden name, Kerry First."

"Kerry First?" The older woman's eyes narrowed. "So you're the one."

Kerry wondered if Craig had purposely not mentioned that his mother was not quite coherent. "May I come in?"

Gina shrugged. "Might as well. No sense in standing out here." She stepped aside for her guest to enter.

She led Kerry through a narrow entryway to a small but pleasant low-ceilinged room that had the feel of a country cottage.

Kerry found herself comparing Craig's mother with her own. Helen First would have been about Gina's age had she lived, and about the same build—a little on the pudgy side. Helen had had to watch her weight because she liked to sample her own good cooking too much. Gina didn't strike Kerry as the culinary type. Her propensity for extra pounds more likely came from chiffon pies and chocolate éclairs. Kerry scolded herself. She had no reason to draw that conclusion. Or to pass judgment.

She waited for the older woman to take a seat in what was probably her regular chair, an old-fashioned platform rocker with crocheted doilies on the armrests and behind the head.

Kerry sat on a love seat at an angle to a television set. "You said I'm the one. What did you mean?"

The lines at the corners of the woman's mouth deepened. "You broke my boy's heart."

"I don't understand."

"The prom."

Kerry had the feeling this conversation was going to be even more difficult than she'd imagined.

"He was smiling. My son didn't smile much then, what with Harry losing his job and everything. We were going through a difficult period. Well, I guess every family does, but then he asked you to go with him to the prom, and you said yes, and he was all smiles."

Kerry had no idea the date had been so important to him. Under other circumstances maybe it wouldn't have been. It was just a date, after all. They didn't know each other, and she wouldn't have accepted his invitation if Rafe hadn't been kicked out of school. She'd been counting on Rafe to take her to the dance.

"He wasn't smiling when he came home that night," Gina said in an accusing tone. "He wouldn't tell me what was wrong, but eventually I got it out of him. You'd run off with some riffraff. Left him standing there, humiliated in front of his friends."

A sigh welled up, but Kerry stifled it. "It was a serious mistake on my part, Mrs. Robeson," she admitted. "I'm sorry."

Gina wasn't mollified. "A little late, it seems to me." She began rocking, the determined, impatient movement of long-pent-up anger. "If it hadn't been for you that night, Harry wouldn't be dead."

Kerry blinked, uncertain she'd heard correctly. Surely this woman wasn't accusing her of being responsible for the death of Craig's father. Patiently, she said, "I'm sorry, Mrs. Robeson, but I don't understand what you're talking about. I never even met your husband, and I only had one date with your son. I understand Mr. Robeson died in a car crash. You can hardly blame me for that."

"Well, I do."

This was surreal. Craig should have mentioned that his mother was not rational. The tragic death of her husband must have unbalanced her. Perhaps Harry's abuse had contributed to it.

Kerry was inclined to rise, apologize for intruding and leave. Clearly, nothing positive was going to come from this visit. She'd made mistakes in her life, hurt a lot of people, including herself, but being accused of killing someone she didn't even know was going too far. On the other hand, she was curious why this bitter old woman would make such an outlandish accusation. Her explanation, illogical though it might be, could still furnish a clue to Craig's hang-ups about seeking forgiveness.

"Would you mind telling me why?" she asked.

Gina climbed to her feet. "I'm going to have a Coke. You want something? I have beer, if you prefer."

"A Coke will be fine. Thank you. May I help?"

''No. I'll be right back.''

Kerry used her hostess's absence to survey the room more closely. Knickknacks, figurines and bric-a-brac cluttered gracefully curved Queen Anne furniture. Delicate lace curtains framed the picture window, which gave a view of a pristine green lawn and a neat stucco house across the street. The intense femininity of the room contrasted sharply with the house Kerry had grown up in. The ranch headquarters had been a decidedly masculine home, with massive leather-upholstered furniture and dark wood. Kerry's mother had worn dresses only to church on Sundays, the rest of the time running around in jeans or shorts and simple blouses, not a belted shirtdress like Gina was wearing.

This room's picture-book tidiness and the woman who lived in it made Kerry uncomfortable, though she couldn't exactly explain why. She tended to be casual about her home, depending on day help to maintain elementary order. There was something compulsive and unhealthy about the precision of this house.

Gina Robeson pressed a cold soda into Kerry's hand, removed a felt-bottomed sandstone coaster from a caddy on a nearby end table and placed it on the polished surface at Kerry's elbow.

''We were having a rough time then, like I told you,'' the older woman said after sitting down. Her strident tone had mellowed to one that was more conversational. ''Harry had lost his job with the telephone company and was mad as hell. You couldn't blame him. After all, he'd worked for them for more than twenty years, then one day they tell him he's finished, just like that. The miserly severance pay they gave him wouldn't last very long, and he'd already borrowed against his retirement fund.''

''I understand he was an alcoholic.''

The widow clearly didn't like hearing her late husband maligned. Her lips tightened before she spoke. ''Harry drank sometimes,'' she acknowledged, ''but he wasn't an alcoholic. He was upset. You would be, too, if you'd just been laid off.''

Having a drinking problem was one of those euphemisms people used when they wanted to avoid the truth. Being an alcoholic somehow smacked of having a moral disease. According to Craig, his father had been fired—not laid off—for being drunk on the job, and not for the first time. Gina must have known that, but like many enablers, she blotted it out of her mind.

''I understand he was abusive,'' Kerry commented, and watched Gina cringe at the statement.

''A man has an obligation to discipline his son.''

Kerry was tempted to ask when discipline crossed the line and became brutality. ''He slapped you around, too, didn't he?''

''That was my own fault. I said things I shouldn't have.''

The rationalization of a victim. Kerry had done the same thing with Rafe, assuming responsibility for the things he did, blaming herself for somehow instigating his violent behavior.

Her father had insisted she and Brian get formal counseling after Adam had run Rafe off the ranch and he'd persuaded her to divorce the louse. It had been the right thing to do, and she'd agreed, but only because of Brian. Adam's good judgment had reinforced her sense of inadequacy. When the counselor suggested to her father that she might also have a drinking problem, Kerry had managed to convince him it had been temporary and that it was resolved with Rafe's leaving. Adam had believed her, and for a long time she'd persuaded herself it was true.

Gina fixed her with watery hazel eyes. "Every time Harry got a little upset, Craig wanted me to call the police and have Harry arrested. Of course I couldn't do that. Harry didn't mean any harm. It was my fault he got so upset, but Craig didn't understand that. He called the police on his own. Naturally, I refused to press charges."

"How long was this before your husband died?"

"A couple of years, I guess. Right after we moved to Coyote Springs."

Her son would have been perhaps sixteen years old.

"Craig started baiting his father, taunting him into hitting him, and when Harry did, he'd phone the police and have him arrested."

"I suppose you bailed him out," Kerry ventured, making it sound as if it was the perfectly reasonable thing to do. What, Kerry wondered, would Gina Robeson say if she found out her son had had Kerry arrested and thrown into the drunk tank?

"Of course," Gina responded, showing satisfaction that her guest understood. "He was my husband. I had to. It was my duty."

Kerry had an urge to shake the woman rocking smugly in the platform chair, to remind her she'd had a greater obligation to protect her son. "What was Craig's reaction?"

Gina's lips tightened into a disapproving scowl. "He got mad at me, as if I had done something wrong. Said his father ought to be in jail. I told him that wasn't right, that for all his flaws, Harry was still his father and deserved respect from his family. I reminded him of the commandment to honor thy father and thy mother. That's the way we brought him up, you know. But it didn't do any good. Craig refused to drop the charges. The judge let Harry off, of course. After all, it wasn't like he was a common criminal."

He was worse, Kerry realized. A common criminal preyed on strangers; he didn't hurt the very people he was morally obligated to protect. "What did Craig do then?"

Gina shook her head. "He kept provoking his father, calling him terrible, ugly names, insulting him, just because Harry took a drink once in a while to relax. It was like he was daring Harry to hit him."

"And Harry did—hit him, I mean," Kerry speculated.

"He was just trying to discipline the boy. That's a father's right...his responsibility."

"Is that why your husband beat you?"

"You said you understood, but obviously you don't," Gina complained bitterly and sped up her rocking.

"I'm trying to, Mrs. Robeson," Kerry replied. She'd already grasped one very important fact. Craig had used the only nonlethal weapons he had available to him to combat his father's abuse and protect his mother. But like all victims, he suffered from guilt that he might be directly responsible for what had ultimately happened. Craig's words and actions had resulted in his father's death, and he would never get to find out if there could have been a different outcome.

"What happened?" she asked, doing her best to sound sympathetic. "Did they keep butting heads and catch you in the middle?"

Gina didn't smile, but Kerry could see hope in the aging woman's eyes that maybe she did understand.

"It wasn't fair. The third time Craig had his father arrested for assault and battery, the judge sentenced Harry to thirty days in jail. He was really mad when he came out. Blamed me for not controlling the boy. I tried to talk some sense into my son," Gina lamented. "I really did. But he had a mind of his own."

"When did Harry get out of jail, before or after the prom?" Kerry asked.

"A few days before."

"And he got drunk again."

"He didn't get drunk." Gina was adamant. "Sure, he had a few drinks. Wouldn't you, after being locked up like an animal for a month?"

Kerry shivered at the recollection of the drunk tank. It had been her wake-up call, and she was grateful to Craig for his courage in giving it to her. Jail could have been an opportunity for his father to reassess, to be honest with himself and assume accountability for the chaos he'd created. But his wife had contributed to his blind spot by making excuses for his brutal, indefensible behavior. Then she closed her eyes to her culpability in her husband's wrongdoing.

Kerry saw this meeting with Gina Robeson as a second wake-up call.

"It was Craig's fault for putting his father there," Gina persisted, "and your fault for making him so unhappy."

It was time to end the pass-the-blame game, Kerry decided. "Mrs. Robeson," she said politely but firmly. "I think you know that's unfair. You should be honoring your son for standing up to his father's violence and trying to protect you, not condemning him or me for what Harry did."

The older woman flinched at the implacable tone. "If it wasn't for Craig's threatening him," she responded in a whiny voice, "Harry would still be alive."

"And he'd still be beating you," Kerry snapped, unable to withhold her anger at the willful blindness of the woman even after all these years, "if by now he hadn't already killed you."

Gina scowled, her lower lip quivering. "You have no right," she declared haughtily, but her protest rang with uncertainty and fear. "How dare you come into my house and talk about my Harry that way?"

Carefully, Kerry modulated her tone. "According to Craig, his father beat you unconscious that last time. Isn't that right? He beat you so badly you ended up in the hospital with a ruptured spleen."

The platform rocker moved furiously. "He was sick, I tell you," Gina insisted. "He didn't mean to hurt me. I should have helped him."

Kerry took a deep breath in utter frustration. "Yes,

Mrs. Robeson, you're right. Your husband was a very sick man. You should have helped him see that.''

''He had problems and sometimes he needed a drink to calm himself.''

Kerry leaned forward and held the woman's reluctant gaze. ''Mrs. Robeson, listen to me,'' she said slowly. ''No matter what words you choose, your husband was an alcoholic, and no matter what problems he had, drinking wasn't going to make them better. It only made them worse.''

''What makes you such an expert?'' Gina challenged angrily.

Craig had asked Kerry once if she talked to women's groups about being abused. She'd recoiled from it, a luxury she could afford at the time but couldn't justify now. If any good was to come of this visit, she had to be absolutely honest—not only with this woman, but with herself. She reached forward and placed her hand on the aging widow's. The rocker stopped.

''I know, Mrs. Robeson,'' she said compassionately, ''because I'm an alcoholic. I've stopped drinking. I'm recovering.'' She felt proud to say it. ''But I'm still an alcoholic. I always will be.''

Gina gaped, stunned by the candor. She was still defensive and hostile, but she was also intensely interested. Kerry glimpsed a shadow of hope, as well. ''I was also a battered wife.''

''Because you drank,'' Gina said smugly.

Blame the victim. ''No,'' Kerry answered, and took a deep, fortifying breath. ''Because my husband was a bastard who got his kicks beating up people who couldn't fight back. Just like your husband.''

"That's not true.'' But there was no conviction in the denial. "Harry was a good man. He fell on hard times, that's all.''

Kerry recognized from the pleading tone that Gina was no longer trying to convince her guest, but herself. No one except Craig had apparently ever attempted to make Gina Robeson face the truth.

"Good men don't beat women and children, Mrs. Robeson. They protect them. Your son tried to protect you from a vicious coward who was hurting you. Craig's a good man. You should be damned proud of him.''

Gina glowered at her guest, or tried to. It came across more as trepidation in the face of resistance. "I think you'd better leave.''

Kerry nodded. "I will, but before I go I want to tell you something. I love your son and I hope someday to be worthy of his love. In the meantime, I can only be inspired by it. I hope you'll reexamine your relationship with him. He cares for you far more than you can imagine. You see, he did learn the commandment to honor his parents.''

Kerry rose. "Thank you for seeing me, Mrs. Robeson. You've been a great help. I think I understand your son better now.'' *And myself.*

She moved to the door, opened it and turned to contemplate Craig's mother. Gina Robeson sat immobile, like a person stunned. Her eyes were brimming as she regarded her departing guest. Soon the tears would fall. They would burn when they did, and they would ache in the old woman's heart. Part of Kerry wanted to stay and console, but Craig had given her the insight to understand that his mother needed and deserved privacy for her epiphany.

Kerry retreated and closed the door quietly behind her.

She drove away in a strange mood of hope and euphoria. She'd sought out Gina Robeson hoping to learn more about Craig, to gain information that would help her understand him. She'd learned far more than she'd bargained for.

He'd told her that as much as he loved her, he would leave her rather than stand by and watch her destroy herself with alcohol. She'd thought it a strange form of love. It was ridiculous that abandoning someone could be a sign of strength rather than weakness. Only now was she beginning to understand it took uncommon courage to step back from the beloved.

If the situation had been reversed and he had been the one arrested for drinking while intoxicated, would she have had the intestinal fortitude to let him spend the night in jail when she could have used her influence to get him out? Her every instinct would have been to come to his aid by saving him from humiliation. Yet he'd had the wisdom and courage to let her stay in that hellhole, allow her to see for herself where she was headed. She understood it wasn't the vision of derelict human beings, wasting their lives, trapped in a vicious circle of dependence and self-destructiveness that gave her the strength to resist the next drink. It was the fear of losing Craig, of losing his love.

CHAPTER FIFTEEN

CRAIG RETURNED to Dallas late in the afternoon. He had plenty to do—get his staff started on a bid for Number One land, then establish a project team for the new development. He debated whether to call Kerry and tell her about his trip to the ranch and the Home Place or wait until morning to visit her. But he was eager to see her, to be with her—now. On the drive from Love Field, he checked with Al Schneider's security agency. The condo was under constant surveillance, front and back, and there was a guard on the service entrance verifying and recording the identity of everyone who sought entry into the building.

A different doorman was on duty in the lobby when Craig entered, a man he hadn't seen before. He gave his name and stood by while the security guard called Kerry's penthouse, then escorted him to the elevator.

She met him at the door wearing jeans and a plaid cotton shirt. A hopeful expression brightened her face. The gleam in her eye told him she was glad to see him, but there was something else there, too. A glow of inner joy. Acceptance? But of what?

She wrapped her arms around his neck and kissed him gently on the mouth. "Welcome back. Good trip?'' She closed the door behind them and threw the chain.

"Very good.'' He drew her against him, inhaled her exotic scent and initiated another kiss, this one more probing, more demanding. "You have a wonderful family, Kerry.''

The tautness that the mention of her family usually stirred was missing, replaced with a gentle mood of agreement. "How's my kid?''

Her reaction surprised him. "He's fine. But he's hardly a kid anymore. He's a mature, responsible young man.''

She smiled. "He'll always be a kid to me.''

"He wanted me to bring him back so he could stay here with you, but your dad, his wife and your brothers managed to talk him into remaining at the Number One and returning to school when it starts next week.''

Kerry closed her eyes in relief. "He's always been very protective. But then, you know about that, don't you?''

He could have told her that being protective of one's parents wasn't always appreciated, but at the moment the observation would have thrown a pall on what seemed to be a positive mood. One considerably different from when he'd left.

She took his hand and led him into the living room.

"No word from Rafe?'' He'd checked with Hank Dawson on the flight from Coyote Springs. The fugitive was, as Kerry had indicated, remarkably adept at keeping a low profile.

She shook her head.

"Hank figures he knows they're after him and may already have hightailed it over the border to Mexico."

"Maybe for a while," Kerry insisted, "but when the heat is off, the lure of money will be too much for him to resist. He won't stay away. It's just a matter of time before he turns up again. I'm getting a Sprite. Do you want anything?"

He declined, then watched the way her hips rocked as she moved toward the kitchen. A soft drink definitely wasn't what he had on his mind.

She disappeared behind the swinging door. He heard the refrigerator open and close, the snap and hiss of a soda can being opened. The next moment she reappeared. Yes, he decided, there was a bounce in her step, one he'd never seen before, the confident stride of a woman who'd made a decision she was happy with.

"We'll keep private security in place as long as necessary. You're safe, Kerry. I'll have someone watching Brian when he returns to campus, too. In the meantime, he's well protected at the ranch."

She sipped her soft drink as she approached. "How did he take the news?"

"About the way you might expect. He was confused, then angry—"

Concern clouded her eyes. "At me for not telling him?"

"At first, but he understands now."

"It sounds like you've made a friend." There was pleasure in her voice.

"I hope so." He thought about telling her what Adam had said—that she was welcome on the ranch at any time, but if she wanted him to keep his distance, he would. Craig decided against it. Not yet, at least. Painful as asking for forgiveness was, she still had to do it. He wondered if she'd already made the decision. Was that what gave her the newfound peace he sensed within her?

He circled her waist with his hands and dragged her against him. "Have you thought about what I said about going to see your dad?"

"Yes, I—"

A crash came from the kitchen. Kerry jerked away from the embrace. Instinctively, though, she continued to hold Craig's hand. Together, they turned toward the archway from the hall. A second later, Rafe stood at the top of the stairs, a pistol in his hand. He'd shaved off his mustache, gotten a conservative haircut and traded in his jeans and T-shirt for a three-piece blue suit and tie. It didn't significantly improve his appearance, but it did change it. Instead of looking like a dissolute road worker, he resembled a dissolute banker. The dark eyes were bleary and edged with weathered crow's feet, and the expression on his face was one of smug malice. He descended into the bright room.

"Rafe?" Kerry whispered in disbelief, and tightened her hold on Craig's hand.

He preened. "My new image. You like it? Your professional bodyguard wasn't expecting a businessman. By the time he realized who I was—"

"What did you do to him?" Kerry cried.

"Don't worry, he'll be all right when he comes to. At least, I think he will." Rafe's eyes narrowed as he leered at her. "We've got some unfinished business, babe."

Smoothly, Craig moved in front of her.

"Big hero," Rafe sneered. "Step away from her." When Craig didn't budge, he went on, "I could shoot you where you are, but the bullet might go right through you into my dear ex-wife, so if you want to protect her, I suggest you move away, because you're the target, not her."

Kerry released herself from Craig's behind-the-back grasp. She might need the freedom of movement. "What do you want?" she demanded.

"What do you think, *querida?*" His grin was lecherous, then he snorted. "Money, honey. To start with. You ditched this loser once. I reckon you can do it again. Together we can have a lot of fun, babe. I'm as good as ever, and I bet you're even better."

"Not on your life." She sneered, too, and moved from behind Craig.

Rafe chuckled. "We'll get back to that in a minute. First, we have some unfinished business. You didn't transfer the money like I told you." He waved the pistol toward the desk.

"No," she said flatly. "I'm not going to."

"Don't play games with me, Kerry." His voice had the gravelly roughness of anger. "This isn't a dare. It's an order."

"You don't give me orders, Rafe," she said casually, and sauntered to the wing chair facing the piano. She knew she was taking a chance, that in his rage at being opposed, he might shoot one or both of them.

Rafe scratched the side of his head like a circus

clown trying to figure out what he was supposed to do. "Let's see." His voice was suddenly unnaturally jovial. "How about this?" He aimed the gun at Craig. "You either call your accountant or broker or whoever and tell him to transfer the funds, or your boyfriend here is a dead man."

Kerry had a nearly overwhelming urge to look at Craig, to ask with her eyes for his advice, his support, his concurrence for what she was about to do. She stifled the urge, and just hoped he'd go along with her.

"You're not thinking very clearly, Rafe." She shook her head like a disappointed schoolteacher. "You knocked out the guard by the service entrance, but you forgot the one outside the front door. You fire that pistol and he's in here in a heartbeat." She worked up a lazy crocodile grin. "And your heart stops beating—permanently. Kill Craig, and there's no reason for me to give you a dime. Kill me and there's no way you can get even a penny. So I guess you're stuck. Nice threads, though," she added cavalierly. "Where'd you steal them?"

Her ex-husband clearly was not happy, nor was he amused. "Shut up," he barked.

"Besides," she rambled on, undaunted, "even if I did tell my accountant to transfer the funds, I'd still have to sign the paperwork. And I won't."

"What about Brian?"

"Brian? Your son? I don't see Brian here." She swung around as if searching for him. "Craig, do you see Brian?"

"I don't see him, either," Craig agreed with a carefree nonchalance.

"That's right—" Kerry snapped her fingers "—you said he's at the Number One visiting the family." She gazed at the man holding the gun. "You could always kidnap him from there." She gave him a twisted smile. "Of course, you know if you go within a mile of the ranch, your ass is grass." Her genial mood changed in a flash, and she glared hard at Rafe. "Do whatever you want to me, Rafe, but if you do anything to hurt my son, I'll kill you myself, and without a moment's regret. And if I can't because I'm dead, someone else in my family will. My father taught us all to shoot. He's really not a vindictive man, you know. After all, last time he only pointed his shotgun at you. This time I guarantee he'll pull the trigger."

There was no hiding the apprehension in Rafe's eyes as he glowered at her. "I want my money," he insisted a little too forcefully.

"It's not your money. It's all mine. I sold out my family for it, remember? And you're not getting a penny of it."

She could feel Craig studying her, but her attention was focused on the face of the man who'd raped her and turned her into something less than human. Even under the circumstances she was amazed it had taken her so long to understand the depth of her collaboration in being a victim.

Rafe's dark complexion had turned nearly black with rage. "I ought to kill you." He was nearly out of breath with hatred.

"You almost did. For years I was a zombie because of what I let you do to me. But I'm not interested in blaming you, Rafe. The fact is, I feel nothing for you, not even the loathing you deserve."

"Shut up," he screamed.

"Keep your voice down," Kerry advised him calmly, amazed that he didn't hear her heart pounding. From where he stood, he couldn't see the front door, couldn't see the chain that would at least slow down a guard if there had been one on the other side. He cast a sharp, fearful glance in that direction, as though he expected a SWAT team to come storming in with guns blazing. Paranoia was a wonderful tool, Kerry concluded.

"You have a choice," she informed him, building on his growing insecurity. "You can leave the way you came and hope no one sees you, or you can put down that gun, give yourself up and we can get this thing over with. Your choice."

"You bitch."

Her only response was a lackadaisical smile. She was in control. They both knew it. Rafe Durgan had lost all power over her. He stared at her, shifted his gaze to Craig, focused on Kerry, then backed toward the kitchen and disappeared. A moment later there was a clattering sound followed by a gunshot.

THE FOUR OF THEM sat at the kitchen table—Kerry, Craig, Hank Dawson and Alvin Schneider.

"Rafe approached the service entrance carrying an attaché case," Al explained. "He reckoned the condo was being watched, but apparently he didn't expect to find a guard on duty. When he did, he told him he had an appointment with Mrs. Wellman on the fifteenth floor.''

"Dressed the way he was," Craig observed, "why didn't he come in the front door?"

Hank chuckled. "We asked him that. He knew there was extra security in the lobby, and he was afraid he'd be recognized. He figured he could slip in the back way without being noticed."

"Not a bad plan," Schneider noted. "If I'd simply had the service entrance under surveillance from a car in the parking lot, for example, we probably would have figured that dressed the way he was, he lived in the building."

"But it backfired," Craig concluded.

"Quint, the guard at the service entrance, was suspicious. Up close, Rafe didn't have the deportment of a gentleman, and visiting lawyers and businessmen don't normally enter fancy condos by the back way. Unfortunately, it took him a bit too long to process the information and see through the disguise. Quint picked up the phone and was about to sound an alert when Durgan rammed him in the gut with the attaché case and conked him on the head with the butt of his gun, knocking him unconscious."

"Is he going to be all right?" Kerry asked.

"Mild concussion, but he'll be okay. Fortunately, he was only a few minutes from his next scheduled security check-in, which he missed. That's why we found him when we did."

Hank nodded and shifted his attention to Kerry and Craig. "Now, tell us what happened up here."

Craig smiled at Kerry, his eyes glinting with admiration. Unmindful of the two men sitting across from them, he pressed her hand between both of his. "Rafe Durgan ran up against a brick wall."

Both Hank and Al politely sipped their black coffee and waited.

"He wanted money, of course," Craig went on. "I think he would have killed one or both us if he thought he could have gotten away with it. But Kerry had him convinced there was an armed guard outside the front door and that if he fired his gun he would be shot dead instantly."

Kerry fingered her cup. "I was afraid he'd see the chain on the front door and realize I was bluffing."

Craig's eyes never left hers. "So she maneuvered him away from the hall to keep him from seeing it," he explained. "Rafe was facing it when he backed into the kitchen, but he was too distracted to notice."

"Thank God," Kerry said. "I was already shaking in my boots."

"Don't believe her," Craig objected with a fond grin. "She was steady as a rock."

The air between them seemed to crackle. Hank broke the silence. "Well, it's over now," he said.

"You're sure he's going to be all right?" Kerry asked. "The gunshot we heard—"

"Was him shooting himself in the foot—literally," Hank explained. "By the time he got to the kitchen, an officer had arrived outside the door. Durgan wasn't expecting anyone to be there. The officer knew he was armed. So he tripped him. There was a brief scuffle, and Durgan's gun went off. He may limp his way through his prison years, but he'll live."

Kerry shook her head. As much as she abhorred the man who'd raped her and made her life hell, she didn't want him to suffer.

"By the way," Hank continued, "I did some checking. His version of the statute of limitations isn't quite accurate. It would have run out if he had remained within U.S. jurisdiction, but when he crossed the border into Mexico the clock stopped. He can still be charged with his former offenses, and I can pretty much guarantee he will be. Rafe Durgan isn't going to be breathing free air for a long, long time."

Kerry and Craig agreed to go to police headquarters the following morning to make formal statements.

"I have some things I need to tell you," Kerry said to Craig after Hank and Al had left.

"Do we really have to talk now?" He slipped his arm behind her back and tugged her against him.

She smiled at him and planted a kiss on his sandpaper-rough chin. "Yes, we do. I do."

They went into the living room. He wanted her to sit on the couch beside him so he could wrap his arms around her and feel the warmth of her soft, feminine body against him. But she took the club chair, instead, and indicated for him to sit on the couch opposite. Somewhat bewildered, he did.

"I visited your mother yesterday," Kerry said, hands laced on her lap. "We talked for about an hour. She's a very unhappy woman, Craig."

"That's my—"

She raised a hand to stop him. "Don't say it's your fault, because it isn't. She's unhappy because of her own unwillingness to face reality. She blames you for what happened to your father. She even blames me. Because she can't admit her own guilt."

"You? But you—"

"She and I have a lot in common. We're both too damned proud to face our faults. We both prefer to blame other people for our mistakes. We're both blind, arrogant and vindictive."

He started to object, but again she put him off. "I know I shouldn't talk about your mother that way. After all, I hardly know—"

"I was about to observe that you shouldn't talk about the woman I love that way, either," he said with a broad smile on his face.

Kerry closed her eyes, savoring the words, but she didn't deserve them, not yet. Taking a deep breath, she opened her eyes and gazed at him. "Please let me finish."

He sensed her seriousness. Respectfully, he wiped the grin off his face and nodded for her to continue.

"Your mother's searching for scapegoats, Craig. She failed you and herself in dealing with your father. It's a bitter pill to swallow, admitting culpability for her own pain, for her son's unhappiness and to some extent for her husband's death."

"It's not all her fault," he objected.

Kerry almost snorted. "No, it's not all her fault," she agreed. "Your father bears the largest responsibility. He was the alcoholic. He was the wife and child abuser. He was the one who lost his job and he was the one driving the car when it crashed. But your mother facilitated his drinking by excusing it. She enabled his abuse by refusing to press charges against him, by not leaving him. She made it possible for him to continue down the path to his own destruction. That's not easy to own up to, Craig. There's a good chance she never will. I wish it could be different. You love her, and in her own way, she loves you. But reconciliation doesn't seem very likely.''

"I realize that," he said, tension salting his words. "I came to terms with it a long time ago."

But had he? she wondered. "Nevertheless, it still hurts. I'm sorry."

He started to rise, to go to her, but she shook her head. "Let me finish, please."

Reluctantly, he settled once more onto the couch.

"I couldn't make her see her mistakes, Craig, but she helped me see mine. Like her, I've had my head buried in the sand. I do have a very loving family, one I don't deserve. I've lied to them and blamed them for not understanding me. I've tried to make my father responsible for my not being loved when all the time I was doing everything possible to make myself unlovable.''

She paused, beheld the expression of admiration on Craig's face and felt her heart skip a beat.

"But it's so much easier," she continued, buoyed by his warm, wordless response, "to take the arrogant way out. To take people for granted. To say, 'They love me, so they'll understand,' and then blame them when they can't comprehend why we continue to hurt them. For years I tried to prove that no matter how selfish and ungrateful I was, they had to love me anyway. The remarkable part is that, through it all, they actually have. I can't imagine why."

Craig wouldn't be deterred any longer. He rose, went to her and offered his hands. She took them and let him pull her to her feet and into his arms. "Kerry, I love you."

She bit her lip. "I know. And that's the greatest mystery of all. I humiliated you in front of your friends in high school at a time when you were in need of a friend even more than I was. I've been ungrateful for all the things you've done for me, Craig, but you've continued to support me. It doesn't make sense."

"I don't think anyone's been able to explain love, Kerry, so I won't try to, either. But maybe I love you because I see a person who cares very deeply but who has had a hard time showing it. I see a mother who's devoted to her son, who wants to help other people overcome the pain and suffering of abuse."

She shook her head. "That's not enough, Craig. Other people do those things and do them better."

"But other people aren't you, that unique combination of qualities that reverberate inside me." He gathered her hands in his. "Let me tell you something. The night of the prom, when you walked away from me and climbed on Durgan's bike, you looked back at me for a brief moment. Yes, you were smirking at me, but in your eyes I saw pain and a terrible kind of loneliness. Your ditching me was embarrassing, but I got over it. What stayed with me was that I somehow felt I understood the void I sensed inside you."

He tented her hands and arms beneath his. "Initially, your beauty attracted me. The sound of your laugh. The way you seemed to enjoy life. I wanted to share that kind of joy. God, Kerry, you can't imagine how envious I was of you, of your family and friends. As time went on, though, and I watched you from afar, I began to glimpse something else, an uncertainty, a doubt that, contrary to appearances, you didn't really have life by the scruff of the neck. That was when physical attraction developed into something deeper, and envy became a kind of longing. That was when I became aware that we shared something. Then you turned away from me that night, and I realized I'd been fooling myself. I was inadequate to the job of making you happy.''

Tears were streaming down her face. "Oh, Craig," she moaned, her heart filled to overflowing with happiness and breaking at the same time. "I wish Rafe had never shown up, or if he had, that it would have been five minutes later.'' At the quizzical expression on his handsome face, she smiled and added, "By then you would have kissed me.''

His eyes lightened. "You knew?''

"That you were hunting for a quiet corner where we could kiss?'' She smiled through her tears. "I'd been waiting all evening for that moment.''

He shook his head in amazement at the opportunities lost. But he wouldn't miss this one.

"I love you, Kerry,'' he said softly. "I'll always love you.''

He wanted to stop the tears coursing down her soft cheeks, but he knew they were a catharsis, the cleansing away of a dark smudge deep in her soul. They were, in a very real sense, tears of joy as much as tears of pain and sorrow, for she had found hidden in her heart the core she thought was missing. It took a long time to discover, but it had always been there.

He relaxed his embrace and held her at arm's length. She gazed at him, acceptance replacing the unhappiness he'd seen in her eyes so long ago.

His hands skimmed up and down her spine, soothing away the tension bunching her long, supple muscles. His fingers ascended the column of her neck, insinuating themselves in her silken raven tresses. He tilted her head up. Their eyes searched and locked, but it was enough. A question asked and answered. He lowered his lips to hers, made reckless, demanding contact. Passionately, impatiently, he deepened the kiss. His loins were on fire by the time their tongues collided. The softness of her body accommodated itself so perfectly to the hardness of his.

"Make love to me, Craig," she said when their lips finally parted.

He chuckled. "I thought you'd never ask." Her skin was smooth, slick, hot; her pulse rapid, tripping. "I've spent all my adult life dreaming about making love to you."

Her tears were drying on her cheeks, and her eyes glowed with a new confidence and self-awareness. "Well, what are you waiting for, an embossed invitation?" She grinned mischievously. "Or do I have to say please?"

He scooped her up in his arms. "I'll have only two words to say if you do." He moved toward the bedroom. "Thank you."

She raised her dark brows. "My words exactly."

"I certainly hope so." In the middle of the bedroom, he lowered her to her feet. "I'll do my best to make sure they are."

She leaned against him, her arms around his waist. "You better."

He began to unbutton her blouse, the backs of his hands lingering on the warm fullness of her breasts. "I love working under pressure."

Lips pursed, tongue in cheek, she released his belt buckle and slowly unzipped his pants. "Yes, I can tell."

He groaned at her touch, and they both grinned from ear to ear. She started unbuttoning his shirt from the bottom to the top, then ran her fingers along the concave ripples of his belly, the firm contours of his chest. He held his breath as her nails combed through the hair and flicked against his tight nipples.

He'd dropped his hands to his sides, but now he touched bare arms, her shoulders, the sides of her neck, her jaw. Bracketing her face, he covered her mouth with his and kissed her hard. When he pulled away, she was breathless.

He reached to unsnap her bra. As soon as he grazed her exposed skin, the pace quickened. In a matter of seconds they were completely naked.

Desire, sweet and savage, raced through Kerry as he picked her up in his arms and settled her on the bed. He lay beside her, his hands stimulating already sensitized flesh, setting off throbbing detonations of heat and panic. Her breathing deepened, became slower, measured, labored. His lips glanced her hardened peaks. His tongue encircled them. Her body arched against his mouth as delicious convulsions

racked her. Surrender was never so inviting or fulfill-
ing.

"I love you, Kerry," he whispered against her flesh.

She closed her eyes to absorb the words. They settled deep inside her, stirred untapped heat and melted
her core. "I love you, Craig," she heard herself say.

Her eyes shot open. She'd never told a man she
loved him. Never. She'd long since despaired that she
could. She'd always felt the words meant subordina-
tion. Capitulation. She never imagined they could
mean sharing.

"I love you so much." She brought his face to hers
and kissed his brow, his nose, his lips. His eyes met
hers and swallowed her. For a long time, they basked
in each other's gazes, until she felt herself floating
beneath him.

But bodies once in motion tend to stay in motion.
She was carried on the crest of a wave.

CHAPTER SIXTEEN

MICHAEL AND BRIAN met them when they landed at the Number One. Kerry had phoned her brother the evening before and told him of Rafe's arrest. It had been Craig's call to the ranch that morning, though, that had brought the two men to the airstrip.

Craig shut off the engine. "You okay?"

Kerry sat motionless in the bucket seat beside him, then inhaled deeply through her nose. "Yeah, I'm fine."

Craig reached over and took her hand in his. "They're family and they love you—almost as much as I do. Remember that." With his free hand he tilted her chin toward him, smiled and planted a soft kiss on her forehead. "Ready?"

She nodded, brought his hand to her lips, turned abruptly and opened the door. Michael was standing at the trailing edge of the wing, his arms outstretched to help her to the ground. Once there, he swallowed her in a bear hug.

"Welcome home, Sis."

Craig jumped down behind her. Michael released his sister and, grinning broadly, shook Craig's hand.

Brian kissed his mother on the cheek. "I'm glad you came, Mom."

"Me, too," she murmured. "Your father—"

"Is in jail, I hope."

"I'm sorry."

"Don't be. I barely remember him, and he wasn't much of a dad."

She was going to ruffle Brian's hair, then realized how high up she'd have to reach. For a moment, she missed the little boy. "He has one good point."

Brian raised an eyebrow.

"He gave me you."

"Oh, Mom." Too embarrassed to say more, he led her to the waiting Suburban.

"We'll talk about this more later, if you like," she said, for his ears only.

"Everyone's over at the Home Place," Michael announced as he grabbed the luggage Craig was unloading from the plane. They put it in the back of the waiting vehicle. "You haven't seen the restoration yet," he commented after climbing behind the wheel and starting the engine. "I think you'll be impressed."

"Brian's told me all about it." She smiled at her son. "I'm looking forward to seeing it for myself."

Sitting in the rear seat next to Kerry, Craig squeezed her hand. He could feel the tension in her and wished he had the power to dispel it, but he knew this rendezvous with her past was necessary.

"You might have noticed," Michael said when they were under way, "the drought is still taking its toll." The land showed the light green tones of spring, but the vegetation was sparser than she remembered from past years. "Here on the Number One, we've cut our herds by nearly fifty percent. Dad's a little luckier. He has more water and fewer head in a less spread out area. He's reduced his steer numbers, but he's actually increased his count of breeding heifers. When this dry spell is over, he'll be in better shape than most ranchers around here.''

Michael was rambling. Livestock and range management had never been subjects they discussed. But Kerry was grateful for the distraction from the natural, embarrassing questions and comments about why she was really here, what she expected from her visit and when she was planning to leave. She surveyed the land on which she'd grown up. Funny, but being back made her homesick for it.

"Any idea when the drought will end?" Craig asked.

Michael chuckled. "When it rains. Seriously, though, if the past is any measure, we still have a couple more years before the pattern shifts. Then Katie bar the door. The next natural disaster will be floods.''

They turned from the high plateau onto a caliche road that led into the shallow box canyon where the Home Place was located. A few minutes later, they were in the shade of ancient sprawling live oak trees. The cool morning air took on a subtle chill.

"Nothing left of the old house on the mesa, I understand," Kerry ventured.

"Not a stick," her brother assured her. "It's as if it had never existed."

The house where she'd grown up had been swept off the top of the butte in a tornado soon after she sold her share of the ranch. Maybe that was as well, Kerry thought. She had happy memories of her parents there, memories that nothing could erase. But increasingly over the years, the headquarters had been the scene of confrontations between her and her father, starting with the announcement of her pregnancy when she was sixteen years old. She'd been married to Rafael Durgan in that house, which was something she'd just as soon forget. Still, for the rest of the family, the old house on the top of the mesa had been home, and for them she regretted the loss.

"Your place is still safe and sound," Michael assured her. "We repaired the roof damage from the twister."

Her father had built it for her and Rafe. It was a good house, even if she had never made it a home. "What are you doing with it now?"

"Not much, really. It's an oversize guest house that rarely gets used. We put a few hunters up there last season. We'll probably do the same this fall."

The ranch house her great-grandfather had built over a century earlier came into view—or as much as the stately trees revealed. She'd never known it as a habitable structure, only as a burned-out ruin. Brian had been right. The restoration showed loving care and attention to detail. To a stranger it must seem as natural as the rocks and brush and the babbling brook nearby.

"The name suits it," she said before she realized she was vocalizing her reaction to it. "Home Place."

"Wait till you see the inside, Mom. The fireplace is awesome."

Michael opened his door and slipped out from behind the steering wheel. Brian jumped from his side

and opened his mother's door. The courtesy took her
by surprise. She'd tried to teach him good manners,
though he hadn't always shown them, but this thoughtfulness went beyond mere etiquette. Her mind drifted
to the way her father had always treated her mother.
Helen might be in dirty jeans and a sweaty T-shirt,
but Adam First always treated her like a lady. Rafe,
on the other hand, had never held a door for his wife,
except perhaps in mockery. Brian had learned the right
things from her father and brothers. Fortunately, Rafe
hadn't been around to corrupt him. It had been tough
enough for the boy to live with an alcoholic mother.

"Thank you, sir." She stepped from the Suburban.
By then, Craig had come around to her side.

She tried to smile, but instead her chin quivered.

Knees suddenly like jelly, she clutched his arm on
one side and her son's on the other. They guided her
around the front of the vehicle. Her brother smiled
encouragement, and together the four of them approached the wide front porch. Kerry was shivering in
spite of the warmth of the men at her sides.

The door opened, and Adam First filled its frame.
With the light coming from behind him, she couldn't
see his face clearly, but she knew he was watching
her. He stood motionless, waiting. Kerry had contrary
urges—to run away and to leap into his arms.

She mounted the steps to the gray shade of the
porch and had to force the words out. "Hello,
Daddy."

"Hello, Kerry," he said softly in his deep, resonant
voice. Its quiet strength had always made her feel se-

cure, safe. Why had she ever rejected him? "How are you?"

Scared, she wanted to say. "Fine." She fumbled for something to add before they went inside. "Thank you for letting me come."

"You're always welcome here, sweetheart."

The natural tendency would have been for them to touch each other, if only in a perfunctory way, but both of them seemed afraid to make the first move.

She could see him more clearly now. He hadn't changed much. If anything, he looked younger than the last time she'd seen him. The worry lines around his eyes had receded, lightened. Michael was right. He was content. His new wife, Sheila, must be a hell of a tonic.

"Come on inside." Adam stood back for her to pass.

"No." Kerry didn't budge.

The other men froze in their tracks and stared at her.

Brian was the first to utter a sound. Quietly, he drawled, "Mom…" There was such anxiety in the plea that no other words were necessary.

Only then did Kerry realize how her response must have been interpreted. She smiled ruefully and turned to Craig. "Why don't the three of you go inside? I need to talk to Dad alone first."

Craig placed his hand behind her neck and kissed her on the temple. In her ear, he whispered, "I love you."

The words washed through her like warm honey, sweet and comforting.

Michael clamped a hand on his nephew's shoulder and steered him through the doorway. Craig followed.

Kerry looked at her father. "Can we go for a little walk?"

He nodded solemnly. "Let's check the springs." He extended his hand.

Feeling both light-headed and as though she were pushing her way through deep water, she placed her hand in his—as she had so many times when she was a little girl, always sure it would be there for her. This coarse, work-hardened hand had been here all this time, if only she'd been willing to accept it.

He released his grip at the foot of the steps, and they walked slowly toward the narrow creek that flowed over smooth rocks on its way to join other streams and form a river. A river of life in this parched land.

"Dry as it is, this spring keeps producing," Adam said. He might have been talking about the love that flowed between them.

Her mother used to bring her here sometimes for a picnic lunch. They'd listen to the gurgle of water over rocks and inhale the spicy perfume of juniper. They'd pick a sprig of the spearmint growing along the pool's edge, crush it in their hands and savor its clean, fresh scent.

Kerry stared at the rippling brook, knowing how disappointed her mother would be with what Kerry had done with her life. *You have to do things for yourself,* Helen would tell her, *not depend on others to do them for you.* But, *Mama,* Kerry wanted to cry, *I tried to do it myself and look what happened.* And what would the answer have been? *There's no shame in asking for help.*

"Daddy, there's so much I need to say to you, so much I want to say, but I don't know how. *Sorry* is such an inadequate word."

Her throat burned. She couldn't face him, though she felt his eyes assessing her. She wondered if he was going to tell her it wasn't necessary to apologize, that he understood she'd been confused and unhappy. When he remained silent, she knew he had the wisdom this time not to give her an easy out, that she had to humble herself to regain her pride and be worthy of his respect.

"I'm sorry, Daddy, for not trusting you to understand what I was going through when Mom died. I'm sorry...for not asking you to help...for not accepting your help when you offered it. And the ranch...I'm sorry I stole it from you."

For what seemed like an interminable minute, the silence between them was broken only by the murmur of the spring that never went dry, even in a drought.

"I'm sorry, too, Kerry," Adam said, "for not hearing your cry for help, for not being the parent you deserved—"

"You were, Daddy," she interrupted. "I was just too pigheaded to—"

"Pigheaded?" Adam questioned, irony in his tone. Kerry raised her head and caught the glint in his eyes. The familiar sparkle, the sly grin had her heart leaping. Her chest swelled with hope and pounded with anxiety. "Seems to me I've heard that term before." The humor in his voice was unmistakable. "You couldn't have gotten it from me, could you?"

She smiled through the tears poised on her lashes. But the ache of regret still lay heavy in her heart. "I know I don't deserve your forgiveness, but I want you to know...how sorry I am for all the pain I've caused you."

He wound his arm around her and cradled her head against his chest the way he had when she was a little girl. "I forgave you a long time ago, sweetheart. We all make mistakes. I've certainly made my share. If you can forgive me for not being the dad you needed after your mother died, you'll make me the happiest man in the world."

"You've always been there for me. I just didn't see it. I didn't understand how much you loved me." She tightened her grip on him. "I love you, Daddy."

They rocked in each other's arms for several minutes as birds twittered in the trees and sunlight sparkled through the thick canopy of ancient boughs and newborn leaves. A lightness came to her spirit, the feeling of redemption she'd needed for so long.

"There are so many people I need to ask forgiveness from," Kerry said when they started up the hill to the house.

"I think you'll find they're all very happy to have you home," her father assured her.

She swung her hand in his, strangely contented. "I never thought I'd miss this place," she admitted. "I always thought I hated being stuck way out here, away from where things were happening. But when Michael was driving us over, running on about cattle and horses and the drought, I realized how much I've missed it. All these months I've been lonely for home and didn't know it."

Adam chuckled. "You've got your mother's fascination for city lights, and that's fine, but she also found contentment on this land. I hope you'll keep coming back and find peace, too."

"As long as you'll have me," Kerry said as they made their way on the gravel path that wound among sprawling live oak trees.

"Always, Kerry. You'll always be welcome." He escorted her around the building.

They took the fork that led to the back door. It opened, and Sheila stepped onto the service porch. Clearly, she'd been waiting for their return. Kerry didn't really know the woman his father had married after almost nineteen years of widowhood. Her step-mother was slender, though not petite, with short, wavy blond hair.

"Are the two of you happy?" Kerry asked her father.

Adam squeezed his daughter's hand reassuringly. "She's wonderful, Kerry. I'm a very lucky man. Yes, we're very happy."

"I'm glad. And Brian? How's he taking this?"

"You've given me a grandson to be proud of."

His crediting her for Brian's qualities was unduly generous, but she savored the compliment nevertheless. He and the rest of the family had been far more instrumental in giving Brian a sense of belonging, a refuge when things got out of hand. She'd hated her father when he gained temporary custody of her son after Brian had been arrested for underage drinking and driving under the influence. Now she realized it had been the best thing that could have happened to him. The juvenile experience meant Brian was less likely to ever spend a night in the drunk tank.

"I'm proud of him, too, but this thing with Rafe..." She paused. "It can't be easy for him to know his father's going to prison for a very long time."

"You'll be surprised at how well he's handling it."

Sheila greeted her when they reached the porch. "Hello, Kerry." The smile on her face was welcoming, but Kerry detected nervous apprehension lurking behind it.

"Hello, Sheila." They'd met only once, and that was at the county courthouse for Brian's hearing. It hadn't been a pleasant time. "Thank you for making my old man so happy."

"He's not so old." Sheila grinned at her husband, a silent message passing between them. "I'm the lucky one."

Adam placed a hand on Sheila's shoulder and answered the unspoken questions in her eyes. Had father and daughter reconciled? Had the breach been mended? "We're fine, sweetheart. Everything's fine."

Sheila nodded briefly, her blue eyes glassy. "I'm glad," she whispered. Impulsively, she gave Kerry a light hug and murmured, "Welcome home."

Kerry reciprocated the embrace. "Thank you."

Slightly embarrassed by their show of affection, they backed away from each other.

"I figured you'd be hungry by the time you got here," Sheila said casually, "so I fixed us an early lunch."

"Hungry?" Kerry hadn't thought about food. She'd been too nervous to eat any breakfast. "How about famished. And thirsty. What do y'all have to drink around here?''

She saw the startled expression on Sheila's face and couldn't help but laugh. ''Like coffee or tea,'' she said lightly.

Sheila visibly relaxed. ''There's always a pot of coffee on.''

''Caffeine. I think she's a saint.''

''Saint Sheila,'' Adam muttered. ''Yep, it has a ring to it, and she'd have to be one to put up with me.''

Kerry had never been in the room she entered—it hadn't existed when she left the Number One supposedly for the last time—but she felt instantly at home. Large and open, with a high-beamed ceiling and a sweeping window that framed a view of the wooded hillside. At one end was the large gray stone fireplace Brian had mentioned. Ironically, it had been undamaged by the fire that had devastated the original structure more than fifty years earlier. It dominated the room and lent a rustic sense of continuity and heritage. On the broad wall opposite it was the restored oil painting that had hung in the entrance of the old headquarters—a wagon train crossing a sun-bleached prairie, rugged mesas cringing below storm clouds in the background. Tough people, those pioneers who risked everything for independence and freedom.

The smiles on the faces of the people in the room, however, made Kerry feel truly at home. Michael stood by the fireplace with his wife, Clare. Kerry remembered her last encounter with her sister-in-law at the ranch picnic to celebrate her father's birthday. Kerry had shown up drunk and obnoxious. Clare had yanked her by her hair and threatened to slap her silly if she didn't behave. To this day Kerry wasn't sure if she would have done it. Probably. Clare was as tough and determined as any pioneer. Nobody messed with Clare First twice. Their four children, three girls and a boy, were also there to welcome their aunt Kerry. She bent and kissed them all.

Kerry's younger brother, Gideon, stood next to their sister, Julie. He was tall and wiry, with sandy-colored hair that bleached out in the sun, a smooth tan and baby-blue eyes. Julie, the smallest of the brood, had hair that was even lighter and skin that was more delicate.

Kerry kissed them both and promised to talk to each of them individually later.

"Neither of you two has gotten hitched yet?" she teased.

"The search has narrowed," Gideon acknowledged happily, "if I can only convince Lupe to have me."

Kerry remembered Lupe Amorado, who was small and dark, a marked contrast to her Nordic brother. Lupe had two children from a former marriage.

"And I've been holding out for Mr. Perfect," Julie told her. "It appears you already have a claim on him, though. I may have to retire to a nunnery."

Kerry chuckled. "He's too old for you, anyway."

Craig's head shot up, and he assumed an offended air. "Who's too old?"

"I've always liked older men." Julie gazed admiringly at Craig. "He looks perfect to me."

"Perfect for *me*," Kerry corrected her. "Find your own Mr. Wonderful."

Craig clicked his tongue in annoyance, tilted his

head and held up his hands. "Ladies, ladies, please stop fighting over me. It's embarrassing."

Everyone laughed, even Brian, who reminded everyone he was still a teenager by adding, "Let's eat."

"Some things never change," Kerry quipped. "Like Brian's appetite."

He extended his elbow and led her to the wainscoted dining room. One entire wall was casement windows that opened to a dark forest of ragged Afghan pines and towering cedars. At the door to the kitchen stood a short, round woman wearing a bib apron over a brown print dress.

"Elva," Kerry cried, and rushed to embrace the woman with salt-and-pepper hair. A scowl stopped her short.

"So you're back," said the housekeeper of twenty years. Elva Hernandez had come to work for the family when Helen First was diagnosed with cancer.

"Like a bad penny," Kerry admitted, standing over her, wondering if she was going to be the single holdout in the welcoming party.

"A shiny new penny, from what I've heard. You still like *chiles rellenos?*" she demanded archly.

"No one makes stuffed chile peppers like you," Kerry insisted. "Did...did you fix some?"

"When your papa said you were coming home—" a smile finally broke through "—what choice did I have?" The sixty-year-old woman opened her arms.

With relief, Kerry stepped into them and gave Elva a hug. "Thank you."

"Welcome home, *niña.*"

They all took their places around the table, which

resembled a groaning board of country foods—barbecued brisket and Elva's cheese-filled Anaheim peppers, *borracho* beans and pan-fried potatoes, biscuits and tortillas, butter and honey. While plates were still being loaded, Kerry, who was sitting next to her father, tapped her knife against the side of her iced tea glass.

"May I propose a toast?" She lifted the glass high. "To the First family. The people who, through thick and thin, have loved me better than I deserved. Thank you, all of you, for being here for me, though I didn't always know it or appreciate it. And thank you for helping my son grow up into the man he is."

The next hour was filled with the clatter of dishes and tinkle of silverware. Everyone wanted to know about life in Big D., about being on television and establishing a foundation.

They were in the midst of helping Elva clear the table when Craig's cell phone beeped. It wasn't an unusual occurrence. He'd received two other calls already from business associates.

"Mother?"

Kerry was immediately on the alert.

"Is something wrong?" he asked guardedly, and stepped into the living room.

Kerry followed. The conversation was one-sided, Craig mostly listening. Seeing the shocked expression on his face and knowing Gina never called her son, Kerry was sure it couldn't be good news.

"Yes, of course, Mom. I'll see you this Sunday." He clicked the instrument closed and hooked it on his belt.

"What is it? Is she all right?" Kerry asked.

He turned to face her, his brows raised in confusion. "What did you say to her?"

Panic rippled through her. Had she made matters worse between mother and son? "I...we talked...I..."

He didn't seem to notice her stuttering. "She wants me to visit her on Sunday. This isn't our usual weekend, but she said she wants us to eat in. She's going to fix meat loaf for me."

Kerry observed the awe on his face and relaxed.

"She's never done that before. She says she wants to talk."

Kerry wrapped her arms around his waist. "Good. Maybe she's decided it's time for her to mend fences, too."

He hugged her tight. "You're incredible, you know that?"

THE SPRING SUN was warm, the perpetual West Texas wind a gentle breeze when Craig took Kerry's hand and led her along the narrow path that climbed through the forest of oak, elm and cottonwood trees behind the Home Place. A contentment neither of them had experienced seemed to envelop them as their fingers intertwined. They came to a rivulet of pure, clear spring water.

"Have you ever considered changing your name?" Craig asked.

"Take back First as my legal name? Several times, but Durgan is Brian's name, and I didn't want to confuse him any more than he already was."

"I wasn't thinking of Brian...or the name First."

Kerry felt a strange fluttering in her chest and a light-headedness that made concentration difficult.

Movement had suddenly become impossible, too. She could feel only the warmth of Craig's hand holding hers, her single tether with the world around her.

He whirled her to face him. His eyes were smiling, his lips curved upward.

"Will you marry me, Kerry? Will you be my wife?"

"I… You…" She was supposed to say something. His arms were around her. His lips were on hers. He deepened the kiss, and she lost awareness with any world beyond the probing swirl of his tongue and the heat of his body against hers. Then, as if suddenly awakening from a long, deep sleep, she joined him in this magical exploration of sensations. Mouth to mouth. Breast to chest. Pelvis to pelvis.

Gradually, reluctantly, she drew away.

"Is that your final answer?" he inquired with a happy gleam in his eye.

"Would you repeat the question, please?"

He kissed her again, a tender tasting this time.

She curled against his chest. "Are you sure, Craig? You'll always wonder…."

"We'll wonder together." Holding her hands, their bodies still joined at the hip, he stretched his arms full length, his gaze holding hers. "I love you, Kerry." He watched her lips quiver and held her tight.

"I promise—"

He put a finger to her lips to seal them. "One day at a time."

HARLEQUIN *Super*ROMANCE®

CREATURE COMFORT

A heartwarming new series by

Carolyn McSparren

Creature Comfort, the largest veterinary clinic in Tennessee, treats animals of all sizes—horses and cattle as well as family pets. Meet the patients—and their owners. And share the laughter and the tears with the men and women who love and care for all creatures great and small.

#996 THE MONEY MAN
(July 2001)

#1011 THE PAYBACK MAN
(September 2001)

Look for these Harlequin Superromance titles coming soon to your favorite retail outlet.

HARLEQUIN®
Makes any time special ®

Harlequin truly does make any time special.... This year we are celebrating weddings in style!

A
Walk
Down
the Aisle

WEDDING CELEBRATION

To help us celebrate, we want you to tell us how wearing the Harlequin wedding gown will make your wedding day special. As the grand prize, Harlequin will offer one lucky bride the chance to **"Walk Down the Aisle" in the Harlequin wedding gown!**

There's more...

For her honeymoon, she and her groom will spend five nights at the **Hyatt Regency Maui.** As part of this five-night honeymoon at the hotel renowned for its romantic attractions, the couple will enjoy a candlelit dinner for two in Swan Court, a sunset sail on the hotel's catamaran, and duet spa treatments.

To enter, please write, in, 250 words or less, how wearing the Harlequin wedding gown will make your wedding day special. The entry will be judged based on its emotionally compelling nature, its originality and creativity, and its sincerity. This contest is open to Canadian and U.S. residents only and to those who are 18 years of age and older. There is no purchase necessary to enter. Void where prohibited. See further contest rules attached. Please send your entry to:

Walk Down the Aisle Contest

In Canada	In U.S.A.
P.O. Box 637	P.O. Box 9076
Fort Erie, Ontario	3010 Walden Ave.
L2A 5X3	Buffalo, NY 14269-9076

You can also enter by visiting www.eHarlequin.com
Win the Harlequin wedding gown and the vacation of a lifetime!
The deadline for entries is October 1, 2001.

HARLEQUIN®
Makes any time special ®

PHWDACONT1

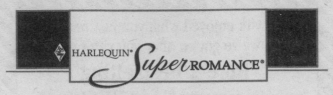